A SACRED GROVE

A SACRED GROVE

CHRONICLES OF AN URBAN DRUID™ BOOK 2

AUBURN TEMPEST
MICHAEL ANDERLE

L M B P N
DISRUPTIVE IMAGINATION®

LMBPN Publishing
PMB 196, 2540 South Maryland Pkwy
Las Vegas, NV 89109

First US edition, October 2020
eBook ISBN: 978-1-64971-256-1
Print ISBN: 978-1-64971-257-8

THE A SACRED GROVE TEAM

Thanks to our JIT Team:

Dave Hicks
Deb Mader
James Caplan
Dorothy Lloyd
Jeff Goode
John Ashmore
Micky Cocker
Kelly O'Donnell
Diane L. Smith
Debi Sateren
Rachel Beckford
Larry Omans

Editor
SkyHunter Editing Team

Beart de Reir ar mbriathar. Glaine ar gcroi. Neart ar ngeag.

CHAPTER ONE

My outlook on life isn't complicated—any day that passes when nobody tries to kill me or someone I love gets put into the "good day" column. Simple, right? Lately, good days have been hard to come by.

Since I totally ignored Da's warning three months ago and flew to Ireland to embrace our super-secret heritage, I've seen the world in a different light—a mythical and magical light. I am a druid.

And yeah, at first, that blew my mind.

Now, I think I have a better handle on it.

Magic is real, and my family is part of the Ancient Order of Druids who have protected nature for millennia. In exchange, we were gifted with preternatural abilities by the fae. Now, if that were the end of it, all would be well in my world, but life, as does nature, demands a balance to all things.

If we're the good guys, there have to be bad guys.

Since grabbing this particular magical bull by the horns, I've had a few harrowing scrapes with the impossible—dragons, leprechauns, Baba Yaga, evil druids, and even a couple of ensorcelled vampires.

I have peed a little on more than one occasion.

But the coolest thing that happened was when my ancient great-great- I have no idea how many greats-grandfather Fionn mac Cumhaill, leader of the ancient druid Fianna warriors, set me on a quest… Return to Ireland and reclaim the Fianna treasures from his ancient fortress beneath the Hill of Allen. To his horror, they're in danger of being discovered or destroyed by the gravel company excavating the land.

While it sounds like a crazy LARPing adventure, it's not. It's real. And that's what brings six Cumhaill druids, a wife, two rug rats, and one bonded spirit bear to the Kerry Airport in the middle of September.

"Jackson, get back here. Emmet, grab him." Aiden jolts from the group to corral his four-year-old as the wily little beast evades Emmet's grip and darts into the flow of arrivals, cackling with glee.

I lean close to Meggie and giggle. "Your brother's getting into trouble again, isn't he, baby girl?"

Meg is turning two, and I have her locked down in her car seat and nestled amongst the suitcases on our airport cart. There's no escape. Not that she's trying to get free. Meg is in what Calum and I call the baby coma. Past the point of exhaustion, she blinks and stares, too tired to interact with the world.

Baby coma is a good thing.

"Over there." Da points to the Customs desk at the end. "Families with kids and strollers go through the desk on the end there."

I turn my cart to follow him, and Dillan spins his to roll along beside me. Yep, we're quite the procession.

"Let me know if you see her." Dillan cranes his neck and searches the baggage area as we make our exit.

The *her* he's looking for is Baba Yaga. I glance around and hope like hell *not* to see her sexy, ebony angel persona anywhere near my family.

"I doubt she still works here. I fulfilled her prophecy, and the queen delivered her box to her sisters in the afterlife. I'm sure she gave up the baggage claim gig the second Patty told her it had happened."

"Maybe she needed the benefits."

I roll my eyes and let that one go.

"And you have no idea what was in the box?"

I shake my head, and my red hair sweeps across Meg's face. When I get nothing, I know she's out. "Nope."

Aiden and Emmet catch up with us, both of them red in the cheeks and winded. "Captured." Emmet flips Jackson upside down to raspberry his belly. "One crazy monkey boy to sell to the Ireland zoo."

"Noooo," Jackson shouts while squirming. "I nots a monkey."

Kinu shakes her head and her brown ponytail swings against her neck. "I really think we should've stayed home."

Aiden bends and kisses her forehead. "Nonsense. If I'm flying to the Emerald Isle to meet my grandparents for the first time, you and the monkeys need to be with me."

I ease my cart behind Dillan's, and we stop in the line behind two other families. "Aiden's right. While we're off on our family quest, you three can keep Gran company and enjoy a week away."

"Och, Fi's right," Da says from beside Dillan's cart. "My mam will be out of her mind havin' the wee miscreants all to herself. Ye'll barely have to lift a finger. I promise ye that."

"Next in line."

Da turns as we're called to the counter.

"It'll be grand." I lay on the Irish lilt as I offer Kinu a smile. My reassurance falls flat, and I sober. "It's important the kids grow up understanding their Irish heritage as well as their Japanese heritage. Then they won't get blindsided like we all were."

Kinu laughs and waves that away. "I wish *I* understood. I'm still in the blindsided stage."

"I get that. I'm relieved Da said Aiden could tell you. It twisted him up to leave you at home all the time to come over for our latest disaster."

Kinu sighs. "That's my point, Fi. I worried enough about him already being a cop. Then Brenny, and now this?"

"It's a lot. I know."

Having a father and five brothers putting on a badge and hitting the city streets every day and night is hard on both my heart and my nerves. Brendan's death last month brought the dangers home hard. "The way I look at it, having abilities gives them an edge on the streets—a shield, a little extra strength, extra speed. It's a good thing."

"I might've agreed with you until I found out the people they chase down won't only be garden variety hoodlums and criminals."

I glance at the people around us in the arrivals lines. Most fae I've encountered could pass as human and blend into any crowd. "Yeah, that part is scary. I'll give you that."

I ease up to the window and hand the officer my passport. Then Kinu and Aiden…then we're through.

Unlike the first time I came through the arrivals doors and felt lost and had no one standing on the other side of the doors waiting for me, this time I find Granda, Sloan, and—

"Patty!" I head straight over to my leprechaun friend. The wispy, snow-white hair he usually keeps tucked under a leafy green hat is currently loose and wild. His cheeks are round with a smile and his mischievous blue eyes sparkle behind rimless glasses.

"Dandylion." Jackson points at Patty's head.

I blink, hoping Patty didn't hear him and move so we turn away from Jackson's observations. "I didn't expect to see you. This is a lovely surprise."

"I wouldn't miss welcomin' ye home, my girl." Patty reaches up to hug me.

Granda's and Sloan's eyes widen as I accept the gesture and hug him back. Sure, touching a Man o' Green is historically an impossibility, but Patty's my friend. He trusts me not to trap him for his treasures because I know his last line of defense. The Dragon Queen of Wyrms chomps anyone who forces him to take them back to his trove of gold.

Problem solved.

"Coming here is so thoughtful." I'm careful not to thank him outright. Not that it matters, I'm already bound to him both in a debt of gratitude and with a pledge of a favor owed. The former was a lesson learned after the fact. The latter was a conscious choice.

Not that I regret the favor.

I smile over at Sloan Mackenzie. He's tall and dark-skinned and dressed like an Abercrombie model and only stands here now because of my bargain with Patty. "You pulled through for me in a big way, Patty."

Sloan scowls, which is his most natural expression. He doesn't approve of me promising Patty an open favor marker in exchange for the restoration of his life. Sucks to be him. He's alive and well, and that's all that matters.

Patty winks and squeezes my hand. "Her Devoted Mothership asks that ye visit yer wyrmlets while yer here."

Oh, hells bells. I'm in the country for fifteen minutes, and it begins. "I, uh, I'm not sure what our plans are yet." My mind balks at the idea of being stuck in that death-reeking cavern in the belly of a cliff. "Places to go. People to see. Besides, I'm not sure I could find my way back. Send Her Fierceness my best though—her and all the little wyrmlets."

Patty arches a brow. "Yer best not to slight the invitation, missy. Grip yer dragon band and focus. Ye'll be able to access the lair when yer ready to come."

I sigh when I hear the finality in his voice. "It won't cost me another two months of my life, will it?"

He waves my concern away. "Och, silly girl. It's a visit. Yer the Mother of Wyrms. Ye must meet yer young."

Right. I'm so proud. I take in his eager smile and force a smile of my own. "Yeah. Of course. Wouldn't miss it."

In the parking lot of the airport, we divvy up the group. Having already thought about keeping Da and Granda apart as much as possible, I send Aiden, Kinu, Meg, and Jackson with Granda in the Land Rover, and Da, Calum, Dillan, Emmet, and I go with Sloan in a black Skoda Kodiaq.

"*Duuude*," Emmet says as we pile in. "Is this your ride?"

Sloan flashes a glance into the rearview. "Why do you sound so surprised?"

Emmet shrugs. "I thought that since you can *poof* everywhere, you wouldn't need a car, let alone a swanky, spank beast."

Sloan's brow arches. "Keep in mind that ye'll likely not encounter any other druids while yer here and almost certainly no other wayfarers. What ye've seen with me is the exception in Ireland, not the rule. When I go out for a pint with mates, I drive, the same as they do. We have to blend in and while yer here, ye'll need to do the same."

I laugh. "Yeah, we're all about blending."

Emmet smiles and clicks his seatbelt. "It must suck to pretend to be normal. I bet you mostly try to hang around with other druids, eh?"

"I try my best *not* to." Sloan pulls out of the airport parking lot and follows Granda. "Around here, most druids our age are entitled assholes with conniving minds and chips on their shoulders."

Dillan chuffs. "Well, I guess that rules out having a party to make new friends."

Da turns in the shotgun seat and casts a glance into the back. "Yer not here to party and make friends, boys. Yer here to help yer sister on her quest, train with Sloan and yer granda, and absorb all ye can while the magic of the isle feeds yer cells. That's it. No pub crawls. No walks of shame. No gettin' into yer usual trouble."

"Hello, fun police." Emmet throws up his hands. "What if we wrap up the quest quickly and have a night off? You never know, Da, my soulmate might be in town waiting to meet me. You might be cock-blocking me from the destined mother of my children and your grandchildren."

I snort. "Honestly, stopping you from reproducing works in favor of Da's argument, not yours. Sorry, Em."

"There, ye see." Da flicks his hand through the air. "Listen to yer sister."

"Rude." Emmet shakes off the jibe and points at me. "Now I won't name our daughter after you, Fi."

"Lucky her. Now, back to what Da said about the magic feeding your cells. You feel it, don't you? The ambient power in the air? You can almost breathe it into your lungs."

Calum nods. "It tingles on my skin."

Dillan smiles. "Does this mean we'll get a steady power- up for the next few days?"

"It does." Sloan speeds up to pass a couple out for a leisurely country drive. "Lugh expects ye'll want to settle in tonight, eat, visit, and rest. We start training in the morning, and I will assess yer skills and yer disciplines before we set off to the Hill of Allen the following day."

"Did you look over the information I barfed out when I was under the influence of the encyclopedia salmon?"

He meets my gaze in the mirror and chuckles. "Yer granda is the historian of the Ancient Order of Druids. He's been pourin' over yer chicken scratches for weeks. He's in absolute awe of ye, Fi. It's killin' him not to share it with the other families."

"But he hasn't, has he?" Da snaps.

"He hasn't, sir. He understands, as do I, that for everyone's safety and the success of the quest, it's best to keep the details to ourselves until after we've made the retrieval and can tell them the whole story."

Da's bristles settle, and I roll my eyes. If the two of them are wound and waiting for the other to piss them off, this will be one very long week.

We're rolling through the green hills of Kerry and are about halfway to Gran's and Granda's house when the Land Rover puts on its blinker and pulls over to the side of the road. "What's the oul fool doin' now?" Da mutters.

"I'm not sure." Sloan pulls off the road behind him and eases to a stop. "Maybe the wee boy needs to piss?"

I frown. "Not likely. I took him before we left the airport to avoid this exact thing."

Granda and Aiden get out of the Rover and head back to stand at the driver's side door. Sloan and I each roll down our windows to hear what's up.

"Change of plans, folks." Granda leans down to see into the window. "I got a call on my wee cellular, and there's been an incident at the Doyle estate. Sloan and Fi, take Aiden's family home to Lara. I'm takin' advantage of the force of coppers I have at hand to help assess what's what."

"What kind of incident, Granda?" I ask.

He scratches a hand over his whitening hair and shrugs. "I can't say as yet. It was Iris Doyle who called, and she's in quite a fit. Somethin' about the death of her trees and terrified sheep and a big hole in the ground. I couldn't make much sense of it. We'll head there now. You two join us once ye get the young ones delivered safe home."

Sloan and I bail out of his SUV and get into the Rover. I look back, and both Jackson and Meg are out cold. "Nice. They'll be all rested up for Gran."

Kinu chuckles. "I hope she's as up for them as your dad thinks, Fi. They can be a handful in large doses."

Granda pulls a U-turn behind us and heads back the way we came. Sloan pulls us back onto the road, and we continue toward home. "Lara has inexhaustible energy and the patience of a saint. She will love them from the first moment she senses their energy. She's hands-down the most nurturing soul I've ever known."

We venture on for another twenty minutes, and I look back to check on them. Kinu is sleeping now too. Good. Sleep when the babies sleep is wisdom for the ages.

I've been thinking about the devotion in Sloan's words and the loving relationship he has with my grandparents. I've met his parents. Janet and Wallace Mackenzie are quite rigid and driven. They approve of the man he's become, but I've never seen any signs of affection.

Which is totally sad.

"How young were you when you started *poofing* to Gran's and Granda's house?"

Sloan checks the rearview mirror, then casts a sideways glance at me. "Five. I was in the car with my father when he stopped in to speak with Lugh. He told me to wait there, but Lara took me by the hand, and we snacked on cookies and warm apple cider on the side patio with the birds and rabbits and mice she invited for a tea party."

"I can picture that. The first day I spent with her, I told her she reminded me of Snow White."

He nods. "That night, I was lying in bed wishing I could see the nice lady again, and I transported into their kitchen. That's when my wayfarer gift first appeared."

"And a grand first adventure." I can picture them finding a

young boy in his jammies in the middle of their kitchen. "I'm glad you've had their love. It's kinda perfect actually."

"How so?"

"Well, they wanted to love us, but we didn't know about them, and my da cut them off. Your parents kept you a bit cut off, and you needed love. Win-win."

He turns off the side road and into Gran's laneway. I smile out the front windshield at the thick hedge that runs the length of the front of the house.

I like to think my grandparents live in the Shire.

"They've been good to me."

Tension rings in his voice, and I know we're getting dangerously close to "feelings." I don't care. Sloan's more than a high-handed jerk. Beneath that crusty exterior is a gooey center I've caught glimpses of a few times. "It must've hurt when Granda asked you to go to Toronto and find us."

"Don't be stupid. Lugh was dying. It was necessary. Why would that hurt me?" He slows the truck and eases through the arched opening into the property's interior.

The place is exactly as I remember: the thatched roof on the house that backs into a hill, the tree that grows out of the center, the intricate maze of cobbled walkways bordered by lush growth and flowers.

For lack of a better description—it's magical.

I can't help but lean forward in my seat and smile. "It's perfectly natural that you might resent the idea of sharing them after having them to yourself for so long. You're an only child, and you haven't had to share much in life. I think it must've sucked for you."

His brow creases. "Fine. If ye must know, it stung my pride more than it should've and I'm not a bit proud of it. Lugh needed ye and yer his family, not me. I had no right to feel slighted."

"Sure, you did."

"I *didn't*. It was petty and beneath me."

I wave at Gran. She steps out the front door and rushes along the front walk. Before I jump out, I reach over and squeeze his arm. "Surly, love is a complicated thing. Don't get your boxers in a bunch. S'all good. In this family, there's always enough love to go around."

CHAPTER TWO

"*Tsumaranai mono desu ga.*" Kinu holds out the jar of authentic Canadian maple syrup she brought. She presents it to Gran as she leans forward in a formal Japanese bow. "It means this is not much, but I bring you a small gift."

"Och, well, thank you, luv. That was thoughtful." She sets the syrup onto the stone half-wall that lines the walkway and holds her hands out for the sleeping baby girl in my arms.

"And you're even more excited for these small gifts, aren't you?" I hand her Meg and my grandmother bursts at the seams. Jackson toddles beside me while rubbing his eyes. "Jackson, this is your gran. Remember what I told you?"

He nods his little head, his russet brown hair standing up like a rooster's comb at the front. "If Meggie and me is good, we can play with bunnies and Gran's skunky."

"That's right." I chuckle. "Is Dax here?"

Gran sends me an admonishing look and fights back a smile. "He's out at the moment. I'm sure we'll have a grand time with or without him while yer gone."

"So, Granda called you and filled you in?"

"He did. He said yer to deliver Aiden's family, then be off to the Doyle's to join them."

I shrug. "That's what he told us too. I'm so sorry to hug and run. I'm not sure what it's all about yet."

"Och, we'll be fine. Off ye go. Safe home."

Once Sloan has carried the last of the luggage inside, he holds his hand out for me. I clasp his palm, and with a squeeze of his hand, we arrive on the manicured side lawn of a country estate. I eye the surroundings and smile at the rolling beige and sage green hills in the background.

I've come to love the backdrop of Ireland.

"Doyle." I follow him around the back of the house toward the open fields. "As in Ciara Doyle?"

"The same."

"Oh, joy. I've been in the country for two hours. I wondered when ill tidings and personal assaults would begin."

We round the corner of the large, gray brick house and head toward the sheep pastures in the back. At first, I'm not sure what we're looking at. A section of the forested area off the back of the house looks odd. Instead of tall trees and green leaves, there's a section that looks crooked and withered.

I don't have to be a cop to realize something bad happened to part of the Doyle family grove. The magical energy of the area feels anguished, and I understand why Mrs. Doyle was in a fit when she called Granda for help.

If she's anything like Gran, her sacred grove is more than a source of fae power. It's a living, breathing part of her.

I rub the nape of my neck and try to ease the tingling.

Following Sloan's gaze, my attention shifts from the destruction of a centuries-old druid grove to the grazing pasture of a large flock of recently shorn sheep. The green pasture slopes away from the house and in the center of the flat plane of grass sits a massive crater of rich, dark earth.

This would be the part of Iris Doyle's tale that mentioned the big hole in the ground.

Da and Granda stand on the near ridge of the crater while speaking with Evan and Iris Doyle. I'm glad to see them working together. From their perch atop the freshly disturbed dirt, it's not a stretch to envision one of them getting shoved in the hole if things got heated.

I push down my anxiety and stop projecting.

Da said his only problem with Granda was not wanting a druid life. I forced that issue, so there's nothing for them to fight about…I hope.

Deciding to leave them to chat, I scan for my brothers. Aiden, Calum, and Dillan are on the far ridge almost sixty feet away. And Emmet is…

"Ew, don't touch that!" I slap Emmet's hand away from stroking Ciara's arm. I've seen him use that move before and it's not happening. "Gross, Emmet. No. Just no. You're not hooking up with this one."

"And this involves you how?" Ciara sneers.

"Cumhaills watch out for one another. I'm not letting you debutante your way into my brother's pants. That's a hells no veto."

Emmet frowns and gives me a look. "On what grounds?"

"Either Bro Code Article 150 or 86, take your pick."

Emmet looks from Ciara to me and back before his face splits into a wide grin. "Well, well, your trip to Ireland was full of firsts. I didn't know you swung that way, Fi."

I roll my eyes. "Not me, dumbass. Sloan."

Sloan's scowl is hilarious, so I put him out of his misery. "Bro Code Article 150 is, 'No sex with your Bro's ex.'"

Sloan arches a brow. "And Article 86?"

Emmet chuckles. "That's the Hot/Crazy Scale. It's to help gauge whether the allure of the exterior is worth the *Fatal Attraction* boiling bunny scene sure to follow."

Sloan eyes up Ciara scowling at us and laughs. "Yer sister is right. That would be a hells no. Is there a Bro Code for running fast and far and never looking back?"

Emmet chuckles. "That's the advice when a chick tips the Hot/Crazy Scale."

"Consider it tipped. Trust me. This one is not pretty; she only looks that way."

"Fuck you, Mackenzie."

"Been there, done that. Got nothing but regrets."

Emmet sighs. "Okay, I guess I'll go help the others with the craters then."

"Are ye daft?" Ciara snaps and casts withering glances among the three of us. "Yer listenin' to them and blowin' me off? We were havin' a perfectly lovely time until they stuck their noses into our business."

Emmet shrugs. "What can I say? You don't mess with the Bro Code."

He turns and strides off to join the others, and Sloan laughs and shakes his head. "Yer all cracked. Ye know that, right? The lot of ye live life a mile off-center."

I bat my lashes at him. "You say the sweetest things."

Ciara looks like she might explode, and I'm glad. After the snide welcome I got at the Tralee dinner and her arranging an attack on me in an alley as a hazing event, my goal is to foil her at every turn.

All my brothers are good-looking, but Emmet and Dillan are the two who are particularly sweet eye candy. The two of them, as well as Calum and Brenny, got our mam's ebony hair and emerald green eyes. Aiden and I got Da's russet-red hair and bright blue eyes.

I'm not surprised she set her sights on Emmet. He's also the only one who would've responded to her.

Aiden's married, Calum's with Kevin, and Dillan's with Kady. So, Emmet is the only unattached Cumhaill man. I guess Da qualifies too, although he's never had anyone in his life since mom died. Well, that I know of.

"Shall we go look at the big dirt hole?" Sloan gestures at the commotion.

"Great idea. I've enjoyed as much of this as I can stand. Careful not to trip on Ciara's pouty lip."

Ciara crosses her arms and her boobs almost bust out of her tight, knit sweater. "Yer a feckin' riot, Cumhaill. Why anyone gives ye the time of day is beyond me."

"I'm sure many things are beyond you. Don't worry. Everyone finds something they're good at eventually. How are you at puzzles?"

Sloan places a hand at the small of my back, and we take our leave. I see the smile he fights to hide, and it's gratifying. My work here is done.

Except…the woman doesn't take a hint, and the bitter, brunette bombshell follows us like a bad fart.

I cast her a glance over my shoulder and raise my hand. "S'all good. We've got this. You can go paint your nails or kill a puppy or do whatever you normally do after a guy drops you like a hot rock."

"Are ye coddin' me? Yer on my land and ye think ye'll prove yerself more useful to the elders than me? Yer a neophyte. What do ye know about fae monsters?"

"Almost nothing." I think about it. "No. Probably closer to nothing. You're right, I'm new to all of this, but I pick things up quicker than most."

The three of us join Da, and the Doyles, while Granda steps off to receive a phone call. Evan Doyle is a short and stout man in his sixties wearing a stern expression that seems quite natural. Iris Doyle is a brunette beauty standing elegant in jeans and a linen smock top. Even with red-rimmed eyes, I see where Ciara gets her silver-screen good looks.

"Is that what ye think this is?" Sloan asks as we join the group. "A fae monster?"

"Um, pardon?" Emmet jogs over with my brothers in tow. "Fae monsters? Seriously?"

"So, it's not just Fi then," Dillan says.

I prop my hands on my hips. "What's not just me?"

Calum laughs. "We wondered if it was Ireland that stirred up the trouble for you or if it was you that stirred up the trouble in Ireland. Our bets were on you."

"Nice. Thanks."

Granda gets off the phone and curses. "That was Brian Perry. He lost his grove last night. Except, he and Gwyneth were away, and the whole thing is gone. Every tree is desiccated. Centuries of life siphoned and destroyed."

"Oh, sweet goddess," Iris gasps. "How awful."

"It's an attack, then." Evan scowls at his withered trees.

"By someone who knows the difference between a forest and a druid grove," Da adds. "That's the groves of two elders of the Nine Families targeted in one night."

"Do druids have standing enemies?" Aiden asks.

We all look at Granda and wait for him to weigh in on that one. "Not as a rule, but Niall's right. It's too much of a coincidence to ignore both targets being the power source of an elder family."

My guts twist, and I see the same discomfort firing in Granda's expression. "Sloan, take the boys home. I don't want Gran alone. Have her walk the perimeter with them. Then they can keep an eye on things until we get back."

Sloan looks at Granda and gets his nod of agreement.

"Don't tell her about the danger to the grove yet, son. I'll speak with her privately about it when we get back. Boys, ye simply want to see the property and explore, all right?"

"Not to worry, Granda," Aiden says. "We've got this."

"Just to be clear," Emmet says. "If we engage with someone on your property, how much force do we use?"

Granda frowns. "If they're targeting the Elders of the Ancient Order, they aren't ordinary humans. Ye'll be facin' fae, dark druids, or powerful creatures. Use whatever force ye need to keep the family safe from harm."

Let me go too, Red.

"Agreed." I focus on releasing my bonded bear from where he lives within me. A flutter builds in my chest, a gentle pressure forces my lungs to expand, then the pressure pops and he bursts free.

My nine-hundred-pound grizzly bear's sudden appearance startles the Doyles, but my family is used to him dropping in unannounced.

"Bruin wants to go too."

"Thank ye, Bear," Granda says. "Keep them safe."

Bruin nods his massive round head, then pegs Ciara with a glare. Lifting his lips off his canines, he lets out a long, threatening growl.

Mr. and Mrs. Doyle look like they might need a pit stop in the house to change their gitch. I feel bad for them. Not so bad I'd defend Ciara, but hey, I certainly don't claim to be perfect. "It's okay, buddy. You go and protect Gran and the fam. Ciara won't try to hurt me again, will you?"

Ciara's lips tighten, and she looks from me to her parents and back again.

"Wait a minute," Emmet snaps. "Is this the bitch who arranged for you to be jumped and beaten in an alley?"

My brothers all puff up into their protective warrior modes, and I hold out my hand. "Off you go, boys. We'll be along soon."

"You coulda said that, Fi. That's our Bro Code Golden Rule. All those who mess with our sister will pay."

"I've got this. Love you. Concentrate on Gran, please."

Aiden, Dillan, and Emmet each grab hold of Sloan's arm and

when he contacts Bruin, they all disappear. I look up at Calum and shrug. "You didn't want to go?"

He shakes his head. "Not yet. I haven't told you what we found by the forest and what we think about this crater and the creature who made it."

Everyone is still scowling at Ciara and looking confused. It's obvious no one will move on until I explain, so I recap for them. "Your daughter arranged a hazing prank and had me jumped in an alley. I fought with all I had, not knowing, and my bear nearly killed two of your heirs. I came out of it a hell of a lot better than they did."

"We didn't know." Evan drops his chin and offers me an apologetic look. "I'm sorry and disappointed to hear this."

"It's old news, and I'm pretty sure that considering how badly it backfired on them, they won't do it again any time soon." I draw a deep breath and point at the massive crater in the tilled earth. "Back to the problem at hand. Calum, tell us what you boys figured out."

"First off," Calum begins, "Granda, did you ask about a dirt crater at the other site? Did the man on the phone mention a hole in the surrounding ground at his place?"

Granda shakes his head. "He said there's nothin' like that on his land."

"That fits with what we put together."

"Which is?"

"We think two separate incidents collided. We found multiple sets of boot prints on the ground along the edge of the grove. They came in from the road over there and did whatever they did to destroy the trees. Based on the Perry grove being destroyed, the perps here were likely interrupted."

"Not that I'm complaining," Evan replies, "but if the entire grove was the target, what happened to interrupt them?"

"That's where things get interesting. There are four or five separate sets of tracks of the men coming in from the road, but only two sets leave. Also, the grass is compacted along that area as if something very large and very heavy slid across the ground."

"Like a car?" Iris asks. "You think they had a vehicle to get away?"

Calum shakes his head. "No. There are no tire tracks. We think it was another creature—a very large creature with a rounded and smooth body, like a massive tube. Also, we don't think the attackers got away. We found traces of blood spatter in the grass. We think they got eaten."

The entire group shares Granda's look of astonishment. "Eaten? By what?"

"Fi? Do you think your dragon friend could've made a hole like that?"

I follow his pointed finger and wander to the top of the ridge. It's massive…but so is the Queen of Wyrms. And she's smooth and heavy and wouldn't leave any tracks. "Yeah, I think she could."

"A dragon?" Mr. Doyle says. "Ye've got to be feckin' with us. Dragons are extinct. And even if there were still such things, they would most certainly leave footprints. Their taloned feet would claw up the area like mulch."

I turn and wave away his denial. "I assure you there are dragons in the area. I was held prisoner in the queen's lair for seven weeks this summer while her eggs hatched. There are at least one adult female and twenty-three wyrmlets in the area."

Da nods. "And the queen would need to feed more often to tend to her babes. Yer thinkin' she tunneled up to snack on some sheep and got the bonus of three vandals as dessert?"

Calum nods. "That's what we think. Have you counted your sheep, Mr. Doyle? I'd bet a few are missing. If the Queen of Wyrms has twenty-three mouths to feed, I don't think a few assholes sneaking around in the dark would sate her hunger."

"Ye can't be serious," Ciara snaps. "Yer buyin' into her

nonsense about a mythical winged reptile that's been the thing of fables for millennia? Dragons aren't real."

"The Wyrm Queen doesn't have wings or legs. She's more like a giant, blood-red serpent with a penchant for chomping humans and a fixation on Elvis memorabilia."

Iris lets out a feminine sound and brushes a hand over her hair. "If Fiona's right and a dragon came up to feast on the sheep and ate the men destroying my trees in the process, then I am grateful. Let the beast feed her young on the bones of those men. The grove is worth far more than their lives."

Granda frowns. "It would've been helpful to know who the men were and who backs them. Have they finished what they started? Are the other groves in danger?"

I sigh, peel off my jacket, and hand it to Calum. "I suppose now is as good a time as any to try and find out. Fingers crossed Patty's right, and this is only a visit."

"Fi, no." Da jogs around the Doyles to get to me. "What if she holds ye again? What if ye can't get free this time? We can find the answers some other way."

I shrug, pull up my sleeve, and wrap my fingers around the infinity dragon tattoo that bands my upper arm. "At least this time you'll know where I am. I'll be fine. Wish me luck."

"Luck," Calum says.

"Slan!" Granda and Da say at the same time.

I close my eyes, focus on the dragon lair, and marvel as magic bursts beneath my grip.

CHAPTER THREE

The lair of the Dragon Queen of Wyrms is located about three hundred and fifty feet below the ground, not far inland from the Cliffs of Moher. It has a massive main cavern with a few offshoot tunnels and glows gold with the shimmering radiance of Patty's leprechaun treasure.

Thankfully, when I open my eyes, I have indeed materialized within the lair. With my sense of direction, I had no idea where I might end up. I consider my first solo teleportation a huge success. Sloan will be proud.

I check things out, and the lair is as it was, except for the stench. The air no longer hangs with the reek of rot and dank of death like it did before.

That's a big checkmark in the win column.

"Yer here!" Patty shouts and sets his controller on the arm of his recliner and jumps up to greet me. "I didn't expect ye so soon."

"Are you kidding? I couldn't wait to get here to see my little wyrmlets and say hello."

Patty arches a brow. Yeah, he's not buying it.

"Also, I wanted to speak with Her Graciousness about something that happened up top last night." I glance around the empty cavern and shrug. "Is she here?"

"Och, of course. She's in the nursery wing with the nest. Come along. She wants to speak with you too."

I follow Patty past where the eggs were stored off the main cavern and through a smooth, dark tunnel. "This is new, right? I don't remember this being here."

"It is new." Patty pushes his glasses further up his nose. "We needed a place for the littles to stretch and grow. Her Mightiness found two of the scamps near the Cadillac and almost lost her temper."

I shudder even to think of what that might look like.

"Wyrms will be wyrms, I suppose. It's good they have a designated play area now."

"Agreed. It took milady a full week of nights working while they slept, but she burrowed and pushed the rock and dirt out the tunnel of death and into the water below."

"Ahh, that's why it smells so much better in here."

Patty nods. "It's amazing what cleaning every half-century can do. And now the young have their wing."

I don't care about any of this but try to muster the appropriate level of enthusiasm. "I'm sure it's safer for everyone to establish boundaries at a young age. There's a chance she could roll on one of them while she's sleeping if they're loose. I've heard of livestock doing that."

"Och." Patty makes a pained expression. "That would be tragic. Imagine the horror."

The hiss and rattle of scales rubbing against stone precede the arrival of our hostess. "Mother of Wyrms, you've come as requested."

"Yes, Majesty." I drop my gaze and pull my sleeve back into place. "Patty mentioned you wanted to see me and talk to me about something. I came as soon as I was free."

She continues forward into the cavern to join us. The muscles in her body tense and release to propel her across the polished stone floor. If I weren't so intimidated by her size and ferocity, I would consider her a miraculous creature.

When she's fully in the main chamber, her body coils and ropes while her head and first sections of her body rear up like a cobra about to strike. As always, I'm struck by my first instinct of melting into a trembling puddle of goo.

If she opens her mouth and descends over me, she'll swallow me in one violent snap.

"I have much to tell you, but first, you must meet the little ones." She tips her head back and emits a guttural screech that harkens a "nails on the chalkboard" pitch. It seems to act as a dragon whistle though, because a second later, the stone is gone and the floor writhes with royal blue, shimmering gold, emerald green, and candy apple red wyrmlets.

"Wow. Look at how much they've grown." My reaction is genuine, although creeped out. When I left a month ago, the newborns were the size and shape of mucousy, slithery ferrets. Now they are much closer to flipperless seals.

"Do they bite?"

I ask because they're now wriggling around my feet and there's no possibility of me stepping away without stomping on one—which I'm sure wouldn't please the Queen Mum.

"Och, every chance they get, the wee rascals. They especially enjoy sinking their teeth into flesh and giving it a good chomp when they're hungry. They fed well last night, though, so your ankles should be spared."

Comforting. "Speaking of feeding last night." I use Patty's comment to segue. "Were you by chance feeding on sheep and discovered men destroying trees?"

"Yes," the queen hisses. "That's what I wanted to talk to you about. When I broke free of the ground, three men cloaked in black were intent on consuming the life force from a fae grove.

They were maliciously siphoning the power of ancient fae magic. I consumed them, of course."

"Of course."

"I despair not all the trees of the hidden ones were spared, but I didn't arrive until after the carnage had begun."

"I'm sure you did everything you could. The Doyles are lucky you were there. Mrs. Doyle asked me to extend her joy that your actions spared most of her forest."

"Tell her that I could not allow the willful destruction of such a well-kept and honored grove. But know this, Fiona Cumhaill, the men who perpetrated the crime didn't act alone. The people they are with are determined to weaken the guardians of nature."

"How do you know that's what they wanted?"

"Because I ate them."

I blink, waiting…but no, that's all the answer I get.

Patty chuckles and takes pity on me. "When a wyrm dragon consumes a creature's noggin', there is a wisdom transfer release into her cells."

It almost kills me not to say the words *brains* and *dragon zombie*, but somehow, I choke that impulse down. "You're saying she ate them and afterward, she could tell what they were thinking?"

"Exactly."

"And they want to destroy the sacred groves of the Elders of the Order of Druids to weaken their powers?"

"Destroying them is of secondary benefit." The dragon queen dips her chin. "Consuming the power of the hidden ones is their primary goal. I wanted to warn you because your people are among the founding nine and surely have a grove to protect, yes?"

"We are, and we do. I appreciate the warning." A particularly assertive baby dragon uses the bodies of his brothers and sisters to climb me. It's a blue one, and I can tell it's a boy because he has the three-pronged spike at the end of his tail. "Hello, there."

"He remembers you. How sweet," the queen coos.

"Is this the firstborn?" I look down and stroke my fingers over his plated face. He has a weird crested ridge across his face that looks like a chiseled, scaly unibrow. It comes down his face into a horned snout, and I realize I'm in trouble. It's a face only a mother could love—and yet I do.

Oh no. I really am the Mother of Wyrms.

"Hello, little dude. Do you remember me?"

He's straining to climb me, so I wrap my arms around him and give it a go. He's not as slimy as I thought he'd be and when I hold him, he stops wriggling and lets out a soft purring noise.

"Och, that wee one's in love." Patty smiles and reaches over to stroke the blue dude's back. "They only purr like that when they're truly content."

"Would you like to take him with you, Fiona Cumhaill? You gave me twenty-three children, but you could have a wyrm dragon son of your very own."

I smile down at the giant blue reptilian slug in my arms and consider it. Briefly. "I'd love him, but he's better off with you and his siblings. I live in a city, and he'd have nowhere to roam. You know how to feed him and keep him safe. I'll visit though, I promise. Whenever I come back, I'll visit."

"Spoken with the love of a true mother," the queen says. "Sacrificing your heart's need for the benefit of your young. I shall continue his care on your behalf."

"Perfect. I'm destined to come back and take my grandfather's place as Shrine-Keeper when he passes, so you never know, it might work out for us in a few years."

"A few years is a blip in the life of a wyrm dragon. It's settled. You may reclaim him then."

I didn't claim him in the first place, did I?

I force a smile and nod. "Okeedokee. I should be going. My family is waiting, and I want to relay your warning. How do I get back to my grandparent's home?"

"The same way ye got here, Fi." Patty taps his upper arm, right above his elbow. "Yer dragon band can be used as a portal to and from the lair from anywhere in the world and at any time."

Okay, good to know.

I rub the boxy snout of the baby dragon and set him down with his siblings. "Bye, little blue dude. Grow up big and strong and be a good boy for your queen."

After I say goodbye to Patty and Her Scaly Scariness, I pull up my sleeve and hope I can materialize in the right place two times in a row. If bad guys are after my family's grove of power, we need to be ready for them.

Gripping the infinity dragon banding my arm, I focus on my grandparent's property and getting there before the men in black cloaks target our family grove.

It's long past dark when I arrive, but the good news is that I'm standing in Gran's kitchen. I'm thankful to be there and that we didn't lose seven weeks this time. I figure if what felt like eleven days in the presence of a greater fae creature was seven weeks, then every six hours is a day, so every hour would be four and a bit… Right?

Does that make sense?

I think so.

Anyway, it's dark outside, but I can still smell dinner in the air, so I think it's still the same day I arrived. I hope so.

"Fi, *mo chroí*." Da jogs in from the living room to hug me. "Yer back. Are ye all right?"

I soak in Da's embrace, and Kinu and Gran join us. "Ye look in better shape than yer last return from that place," Gran says. "And ye smell a great deal better too."

"Are you hungry, Fi?" Kinu moves toward a ceramic cover and

lifts it to show me a stacked plate. "We fought off the fiends and saved you some dinner."

"Starving, thanks. And yeah, it went fine. Just like Patty promised. It was a quick visit with friends."

"Ye've been gone for hours, luv." Gran punches time into the microwave.

I head over to the sink and wash up. "From my perspective, it was much faster. It felt like a half an hour, maybe an hour tops, so it probably was about four here if my math works out."

"About that." Da points at the table.

I take my cue and plunk down on the end chair. "And the boys are out there with Granda and Bruin?"

"They are. Sloan went home to update his parents and help safeguard their grove."

"Good. That's good."

"So, what did ye find out from the she-dragon?"

I fill Da in on what the Queen Dragon said and thank Gran when she sets a steaming plate of coddle in front of me. I smile and breathe in the succulence of sausage, potato, and bacon. "And when she said the men were all wearing black cloaks, I couldn't help but think of Barghest."

"Ye think they're global?" Da's tone seems skeptical.

"Who are these Barghest fellows?" Gran asks.

"The ones who came after me in Toronto. The ones who kidnapped me that day and took me to the stones, remember?"

"Och, I remember. I was scared out of my wits for ye."

I blow on a forkful of dinner. "That was Barghest."

"Did ye mention that name to yer Granda, luv? Because I'm sure I've heard the term before." Gran gets up and heads out of the room. A few minutes later, she returns with a big old book called *Magical Creatures of the Ages*. "See here. The Barghest is a massive, mythical black dog thought to be a demon or a ghost or perhaps a goblin of some kind. Whatever its origins, it's known to be vicious and deadly."

"So, the clandestine group trying to get rid of druids in Toronto and possibly here as well named themselves after a big black dog. That seems less scary than I thought."

"Maybe." Da grips the handle of the water jug and fills me up. "But it doesn't change a thing. We still don't know who's behind them or why they're set on bringing down the Order."

"True." I try to chew and swallow at a normal pace, but I'm ravenous, and this coddle is *soooo* good. "But it's still information we didn't have a few hours ago. When I finish, I want to go out to the grove and talk to Bruin. I think I might grab a sleeping bag and stay out there with him tonight."

Gran nods. "I'll put together another bedroll and pillow for ye to take out after ye've had yer fill."

Red, wake up.

I hear Bruin's deep, rich timbre in my mind. He's speaking to me using our internal connection, and I blink awake. By the burning behind my eyes and my lead-laden lids, it couldn't be more than three or four hours since I laid my head down.

Don't speak, he directs. *Don't startle, but yer not alone.*

Is it Black Dog?

No. It's the hidden folk. The fae of the forest have come, and they seem quite curious about ye. They're creepin' close and are timid wee things. Ye don't want to give them a fright.

Should I sit up and talk to them?

I don't know. I've never seen so many gatherin'. What do ye think they want?

I won't know unless I interact with them. I lay there still for a moment longer before I crack my eyes open. The three-quarter moon casts a silvery light on the mossy clearing we chose to hunker down in. When my eyes adjust, it's enough to see about fifteen feet in every direction and not much more.

At first, I simply look and smile, but don't move.

Bruin's right. Gathered around our sleeping bag grouping, a dozen fae folk are checking us out. I wish I knew more about the different fae species to be able to identify what they are, but some are winged people as tiny as hummingbirds. Others are no bigger than Meg and have bobbing antennae and globe eyes, and others are the size of small humans but gaunt and with branches and leaves growing out of their arms and head.

I tilt my head up a little and smile. "Hello."

Some of the hummingbird people flit back a few feet, but one of the tree ladies steps closer. "Merry meet, fleshy one."

Very slowly, and with my smile still firmly in place, I roll to sit up. Calum and Emmet are sound asleep in their sleeping bags beside me. Two of the hummingbird people seem particularly interested in Emmet's snoring.

"I'm pleased to meet you all." I keep my voice quiet and my expression friendly. "I am Fiona."

"Lady Cumhaill, kin come from afar. Descendant of Fionn, we know who you are. You wear his mark. It is there on your back. He stood our warrior, but your skills lack."

Okay, ouch. The Tree of Life tattoo on my back appeared the morning after I first encountered Sloan. He assessed my latent druid abilities and found me with the strongest affinity of those in my family.

I've thought about it a hundred times and believe that something he did triggered Fionn's attention because it was then that my ancestor marked me with the Fianna crest and my life began to change.

"I am not the warrior he was, no. The druid world is new to me, but I am honored and determined to follow his path."

"Fledgling are you. A great eagle was he. Yet you sleep on our roots to safeguard our trees?"

I'm not sure what Fionn did to safeguard the fae folk, but I can't imagine I would do any less. "I do. There are bad men intent on harming the druid sacred groves. One has already been destroyed and another damaged."

The tree lady dips her chin. "We mourn the slaughter of life and land. But viler still to be bound to command."

I realize then, Emmet has fallen quiet and the two of them have grown eerily still. I don't look over, but I know they're awake and listening.

"Bound to command? I don't understand." Okay, now she has me rhyming. "Who's bound to whom?"

"Not all druids value nature and life. Others gain power through death and strife."

Right. The Black Dog are dark druids. They are definitely the death and strife types.

"And that's why they're destroying the druid groves? It's not to weaken the Nine Families as we thought. It's to access the power of the fae folk living within."

She dips her head again and gestures a leafy palm toward the surrounding trees. "The dawning of truth begins our defense. Free the dead taken and right the offense."

I'm not a hundy percent on what she's saying, but I get the gist of it. "I'll do my best. Your insights are well received. I value your trust in me."

"Trust is earned, and this is your test. A warrior grows most on a quest."

They need me to stop the Black Dog from destroying the fae forests and free the ones taken. I survey the hopeful glances of the fae folk and nod my understanding. "Namaste."

"Namaste."

The tree lady bows her twig antlers and backs away. Soon after, the rest of our gathering follows suit. A moment later, the mossy clearing is empty, and Bruin materializes to sit with me, Calum, and Emmet.

"Always an adventure with you around, Red."

"Holy shit," Emmet exclaims. "Did that happen?"

"Geez, Fi. What is it with you and the fae strange and unusual? You're like a beacon for the bizarre."

I flop back down onto my pillow and snuggle deep into my sleeping bag. "It's my stupid Fianna mark. It's a magnet of mayhem."

Calum scrubs a rough hand over his face and exhales. "Da and Granda will crap themselves when we tell them what happened. Free the dead taken to be bound by command…are we talking necromancy?"

I chuckle. "That's your geek gamer showing. Is that even real? And how could we see them?"

"I have no idea about either question. Should we go find out now or wait until morning?"

"Wait until morning." My mind spins. "There's no sense in getting everyone spooked in the middle of the night. Maybe we can get some sleep."

Emmet barks a laugh. "After that little meet and greet, I may never sleep again."

I close my eyes and try not to think about it. "Believe it or not, I'm getting used to shit like this."

CHAPTER FOUR

"Necromancy?" Granda snaps and reels back in his seat at the head of the table the next morning. "And yer just gettin' around to tellin' us now?"

I scowl at the old man and finish stirring the juice I'm making in the jug. I pour Jackson a half-glass and set the pitcher on the mat in the center of the table. "What could we have done at four in the morning other than rant and stew? I opted to let everyone else sleep and have only the three of us up all night."

"Regardless of when we found out," Da finishes his plate and rises to give Calum his spot, "we're all up to speed now. We know that the attacks aren't about the groves themselves but the link between the groves and the fae folk who inhabit them. Black Dog captured the hidden ones and will drain them for their power and control."

"It's sickening," Gran says. "Where do people like that come from? Have they no sense of honor?"

"I'm afraid not, Mam." Da squeezes her shoulder on his way to the sink. "Fi and Sloan came into contact with the dark magic of the Toronto group, but had never felt the exploited energy of the dead and so didn't recognize it for what it was."

Calum sits at the table and starts in on his breakfast. "It also explains why they wanted to drain Fi on the altar stone and why the human bodies we discovered in the woods were desiccated and drained as well."

"What power did those humans have?" Dillan asks. "This is going to sound horrible, and I don't mean it to, but they were only human."

"Every living thing has power, lad," Granda says. "Druids protect the cyclical balance between death and life. A tree grows strong, dies, decays, nurtures the soil, and spawns new life. It's a slow and powerful sequence of events that progress with the natural order and a rhythm. The same goes for the life spans of animals and humans."

"But the fae hold much more power," Aiden states.

"They do. They offer raw power on an elevated scale."

Aiden leans against the edge of the counter and frowns. "So, these guys are what, druids who want to consume more life so they can stave off death?"

Da nods. "That's a succinct way to look at it, son. Druids who turn to necromancy are looking for instant gratification magic. They believe that out of death comes life, the same as us, but if they can drain and possess that life power they can enhance and extend their life stores."

"What do they think that gets them?" Calum asks. "Superpowers? Immortality?"

"Well, if they have a host of fae to drain and feed off, it's possible. Many fae are immortal. If they captured and bound the creatures from the Perry forest, they already have an undying supply of power."

"And still they wanted more? If the Queen of Wyrms hadn't been appalled by what they were doing and eaten them, they would've drained the Doyle forest too."

"How do we stop them?" Dillan takes his and Aiden's plates to the sink to wash up.

I take his spot and fill a plate. "The fae I spoke to said Fionn had always acted as their champion. She called him their warrior. Maybe there's something in the fortress that will help—a weapon or a spell in a grimoire or something."

"That's likely our best option." Granda pours himself another coffee. "I'll call around to the other families and make sure they know what we're dealing with. Maybe one of them has an ancestral spell to ward against necromancers trespassing onto their property."

"In the meantime," Da rubs his palms together. "We need to train today as planned. Even with the information Fi was given about how to access the fortress and where the traps and wards lay, you all need to know your strengths and limitations before we head off on the quest."

I swallow and reach for my juice. "I texted Sloan this morning and filled him in. He's meeting us in the rings at ten to work on assessing you guys now that we've got real fae energy to power us up."

"Och, luv." Gran restocks the fruit on the bird platform beneath the open skylight. "It must be so difficult for ye to get anythin' done in the city. I wish ye'd all consider comin' home and bein' at one with yer heritage."

I take a couple of sips of juice and set my glass on the table. "I'm more determined than ever that we can be urban druids, Gran. Our grove is starting to take root. And I work for a meliae, and she has power."

Granda sighs. "Tree nymphs get power from their home tree, Fi. Druids get power from our surroundings at large. Yer Gran's not wrong when she says ye'd find greater success here than ye will there."

"Easier and faster success, definitely, but maybe not greater. Toronto offers us things too, and while they might not be the same as what the countryside of Kerry offers, I have no doubt we'll figure it out."

"Besides," Calum points out as he finishes his breakfast. "If the Black Dogs within Toronto have established a base and built druid stones and are thriving there, we can too."

"And we have to," Aiden adds. "If there are dark druids using necromancy to foul our streets, we can't walk away. We've all sworn to serve and protect. Those aren't simply words on our badge. It's our calling."

"Och, I know." Gran hands Granda the cream and sweetener. "I worry, is all. And I hate the thought of ye bein' there alone and facin' darkness without the aid of the Order."

Aiden squeezes Kinu's hand, wipes Jackson's face, and kisses the top of Meggie's ebony mop of curls. "We're Cumhaills, Gran. We don't face anything alone."

Emmet holds out his hand, and I pass him my plate. He goes around the table collecting and stacking the dishes, then hands them off to Calum and Dillan at the sink.

I smile at my brothers, priceless treasures each of them. "We'll make it work, Gran. You'll see. And you never know. Maybe if we prove we can do it, other descendants who left their druid roots behind to live a different life will circle back around and reclaim their heritage."

Gran's smile is indulgent and not at all convincing. "I'm sure you're right, luv. And by the sounds of things, you're off to a grand start."

"Off ye go, now," Granda urges. "It's going on ten, and it's rude to keep people waiting."

I kiss Jackson and Meg and bring my glass to the counter. "Okay, let's see what we have to work with, boys."

The training ring on my Granda's property is something to behold. At first glance, it seems like nothing more than a simple set of round, stepped plateaus sunken into the ground. When you spend a moment studying it, you see the beauty—or at least, I do.

Three cylindrical rings styled after an ancient Greek amphitheater cut deep into the ground and tighten in diameter. With each three-foot drop into the descending landscape, the rings narrow. At the bottom, a flat circle of manicured grass acts as the training floor.

Although it's grass and not sand, and we're druids and not gladiators, the marvel doesn't diminish. It's cool.

Over the next hours, my brothers and I fill the rings with laughter and grunts and more than a few curse words. Da reunites with his old competition staff and challenges us, three on one. It's no contest. He's a phenom.

His prowess is both surprising and not. I've long believed there is nothing Da can't do. He tends to prove me right more often than not.

Sloan assesses each of my brothers individually and off to the side while we train. Aiden's primary discipline is Physical, like Da. Calum's is Communication, Dillan's is Illusion, and Emmet's is Healing. He retests me, and while my physical strengths are still dominant, my connection with nature and weather are close runners-up. Communication is strong too.

"Watch yer guard, Fi," Da shouts.

The end of Calum's wooden sword whistles past my cheek. It's close enough that it catches my hair as I spin my head and my heart thunders in my chest. I anticipate what's coming next though.

After Calum swings, he lunges with his left foot. I'm ready for it, swipe his leg, and launch at him, taking him to the ground. His back hits the ground hard, and he lets out a breathy grunt.

I hold my practice sword to his throat and grin. "Say it, Cumhaill. Let me hear the magic words."

"Mercy," he wheezes. "Fi is the Queen of Amazeballs."

Bruin's burly laughter rumbles from the sidelines.

"Yes, I am. Thank you for noticing."

Calum laughs, and I bounce, perched on his chest. "You're also so incredibly humble."

I roll off him and allow him to get reacquainted with respiration. "You are a wise and perceptive man."

"Cumhaill. Are ye ready to take off the trainin' wheels, then? Do ye think ye have what it takes to best someone *not* in the infancy of trainin'?"

I straighten and meet the challenge in Sloan's mint-green gaze. "You sure you're ready for what I've got going on? I am reigning Queen of Amazeballs."

He adjusts his workout pants against his muscled thighs, crouches into a ready position, and flicks his fingers in invitation. "Then ye can consider this a coup against the queen. Defend yer crown, Cumhaill."

His hands are empty, so I toss my practice sword to the ground, and we circle. My muscles are already fatigued and quivering from taking on Da and Calum, but there is no way I'll give in to a direct challenge from Sloan.

"I've been practicing." I shift my bare feet in the grass as we circle. "I'm not the same fighter you took on in Toronto last month."

"Yer still as mouthy and cock-sure."

"And you're as autocratic and rude."

He flashes me his GQ supermodel grin, and I curse myself inwardly. It galls me that I melt a little when he looks at me like that, but I refuse to give in.

I am woman. Hear me roar.

"What do you do around here besides stomp and strut around like the peacock prince?"

His grin widens. "Stall all ye want, ye wee girl. Ye won't find a weakness. If yer scared, say so. Ye've admitted as much to me before."

Laughter bubbles up my throat, and I burst out laughing. "I

confessed I was afraid to face Baba Yaga alone. That's not fear, that's intelligence."

"Whatever ye say."

I shake out my hands, ready to get this show on the road. "Show me what you think you've got going on, big boy."

Emmet hangs his head forward and groans. "We get it. You're both aces. Can we fast-forward through the bravado and get to the ass-whooping?"

"Exactly." Aiden folds his muscular arms over his chest. "You're wasting daylight, you two."

I lunge forward and feel Sloan's magic tingle over my skin a second before I fall to the ground stiff as a board. "Stop thinkin' like a civilian, Cumhaill. Yer a caster—so, cast!"

I hear the frustration in his voice, and it lights my temper.

Sloan picks up the wooden sword and points the tip against my chest. "If this were a battle, I'd have ye dead to rights. Raise the bar. Figure out what I cast against ye. Break the spell and defend yerself."

I growl and focus on breaking his hold on me. Heat burns my cheeks, and blood rushes in my veins. I'm spitting mad by the time I roll onto my hands and push up onto my feet.

Gone is my playful mood. I want to take him down.

Focused on my next attack, I cast a confusion spell and push it out at him. He raises his hand and mutters something in tongues. I lose focus immediately and blink at the worried faces of my brothers.

Why do they look sad?

"Come on, Cumhaill. Ye may have managed to live through the assault of the Black Dog when they underestimated ye, but another surge is comin'. Ye need to be better."

"All right." Dillan steps into the ring. "Enough."

"Leave them." Da holds up his hand. "Better she learns the lesson here than at the hands of the enemy."

What lesson? Why is my head swimming in a brain fog?

Damn it. I focus on breaking my rebounded spell and ball my fists at my sides. As I fight myself free of the confusion, my eyes sting with the fury of traitorous tears.

Sloan watches me, his palms up and at the ready, his gaze appraising. "Focus, Fi. Control yer temper and come at me with a clear plan."

I plan to make him pay for making a fool out of me in front of my family. I swipe my cheek as the wind gusts and picks up around us. My hair whips against my cheeks and his eyes widen as a gale wind gains strength.

"If yer not in control of yer offense, yer out of control and no good to yerself or the others. Don't let yer hubris be the death of one of them."

Emmet curses and throws up his hands. "Yeah, let's piss off the Irish girl. Said no one—ever."

"Yer out of control." Sloan lowers his chin and meets my gaze with a focus I feel right to the core of my chest. "Yer a danger to them. Yer not ready and ye know it."

A crack of lightning splits the sky.

Before it hits the circle where we're standing, Sloan lunges forward and portals us out of the strike zone. The moment my feet touch the ground, I punch him in the gut and push away.

I want him to shut up.

I want him to be wrong.

He's not. I'm not ready, and now it's not only dark druids coming at us, but they're also life-sucking necromancers. It's not only me in the line of fire. It's my family.

"Fiona, ye've got—"

"Not another word." I point my finger at his stupid face. I swipe at the moisture on my cheek and feel the fall-apart barreling down on me. "You made your point, asshole. I'm in over my head, and you're a thousand times better than me at everything. Congrats. I vote for you to take it from here. Problem solved."

He opens his mouth to speak, but whatever he sees in my face cuts that shit off quickly. I turn on my heel, then stomp to the steps and leave the training rings in my dust.

I'm halfway back to the house when I remember Aiden, Kinu, and the kids are using the spare bedroom I consider my private space. I have nowhere to run and hide. I take a hard left and step into the grove.

The trees still hold their full foliage from summer, and it's cool and peaceful. Nature surrounds me with its blanket of calm and I can breathe again. Deep in the trees, I call on Feline Finesse and climb forty feet into the canopy.

Alone at last, I sit in a wide intersection of branches and bring my knees to my chest.

Imposter syndrome is real, and I've been outed.

Sure, in an hour or two I'll pull myself together and lift my chin. For now—alone in the strong arms of this tree—I'm overwhelmed. I wrap my arms around my shins and release my insecurities.

It's dark when Da climbs up my tree and perches on my branch. My ass is long past numb, and I've finished my pity-party. I'm just too stubborn to face the humiliation of worried glances and turning heads of a well-meaning family.

"That bad, is it?" He holds out his arm.

I scootch over on the branch and sit beside him so he can rest his arm over my shoulder. "Worse."

"Ye think so?"

"Sloan pushed every button I have, and I completely lost focus. He always tells me to stop fighting like I'm in a city alley and start thinking about things like a druid. I never do. It doesn't come naturally to me."

"Ye've been a normal, human scrapper for twenty-three years and a druid for three months, Fi. Give yerself time."

"We don't have time. I blew it today."

"And tomorrow, ye'll do better."

I stare up between the overlapping leaves at the moon and wish I could go back six months to when a night out was a few drams of whiskey with the boys and a spin on the dance floor with Liam. "How stupid was I to think I could do this?"

Da chuffs. "Fiona Kacee Cumhaill, in all the years of bein' yer Da, I've known ye to be a great many things—stupid has never been one of them."

I lean my head back against the trunk of the tree and draw a deep breath. The ambient power is strong. It makes me feel strong. It's a placebo effect, and I have to remember that.

"I think the reason it stung so much is that he's right. I'm not ready, and I'm going to be the reason one of you gets hurt, or worse. We lost Brendan. I can't lose anyone else."

"Och, now, I'll disagree with you there. Sloan meant well, but that boy has the social grace of a blind rhino in a crystal palace. Despite bein' the center of our world, ye can't take on the responsibility of our health and safety."

"Why not? You're all here because of me and the decisions I made. Sloan is an ass, but he's smart. He knows how much I love all of you and what it'll do to me if I screw up and one of you gets hurt."

"And how do ye think we'd feel if ye went it alone and yer the one who gets hurt? We lived through seven weeks of that hell. Not one of us ever wants to suffer that again. I saw Sloan's face when ye ran off. He never meant to cut ye so deeply or embarrass ye in front of yer brothers. He wants ye to understand that thinkin' yerself ready is dangerous. Ye don't know what ye don't know, and those who know more will exploit yer confidence."

"I get that, but we were training amongst ourselves not fighting the enemy. He didn't need to be such a douche."

Da shrugs. "His parents are strict warriors, luv. Harsh reality is what he knows. When ye train, ye teach yer mind and yer muscles how to react. If ye don't train as if yer life depends on it, ye won't be ready when it does."

I sigh. "Fine. I'll give him that, but I'm still mad."

"As is he. He's scared for ye, *mo chroi.* We all are. Since Fionn marked ye, it seems yer in the sights of the entire fae realm. Hard truths are what Sloan knows. In his way, he was tryin' to help ye grow."

I blow out a long breath. "He's still an autocratic dick."

Da chuckles. "I'll not argue with ye there. Come now. Yer brothers are havin' a few beers around the bonfire. It's not the same without ye there to razz them. And ye needn't worry. Sloan has long since given up waitin' to apologize. He went home with a storm cloud over his head and shadows in his eyes. If ye wanted him to suffer, I'd say ye got yer wish."

"It's not about that. I just..." I shake my head and sigh. "I want this, Da. I want to be great at it. I want to live up to what everyone needs me to be, and when I fail, it hurts."

"I know, *mo chroi.* Come now. Drink a few drinks and tomorrow will be a better day. Look at it this way. Ye called a lightning strike. That takes juice. Take the win."

CHAPTER FIVE

As Da predicts, a full night of sleep does improve my outlook. I have a nice family breakfast, play outside with the kids for an hour, then Kinu and Gran take the monkeys on an exploring tour of the property while we get out the notes I scribed about how to find and access the Fianna fortress.

I study the faces of my family as the discussion progresses and settle into what's to come. I push my worries down, and although they push back up at me like an underwater beachball, I'm determined to keep them buried long enough to get things done.

Someone suggests that either Granda or Bruin should stay behind and guard the grove and the family while we're gone. Since Granda is a historian and well-versed in druid practices and spells—and because I can call Bruin to me if we need him—my bear gets assigned to guard the homefront.

He's annoyed at the idea of missing an adventure but appeased when I tell him he can Killer Clawbearer any black-cloaked intruders to his heart's content.

After lunch, we stack the remaining road trip supplies and medical gear on the driveway and wait for Sloan to make his appearance. The Land Rover won't fit all of us, so we'll also need his Kodiaq. I'd rather make the trip in one vehicle but eight people in seven seats won't work well for a lengthy trip.

I hear the crunch of his tires on the gravel lane before the truck passes beneath the arch of the shrub hedge. His absence has held a looming tension for me, but his arrival spikes my anxiety meter's needle into the redline.

He stops in the middle of the driveway and hops out.

My brothers scatter like ants, and I let out a long-suffering breath. That's not awkward at all.

Fine. I'm an adult. Here goes nothing.

I stride straight for him and stop. "I get what you were saying. I'm still mad about how you said it. Today is about the fortress. The end."

I turn to leave, and he catches my wrist. I refuse to look at him and focus on pushing my beachball of worries back down. "Sloan, don't. I need to focus."

"Then let me apologize so I can too."

"You apologized by text."

"And ye likely didn't read past the first line."

No. I didn't. "Still, you apologized."

"Fiona, look at me."

I pull up my big girl panties, draw a deep breath, and face him. Before he can speak, I take control of the convo.

"I get it. You want me to go into things with a realistic view of my abilities and my shortcomings. You suck at communication, and you duffed the delivery. Point made. I'm well aware I have a long way to go, but if you think humiliating me was the best way to explain that to me, you don't understand me at all. You hurt me, Sloan. Don't do it again."

I pull my hand free from his grasp and head to the Land Rover. "All right, family. Let's head out."

When I Google the drive distance from Granda's place in the Kerry countryside to the Hill of Allen north of Kildare, I get a travel time of between three and four hours depending on the route. I don't know the roads, so I can't give an opinion about which way we go, but thankfully I don't have to. Granda and Sloan know where we're headed so I'm free to sit in the back and read over my notes.

"Sloan spoke to me last night about the assessments of yer skills and where the boys fit into that," Da says. "He's impressed by the diversity and thinks once ye develop into yer own, we'll have one hell of a collection of skills in Toronto."

"I wondered about the diversity too. Do most children follow in the disciplines of one or both of their parents? He has the warrior from his mother and the healer from his father. Is that normal?"

"As a rule, it goes like that, although it's by no means uncommon to get outliers."

Granda joins the conversation. "Sloan's powers may be indicative of his parents' disciplines, but he's different too. There was never a wayfarer in the Mackenzie line, and then, there he was."

I picture him again as a five-year-old standing in the kitchen in his jammies. I lean closer to Granda while Aiden and Da talk. "You and Gran mean the world to him."

"And he to us." Granda meets my gaze in the rearview. "Ye must forgive him his shortcomings, *mo chroi*. He's taken a great many knocks to his confidence, but I've never seen him as lost as he was last night. It's not only yer gran and I who mean the world to him."

I lean back into my seat and gaze out the window at the passing scenery. "I'm focused on being a druid, Granda. I'm clear on that. Sloan made it crystal clear that I've got a long way to go in my training. I'm not interested in taking on anything else until that's finished."

"Message received." He focuses on the road ahead. "We should arrive in Kildare an hour before the quarry shuts down. We'll get some dinner at a local pub and get situated before dark. Once we're sure the workers are clear for the day, we'll move in."

"Sounds good."

The Hill of Allen is a seven hundred eighteen-foot mound of forested earth. The west side has been heavily quarried, and the construction is eating into the core of the hill.

"According to Trip Advisor," I flip to the next screen on my cell, "if we approach from the northeast side of the hill, just off the roadside, there is space enough to park. From what Fionn's fish wisdom told me, there is a row of large boulders there, and through them, we'll find a clearing with an old stone altar."

Granda looks back at me and frowns. "I'm surprised that we're stopping there and looking for the entrance. There's a stone tower farther up the hill believed to be part of Fionn's fortress."

I shake my head. "That was built later. Fionn's fortress is underground. I figure the trick will be finding the entrance after all this time."

The trick isn't finding the entrance but figuring out how to access it. The information I wrote down, most specifically the coordinates, leads us straight to a crevasse in the rocky stone of the ground. Dillan finds the opening, and we all sense the rightness of it as the access point.

After staring at it and wondering what to do next, Dillan clears away a layer of old growth to expose a stone chiseled with a message. "Damn, and me without my decoder ring. Granda or Sloan, you're up."

The two of them kneel over the missive and mumble about the ancient Celtic symbology. When I'm beginning to wonder if we'll be stuck here under analysis paralysis for the rest of our lives, Sloan nods and straightens. "The inscription translates to…

Passage gained at end of day.

Sacrifice of blood to pay.

Aiden's brow arches. "Seriously?"

I make a face and look back down into the dark crack in the earth. "Sloan, whose affinity is strong in paying the blood sacrifice?"

Sloan lifts his palms. "I would, really, but since it's Fionn's ward, and he's demanding blood, I'd say ye have the best chance of success if the plasma comes from Clan mac Cumhaill."

Dillan laughs. "Nice. You tried to sound intellectual there, but it still smells like chicken."

Emmet lets out a couple of clucks and pumps his elbows.

Sloan doesn't engage.

Unfortunately, I agree with him. "Okay, Aiden, slice my hand with your pocketknife."

"What? Why?" He looks at me like I've grown a couple of extra hydra heads.

"Because I want to be bleeding when I stick my hand down the creepy booby-trap hole."

"Ha! You said booby," Emmet laughs.

"It doesn't have to be you." Da throws Emmet a look. "If Sloan's instinct is right, and I believe it is sound logic, the blood could come from any one of us."

I wave away his fatherly concern. "If Fionn came and went from this place regularly, it stands to reason that the blood sacrifice doesn't have to be big. It's simply to prove that we belong here. Aiden. Your knife."

The oldest of the six of us, he's only slightly less protective of me than Da. He pulls out his knife, then looks at the crack. "I honestly would do it, but I couldn't get my hand down there if I tried."

"It's fine." I hold out my hand. "Getter done, Cumhaill."

"Let me do it." Emmet thrusts his hand forward. "We all know I have freakishly delicate girl hands and if my affinity is healing, I'll mend faster than Fi. Right, Sloan?"

"Having an affinity for healin' means ye can heal others. It doesn't give ye regenerative powers like Wolverine."

I frown. "And your hands are not freakish girl hands. Besides, if your power is healing, you can help Sloan heal me if things go badly."

Emmet looks like he's considering that, then shakes his head. "No. Let it be me. I'm good."

Sloan agrees. "My vote's on Emmet. No offense, my friend, but this is yer sister's quest. She should remain whole and unscathed as long as possible for the trials to come."

"Agreed." Da gives us the nod of final decision. "Emmet, it's you."

I roll my eyes and give them all a look. "Fates protect me from well-meaning men."

"No need," Da counters. "Yer well-meaning men will do the protectin' for ye."

I blow Da a kiss and watch as Emmet grips his fingers around Aiden's knife blade. With a grimace and a hiss, he pulls the steel free of his grasp and kneels over the crevasse.

"Okay, Granda-Fionn, here's the sacrifice of my blood."

As he reaches toward the crack in the earth, the stone shifts, widening the opening to accept his hand.

"Well, there," Calum says. "We didn't need Emmet's freakishly girly hands."

Emmet scowls and continues lowering his arm. "Yeah, good to know for next time, eh?"

We all wait, wondering what's supposed to happen. When

nothing does, we end up staring at one another with blank expressions all around.

"Okay, what now?" Emmet asks.

"Feel around in there?" I suggest. "Is there a button or a lever or something that will unlock the door?"

Dillan snorts. "You think there's a doorknob in the earth to unlatch the booby-trapped entrance to a druid fortress?"

We all look at Emmet, who's chuckling. "Booby."

I shrug. "What's your suggestion, Einstein?"

"Wait," Sloan says.

We all freeze and stare at Emmet.

"What wait?" I'm afraid of what's happening. "Why's your face screwed up weird like that?"

Sloan scowls. "I was thinking. And this is what my face always looks like."

Thankfully not, but I don't voice that opinion. "Okay, wait for what? Did you come up with something?"

He points at the tangerine skyline behind the trees bordering the clearing. "The first part of the inscription is, 'Passage gained at end of day.' It stands to reason that now that the sun is setting…"

"Yep. I feel it," Emmet says. "Got it."

Something rumbles in the earth below our feet. I'm staring at Emmet—armpit deep in the rock crevasse—when my footing gives way. Instead of a doorway appearing, the ground beneath me is suddenly gone.

"Oh shit—"

I freefall into the depths of the hill.

Slow Descent!

Sloan and I crash-land in a heap of tangled limbs and I hear the "oof" as Sloan hits the ground with me on top of him. We're at the base of a steep set of roughhewn steps, and my brothers are racing down the treads, calling my name.

"I'm fine." I roll off Sloan and rest on my knees for a sec while

I catch my breath. "Sloan caught me. Well, sort of caught me. Mostly, he broke my fall."

Calum and Aiden help Sloan up, and Da gets me to my feet. "Are ye hurt?"

I brush the dirt off my palms and wipe the side of my face with the back of my wrist. "I'm fine. Good job on releasing the door, Emmet. We better get our lights out before—" I almost finish my warning before the door reforms "—we're sealed in pitch darkness."

"On it." the sound of a zipper, some rummaging, then a *click* accompanies Aiden's reassurance. A wide beam of light streams from a four-inch square, handheld spotlight. "Let there be light."

Dillan's backpack has the super bright penlights, and we each take one and wrap the strap around our wrists. It may not be very druid in Sloan's eyes, but hey, we can't all cast illumination spells, so it works.

"Okay, so, we're in." Da wraps Emmet's palm with a roll of gauze. "Lead the way, Fi. We're all with ye."

"Do you want me to heal that?" Sloan asks with less gusto than usual.

"No, son." Da tests that Sloan's steady. "Catch yer breath. We appreciate yer quick thought, by the way."

"Yeah," Aiden adds. "We owe you one for being her landing pad."

"I'd say it was my pleasure," he twists his back a little and winces, "But Mam taught me never to lie."

"Are ye hurt, my boy?" Granda asks.

"I'll be fine, Lugh. Just tweaked my back a bit. She was a bit of a flailing mess on the way down."

I snort. "Sorry. The next time I fall to my death, I'll try to have better form and stick the landing."

CHAPTER SIX

"And around this corner," I flash my penlight on my notes, "there should be an upright chest on the left that releases poisonous snakes. We have to render them harmless to pass. It says they'll spill out onto the stone of the floor and need to be tamed or convinced we belong here."

"I'll take this one," Granda states.

I move to let him pass. We've been making our way like this, each intruder alert taken on by one of my brothers or Sloan, in turn. That's the problem with being surrounded by heroes and adrenaline junkies. If you don't keep them from getting bored, they'll get into trouble.

"Will they still be alive?" Dillan asks. "Fionn has been dead for centuries."

"They're magical snakes lying in wait," Da reminds him. "If Fionn was as skilled and powerful as he's said to be, the spell will activate after millennia."

"Is anyone else getting an Indiana Jones vibe here?" Calum asks. "Snakes. Why did it have to be snakes?"

Emmet nods. "We named the dog, Indiana."

"That's why they call it the jungle, sweetheart," Dillan adds, putting on the accent.

"Quiet, now." Granda shakes out his hands.

We all grow still and watch. I saw Granda in action when we were attacked on his back lawn a few months ago. He's much more powerful than he looks. Still, I have no idea what kind of skill it takes to calm killer guard snakes.

Granda inches forward, his boots crunching on the pebbled stone floor. When his weight shifts and he steps beside the upright chest, there's a pregnant pause and a breathy hiss. The doors of the cabinet swing open, and a landslide of slithering snakes hits Granda.

I feel both the magic of the spell and Granda's signature energy tingle over my skin. His palms are down, his fingers spread wide. Like Sloan, Granda doesn't need to cast aloud, so I don't know what spell he's using.

Doesn't matter. After a few tense moments, the snakes calm. Then *pop,* they're gone.

"Good one, Granda," Emmet says.

I catch the glint of pride in Sloan's eyes as he smiles. "Well done, Lugh."

"All right," Granda says. "Off we go. We've got a long way to go and a short time to get there."

"Wait," Dillan says. "Isn't that a Foreigner song?"

"It's not," Da corrects. "That's *Long Long Way From Home*. Yer thinking of *Eastbound and Down* by Jerry Reed."

"I thought the Road Hammers did that one."

"*Eastbound and Down,* is that the one from Smokey and the Bandit?"

"That's the one."

I blink at them and wave. "Hello? Can we rein in the mental meltdown? Evil poisonous snakes are taken care of, but we're still on a quest here."

Da smiles. "Sorry, *mo chroi.* Letting off some tension."

I chuckle and get back to my notes while leading the way. We pass the upright chest and follow the corridor down and to the left. When we make the next turn, I frown at the landslide of rubble and stone blocking our path. "Well, crap. Things were going so smoothly, too."

Aiden frowns. "Do you think the vibration from the gravel quarry shook this loose? This is the westernmost end of the fortress, isn't it?"

Dillan nods. "It is. I think yer right."

"Do we double back or dig?" Emmet asks.

I flip through the notes and find the layout map. After I look at it, I hand it to Da and draw a line with my finger. "If we go back to where Sloan disenchanted the broken swords from impaling us at the armory, we might be able to use this back hall to get to the Grand Hall."

"Do we have the booby-trap cheat sheet for that back section of the fortress?" Aiden asks.

We all look at Emmet, but he waves off the attention. "I'm done now. No more booby giggles. I'm over it."

So, back to Aiden's cheat sheet question. "No. I'm guessing Fionn's plan was us taking the most direct route."

"There were rudimentary tools in the repair room of the armory," Calum says. "Maybe it's better to dig and stay the course we know versus exploring blindly."

"I agree with Calum," Dillan says. "It puts us back on time, but that's better than a poison dart to the throat. Besides, we're not sure how to get out of here. Did anyone else worry about that when the door sealed behind us?"

Everyone's hand goes up except mine.

"Okeedokee, well, I'm worried *now*. Thanks for that."

"It's decided then," Dillan says, "we'll dig and try to move forward instead of wandering around and getting dead."

I nod and tuck the map away. "Perfect. Luckily, that works with my plan."

When the boys turn to go, Da puts up his hand. Granda and Sloan are looking at us like we're daft and they're deciding whether to be annoyed or amused.

"What?" I ask.

Sloan shrugs. "Well, yer obviously not the only one having trouble connecting with the fact that yer druids now. Guys, it's a dirt slide. And what domain do druids possess power over?"

"Nature." I turn to look at the rubble. "*Ohhhh*, so we don't have to dig?"

"No, Fi," Granda agrees. "We don't have to dig."

Da cracks his knuckles and steps forward. "Ye'll get there, kids. Ye've had to rely on yer strength and wits yer whole lives. Switching yer mindset to use yer powers will take time and practice."

He steps into the center of the corridor and raises his hands. "*Move Earth*." He gestures with his hands where the dirt should go. He makes great progress, and the soil shifts and splits. In no time at all, the dirt lines the outer edges of the corridor. We follow behind him as he clears our path, and we move another twenty or thirty feet deeper into the hill.

That's when things get mucky.

"Okay, where's the water coming from?" Aiden stares down at the wet sludge advancing on us.

"It's magic." The rightness of my words rings true as I say them. "It has the same energy behind it as the dirt slide. We need to use druid magic to pass this test, too."

"Mr. Cumhaill." Sloan moves in behind him. "Can ye pull the soil from the top? If I can see what's on the other side, maybe I can portal through and see what we're dealing with."

"Is that safe?" My gut says no, but my Spidey-senses aren't tingling. "Don't do anything you're not sure about. We don't want you trapped or hurt by the next trial and us unable to get to you."

"Fi has a point," Granda says. "Take me with you, and we'll work on things together."

"I don't like it."

Granda looks at me and shrugs. "That's it? Do ye have a specific reservation or just that?"

Just that. I don't want them in harm's way. But saying that to druid warriors would not only have them rolling their eyes at me but also insult them and their ability to take care of themselves in a crunch.

"Please be careful."

Da nods at them and raises his arms as he focuses his Move Earth spell toward the top of the sliding, sludgy goo. After a minute or so, Aiden shines his light through to the corridor behind. "Take a look, Sloan. It looks like ten feet of dirt, then a massive chamber. I see tables and chairs."

Sloan nods and holds out his hand, his gaze fixed on the Grand Hall hiding behind the living mud wall. When Granda's hand clasps his, they both disappear.

I'm standing on my tippy-toes and trying to see when Da gets the mud down another foot. He's there. They're there. Safe and sound.

"All right, Niall," Granda calls from the other side of the muddy mess. "I'm going to cast Mud to Stone. When ye feel the shift in form, release yer spell and get the kids through the opening."

"Ready," Da says.

The energy in the air doubles and the creeping progression of the sludge wall slows. A moment later, the mud is solid stone.

"All of ye, up and over," Da orders.

Aiden grabs my hips and lifts me until I can get my knee over the stone dirt pile's top edge. I climb through, followed by Calum, Dillan, and Emmet. Aiden is halfway through when the stone starts to shake.

A rumble beneath my feet has my heart tripping into double-time. "Get out of there."

I rush toward my side of the stone wall. I'm imagining the

horror of the wall turning back to mud and swallowing him when it disappears completely.

Aiden falls to the stone floor and lays prone. I drop to my knees beside him and lean to see his face. "Aid, are you all right? Are you hurt?"

"Ow," he says, breathless.

He doesn't move, so I give him a minute. Da helps him up, and I dust him off.

"You okay, Bro?" Calum checks in.

"Yeah. I'm good." He's holding his left side, and by the pained expression on his face, he's not.

"What is it?" Sloan steps close. "A rib?"

"Maybe a couple." Aiden places a flat hand against his side and grimaces. "I felt them snap when I hit."

I wince, feeling a little woozy. "Sloan? Can you fix it?"

Sloan grins but doesn't look at me. "Of course, I can. Knitting bones is child's play. As long as the bone hasn't punctured a lung or torn an aorta, everything will be grand."

My mind completely skips the grand part and stalls out at the punctured lung or torn aorta. I want to ask what will happen if we're dealing with one of those scenarios but can't bring myself to speak the words.

Aiden will be fine. Next to Da, he's our biggest and strongest hero. He has to be okay.

My woozy feeling grows in strength, and I blink against the hot flash taking hold. I try to focus on what Sloan's doing, but he's blurry and a bit spinny.

"Calum, she's going over."

"Crap on a cracker..."

One minute Sloan's working on Aiden—he's lying on the ground, and I'm standing over him—and the next minute, Sloan's leaning over me, and I'm on the stone floor with Aiden and everyone else leaning over me.

"There ye are." Sloan's hand is cool on my forehead. "Just a faint. Yer fine."

I blink and my cheeks heat. "I fainted?"

"Ye did."

I push him back and sit up. "I don't faint."

"Says the girl drooling on the floor."

I wipe my mouth and glare at Emmet. "I'm not drooling, you dork."

Emmet chuckles and checks the screen of his phone. "Let me see...oh, no, you're right."

"I passed out, and you took pictures of me?"

He pegs me with a look and laughs. "Duh."

"Okay, enough." Da lifts me to my feet. "Ignore yer brother, Fi. Are ye all right, *mo chroi*?"

"Yeah." I move to Aiden and hug him. He's upright and whole and perfectly healthy. "I didn't like seeing Aiden hurt. I guess my panic got away from me. After Brenny..."

Aiden tightens his muscled embrace and kisses my forehead. "I'm good, baby girl. I'm not going anywhere."

I'm shaking and take an extra minute to absorb some of Aiden's strength. "I miss him so much. We can't lose anyone else."

"And we won't," Da says. "That's why we're here, right? We're working on being the strongest and most prepared for the adversity to come. We're leveling up."

I kiss Aiden's dirty cheek and pick at the grit on my lips. "Okay, yuck. Let's get back to it. Just know I love all you knuckleheads and if you die, I'll kill you."

"Back atcha, girlie," Aiden says, and my brothers all nod their agreement. "Now, let's finish this quest and go home. I, for one, need a shower."

I laugh and cast a searching gaze to the ground. "Where are my notes?"

"I've got them, luv." Granda points at his backpack. "Ye won't need them for a bit. We're here, ye see. We're in the Grand Hall of the Fianna sanctuary."

By the light of eight flashlights, the Grand Hall of the Fianna warriors appears to be a forty-foot room, organically shaped with a table-and-chair setup in the middle, statues of warriors along the curved wall behind, and cubbies filled with horn goblets, stone carvings, books and scrolls opposite that.

As cool as it is, there's an eerie feel to it too.

It's like the lives of these ancient men ended and their reality was held in stasis for us to find thirteen hundred years later. Their goblets and cutlery are strewn on the table. The trunks are stacked against the wall by the books.

"Did anyone bring Febreze?" Emmet asks.

I wrinkle my nose. He's not wrong. It smells pithy in here. It's an olfactory trifecta of stale earth, old air, and death.

Awesomesauce.

"Can someone get the lights?" Dillan pans his flashlight into the corners and darkest recesses.

"Are you imagining evil magical spiders coming for you, D?" Calum needles. "I heard Fionn had a thing for spiders."

I catch Sloan's creased brow and lean close. "It's Dillan who has a thing for spiders. They're tormenting him."

Sloan chuckles. "Spendin' time with yer family makes me glad to be an only child at times."

I shake my head. "Never. Tormenting your siblings is the milk of the gods."

"If ye say so."

"Here we are, Dillan," Granda says. "I've got ye, son."

On each side of the entrance stands a metal fire dish held between a tripod of wooden staffs bound by leather thongs.

Granda passes his hand over the container on the right, and it ignites, releasing a glow of golden flames. He repeats the process over the one on the left and continues with the five others around the room.

When all the fires are lit, I turn off my flashlight.

The space emits a different feeling when it doesn't feel like we're sealed inside a gray, lifeless crypt. I study our surroundings and let it soak way down deep.

"Ha! We're in the Fianna-freaking-fortress, bitches!"

My family laughs. They're long used to me. Granda raises a brow, and I'm not sure what the look is that Sloan flashes me. Honestly, I'm so jazzed that I don't care.

I study the room and go for the trunks. "Dibs on anything that fits me."

Aiden and Dillan join me by the iron-bound wooden trunks and start pulling them down from the stack and laying them on the floor. "The Fianna were male warriors, Fi. Unless they had a junior apprentice, I doubt much will fit you."

"These statues are freaking cool," Calum says.

Da and Emmet go over to check those out with him. Granda and Sloan are all about the books and nooks on the opposite wall.

"Dillan, help me lever this sucker open."

As I watch, Aiden and Dillan work on getting the first trunk open. My mind whirs with ideas of what might be inside: treasure, clothes, weaponry, journals, armor…

"Give it up, you bastard," Aiden grunts, really giving it.

"It's not budging," Dillan says.

I chuckle as Sloan's voice speaks in my mind. "I just had an Obi-Wan moment." I avoid any credit to my surly mentor. "It's a druid's chest. Maybe the brute force route isn't the way to go here. All things of nature have intention and purpose. Maybe we need to appeal to the trunk's sense of honor and duty."

I push in and set my hands on the chest. Closing my eyes, I focus my intentions. "Hello, mighty chest." I run my hands over the wood planking and feel the metal barbs of ancient metalwork. "My brothers and I are Fionn's kin and are here on his behalf. I know you're big and strong and supposed to guard his things, but it's okay to let us see what you've got under the hood. We're friends."

"What's she doing?" Emmet asks.

Dillan laughs. "I think she's seducing the chest."

"Kinky."

Aiden chuckles. "Keep at it, Fi. I think you've got it hot and bothered, so don't let him down now. He's panting. Take him home."

I roll my eyes and focus on the chest. "Okay, show them how much you appreciate a little attention. Open Sesame."

A tingle of energy runs up my fingers from where I'm touching the chest and into my wrists and arms. It's a connection, and I allow the magic to assess me. A moment later, the magic quiets and I open the lid.

"Suck it, all ye naysayers."

Emmet snorts. "Fionn was a druid, not a swashbuckler."

Calum laughs. "Oh, good. I'm not the only one who wondered about her going pirate."

Dillan points at the other five. "How much have you got in you, little seductress?"

CHAPTER SEVEN

In the end, the chests hold little more than the dust of old clothing, a few pieces of turned metal Granda says would've been ancient keys and a couple of rudimentary knife blades with no hilts. He says those were likely wood and long ago disintegrated with time.

"Well, that's depressing." I join Sloan and Granda over by the cubbies. "Did you guys find good stuff over here?"

The two of them have cleared the book nooks of all their contents and look like they might burst with excitement.

Granda grips my shoulders in a state of giddy delight I've never seen with him before. "Och, Fi. Ye have no idea the treasures these pieces will be. Even to have a sample of the written word of Fionn…a journal…his thoughts… It means more to me than I can ever express."

"I'm glad you're happy, Granda." And while the historian in him obviously is, that doesn't mean we've scored what we need. "Did you find anything about safeguarding the groves and the hidden folk from necromancy?"

"It'll take time to go through the texts. Ye have to understand, while I read and speak some of the ancient dialects of the Celtic languages, there have been changes over the centuries. What we found here today will take me years to fully understand."

I scratch the tingle at the nape of my neck. "We don't have years, Granda. We have days. The Black Dog wants to consume the life force of the fae creatures in the sacred groves, and I promised the tree lady I'd figure out a way to help."

"We'll figure it out." Sloan sets a couple of scrolls aside and flips through a journal. "Patience is a virtue, remember?"

"Not one of mine." I hear the edge in my voice and let out a heavy sigh. "Sorry. I'm cranky. I thought there would be something cool in those chests. Where are the enchanted weapons and keepsakes Fionn wanted us to collect? If there's nothing here, I failed him."

"Och, yer not going to fail him. Fi, come here to me."

I don't go. I don't want a fatherly pep-talk right now. "Da. There's nothing here. Fionn said the Grand Hall, but there aren't any weapons or keepsakes."

"Fiona Kacee, come here." I give up my obstinance and do as Da asks. He's standing fifteen feet from the statues and staring at them while smiling. "What do ye see?"

I draw a deep breath and look at them. They remind me of the dozens of white marble Greek and Roman statues I've seen at the Royal Ontario Museum. Every year, in every grade, our teachers would take us there for one reason or another. A historical exhibit, dinosaurs, rocks, and minerals, sketching for art class.

These are like those, except all of them have their arms and heads. "I see six stone statues of men—Fianna warriors would be my guess—staged in poses of their strengths and holding stone weapons. The one in the center with his arm raised above his head and wearing the druid crown is Fionn. I recognize him from when we hung out by the fire. I assume the others are his men."

Da nods. "I agree, the man with the bow and quiver would be the range fighter. The one with two daggers is the stealth fighter.

The big boy with the curved blade sword and buckler is a defensive fighter, and so is the one with the staff."

"Who's the streaker?" Emmet points at the naked guy. "Did Fionn mention anything about a kinky love slave?"

Calum laughs and takes a closer look. "My gaydar isn't ringing. I'm going to go with no."

"A nudist, maybe," Dillan muses. "Did druids do the full monte in the seventh century? You know, embrace nature in all its wonder and glory?"

"Maybe his loincloth was at the cleaners when the sculptor stopped by," Aiden offers.

I chuckle and step forward for a closer look. "Do any of you guys feel a draw to any particular statue? Maybe it's because I met Fionn and wear the Fianna shield on my back, but I'd swear his statue is calling to me."

"Now that ye mention it..." Da moves to stand before the defense fighter with the staff. "I thought it was because his staff looks wicked sexy."

"I don't think that's all it is." Dillan lines up with the stealth fighter with the twin daggers.

I watch as Aiden nods and moves to face the defensive fighter with the sword and Calum's grin splits wide at the sight of the bow and quiver. "Please tell me this means something big because *dayam* I've always had a hard-on for Robin Hood."

I laugh and check out the only one of us not enthused.

"Seriously?" Emmet points. "I'm the naked guy? What the hell?"

I bite my bottom lip and try to sober. "Do you feel the draw, Em? Do you want to touch him?"

He cants his head to the side and frowns. "Not in a weird way, but yeah. Shit, Fi. Why can't I be the badass with two daggers? My guy doesn't have weapons."

"Maybe he's the healer, son," Granda offers. "Maybe he didn't need weapons because he was their savior. Sloan, ye did say Emmet's primary discipline was Healing, did ye not?"

Sloan nods. "It is."

"Okay, Emmet." I gesture for him to line up. "That sorta makes sense. Go ahead, touch the nakey man."

I press my fingers over my mouth to keep from laughing, but my brothers don't even try.

"You're all a bunch of fecking eejits," Emmet snaps. "Look away. Nothing to see here."

I wipe the tear that's escaped my eye and focus on Fionn's statue. "Okay, here goes everything."

I don't know how I know it with such surety, but I do. I need to touch the statue. No, it's stronger than need—it's a compulsion.

I reach forward and touch the stone of his torso, and feel the burst of magic invade my body. It's like a download of energy, knowledge, and instinct. I stumble back, and my world spins. I bend at the waist and prop my palms on my knees while I wait for the funhouse ride to stop.

After drawing a deep breath, I straighten and check on the others. They look equally shaken. "Wow. That was something. Is everyone alrigh—Emmet!"

I close the distance between the statues and where Emmet lies starfished in the dirt twenty feet away. Sloan is kneeling over him, and I drop beside him. "Are you okay? What happened?"

"He's out cold." Sloan's hands move over him, but I don't see any blood or injuries. "I think that's all it is, though. He got a jolt—"

Emmet's eyes pop wide, and he launches from his back to his feet. "Did you *see* that! That was incredible. Holy shit, it's like… You know that scene in *The Matrix* in the techno dentist chair? It's that… I downloaded everything. Like, seriously, everything."

Emmet bounces off, rambling like he's high on magic, and my heart starts to beat again. I flop on my ass in the dirt and drop my head, focused on calming the thundering rush of adrenaline pumping through me. "You guys are going to give me a heart attack, I swear."

"Fi, yer gonna want to see this."

"I honestly don't know how much more excitement I can take for one day." I accept Sloan's hand, and he pulls me up. "Thanks, surly. You got to him first to take care of him. I appreciate that more than you know."

Sloan's smile is a little sad. "I do know. Now, go on, see what yer da has to show you."

Da doesn't need to show me. I see it as I'm walking back. What was stone two minutes ago is now not.

"The enchanted weapons." I watch as Dillan takes possession of the stealth fighter's daggers.

"The handles are carved out of bone." He grips them and spins them in his hands like they're a natural extension of his arms and not something he picked up for the first time this instant.

"And look, you get a leafy cape."

"It's a cloak." Sloan lifts it off the stone statue of the warrior. He eases it over Dillan's head and adjusts the shoulders to sit squarely. It's pieced with layers of different green, brown, and copper tones and when the light catches it, it looks almost like a living forest. "If the hood does what I think it does, tell me what happens when it's up."

The fabric barely covers his mop of ebony hair before Dillan squeals like an excited little boy. "Holy-schmoly! This is so cool."

"What? What does the hood do?"

"It's hard to explain." Dillan looks around the room in wonder. "It's like I know everything about my surroundings: what will make noise if I disturb it, what I can use as a weapon if I need one, what each of your strengths and weaknesses is at a glance."

"It's a rogue's cloak of concealment," Sloan says. "The hood brings a greater depth of perception."

"That's so cool, D. Congrats." I leave him to get back to Da. My father is waiting patiently by the statues, and I eye the wizard's staff he's holding. It looks like a solid shaft of oak with a twining twig running and twisting around its length like a protruding vein. And at the top, the solid knot of a burl acts as a club. "Cool staff, old man."

"A souvenir I picked up on my trip."

"That's neat wood. Freaky, really."

"It's snakewood. One of the hardest woods and insanely rare and expensive." He waggles his brow, then points at the Fionn statue again. "Yer so caught up in everyone else's windfall, ye haven't taken a look at what Fionn intended his young apprentice to have."

Right. "Cool. I always wanted an iron crown and arm guards made of bark. I take it by Fionn's stance that he's supposed to be holding Birga."

"Well, ye already found her, so yer ahead of the game."

Fionn's spear is wicked cool. She's enchanted with necromancy magic, so as she cut through the Black Dog enemy during our battle, she transferred their life force to me, to heal my wounds and bolster my strength.

"Yeah, Birga is awesome. I'm okay with what I got."

"What did you get?" Aiden comes over to check out my haul. "Huh, a metal headband and chunks of wood. Not what I expected for the leader of the pack."

Dillan steps around the statue and shakes his head. "Nope. These aren't simply chunks of bark. They're enchanted up the ying-yang. They're bracers cut from a branch of the Tree of Life and hollowed through the core to retain the integrity of the bark's magic. They offer wicked protection."

Aiden looks at him and blinks. "When did you become an encyclopedia of ancient artifacts?"

"His hood's up." I point at the hood of his cloak. "It gives him tactical wisdom about his surroundings."

Aiden grins. "Okay, that's freaking cool."

Dillan waggles his brow. "I know, right?"

"Go on, Fi." Da takes the bracers from the statue to slip them up my arms. "Time to try them on."

I hold my hands out, and he slides the guards past my wrist and up my forearms. Honestly, I'm not sure what to expect, but what I don't expect is for them to suction to my skin and spread up my arms and down my fingers. "What's happening?" I shout. "What are they doing?"

"Relax, Fi," Emmet says. "It's fine. I think they're bonding with you."

"Bonding how?" I look at Da. He seems equally alarmed.

"Taking root is more accurate." Sloan grabs my fingers and turns them over in his hands. "Look. It's forming a tattoo. Roots inking into the skin of yer hands and branches moving up yer arms."

"Why? Why do I want that?" My breath comes fast, and I wonder if I might faint again. "Guys, am I becoming a tree lady or something? I don't want to be a tree lady."

"Lift yer shirt," Sloan directs while shifting behind me.

"Watch it, buddy," Calum warns. "Now's not the time."

Sloan mutters something about us all being cracked and huffs behind me. "Cumhaill, lift yer shirt. I need to see where the branches are going."

I pull my shirt over my head and stand there in my bra. Now is not the time for modesty, and I'm not shy to begin with. "What's happening? What does it look like?"

"The branches are merging with yer Fianna shield. I think Emmet and Dillan are right. I think the bracers are protection and are bonding directly to yer shield. Aiden, give me yer knife."

There's a resounding growl of disgruntled men, and Sloan gets shoved back a few feet.

"You're on the bench, hotshot," Calum says. "We're not giving you a knife so you can test your theory and stab our sister to see if she bleeds."

He shakes his head. "Don't be daft. I don't want to hurt her. I want to see if the protection acts as a shield for her. If I'm right, her skin is impenetrable while she's got them on."

Impenetrable? Well, that doesn't sound so bad.

"But do I have to be tattooed like a tree over my entire body? I'm already freaked about the shield on my back, and people don't even see that one."

"Uh...yeah, I think ye might—"

"Holy shit!" Dillan draws everyone's attention. "Check it." He pulls off his shirt and shows us his forearms. There's a tattoo of his daggers up the inside of each arm. "Now watch." He flexes his hands, and the tattoos are gone, and the daggers are in his hands.

"What. The. Serious. Fuck." Calum says. "How'd you do that? Do it again."

He does. One second the daggers are in his hands, and the next, they're tattoos on his arms.

"It's like Emmet says. With my hood up, I felt they wanted to bond with me. They needed me to accept them as my weapons fully, and they accepted me as their wielder. It's ink magic. Now they're a part of me. Go ahead, Fi. Relax and accept what the bracers are trying to do."

"Bam. Drop the mic!" Calum whips off his shirt. He has a quiver strap inked across his chest, a bow on his left forearm, and yep, when he turns around, a quiver on his back. "Best day, *evah!*"

I meet Da's gaze. "Yeah?"

He dips his chin and takes my hands. "Yeah. Aiden, give me yer knife."

I laugh when he first presses the blade against the fleshy pad of my finger, and I feel nothing. When he pokes me, the blade doesn't penetrate. Then, he draws the cutting edge across my palm. Nothing.

"Sloan seems right about the shielding," Granda observes. "I'm not willing to say impenetrable, but certainly as tough as bark. Now see if ye can bond with it, *mo chroi*. My thinking is the tattoo will only cover yer flesh when it's active. Otherwise, it'll go inside ye like the boys' weapons."

Thank you, baby Groot. That I could handle.

So, if accepting the gift of impenetrable flesh is my reward from Fionn, I accept, and I'm grateful to the Tree of Life for her magic bark bracers.

I peek one eye open and look down at my skin. "Nothing happened. Why do I still look like I live in a tattoo parlor?"

Sloan frowns. "Yer granda's right. I think the inking will disappear when the magic of the bracers is dormant. Are ye sure yer accepting of the gift?"

I sigh. "Yes. No. I don't know."

"It's a lot all at once." Da grabs the metal band off Fionn's head and places it on mine. "Come now, let's figure out how to get out of here. We can worry about Fi's tattoo later."

"Not a problem," Dillan says. "Follow me. I sense the hidden exit. Damn, can you believe how cool I am?"

I snort. "And humble, too."

CHAPTER EIGHT

It's late by the time we make our way out of the fortress and breathe the crisp, clean night air. The moon is high and casts a silver glow through the canopy of the trees. Although the group vibrates with newfound powers and awareness, our travel is quiet. Silent. Not a whisper of a sound.

Dayam. It seems our upgrades have improved more than our knowledge. Although sticks and leaves litter our path, there's barely a stir in the air.

"To paraphrase Dillan," I say, my mind spinning. "Can you believe how freaking cool we are?"

Da snorts. "It's less impressive if ye've spent yer life among the Order. Enchanted weaponry and heightened abilities are part of this life. The amazing part is that it didn't take ye forty years of study and practice."

I'm not keen on the implication that we got off easy. "We will. Just because we've been dipped in awesomesauce doesn't mean we're going to rest on our laurels. We'll study and practice like everyone else, won't we, guys?"

There's a resounding grumble of affirmation.

Granda points out, "If ye think about that, perhaps it's the will of the gods somehow that the six of ye be brought up to speed quickly so yer ready to face what's to come."

"And what do you think is coming?" Da asks.

Granda shrugs and steps around a large rock in the center of the path. "I can't say. It was a thought."

I cast a sideways glance at Sloan and frown. He's been awfully quiet since we touched the statues. I drop back and walk beside him. "Hey, you okay?"

"Right as rain. Why wouldn't I be?"

So, *not* okay. I recap the night and come up empty. Is he upset that my brothers harassed him about looking at the tattoo? Is he still hurt from me falling on him? Does he feel left out since he didn't get an item gifted to him?

"Thank you for coming along and for catching me. I hope your back isn't too sore."

"It's fine."

We carry on in silence, him brooding, and me listening to an animal foraging in the scrub and an owl in the trees somewhere close by. "There was tension between us this afternoon when you came to pick us up, but I hope we ironed that out. I'm over it. I get pissy and hurt sometimes. I'm sorry about that, and hope you're not still put out."

"There's nothing to apologize for. Everything's fine."

"Clearly not, but I won't push. I just want you to know that I value everything you've done for us. I appreciate you."

He slows and lets me pass through the large boulders ahead of him. When we get back to the vehicles, he pulls out the keys and tosses them to Da. "If it's all the same, I think I'll transport home. I'm tired, and I want to check on our family grove. I'll pick up the SUV tomorrow when Lugh and I start going over the scrolls and journals we found."

"You're leaving?" I give him a sideways glance.

"No offense meant, but I have things to worry about aside

from the Cumhaill chaos. I needn't spend the next four hours in transit. I'll see ye tomorrow."

I'm about to respond, but there's no reason to. He's gone.

"I guess that's the end of that convo."

Emmet chuckles. "He kinda kicks ass at dramatic exits."

The quest team is slow to rise the next morning, and I feel bad for Aiden. The kids don't seem to care that daddy was up late. They want to climb on him and give him hugs. "How much sleep did you get?" I ask as we meet at the counter.

"Three hours."

I groan and take the mug from his hands. "Go back to bed. I'll play with the kids outside and keep them occupied for a few hours with Gran so you can get some rest."

"If you don't need Kinu, can she join me? She was up worrying all night and could use some time relaxing with me too. The druid stuff has been hard on her. I'd like to smooth out some rough edges."

I submerge his mug in the dishwater and shoo him toward Da's old bedroom. "Off you go. I'll find Kinu and tap her out so the two of you can have some private time. But please make sure you get at least *some* sleep."

Aiden kisses my cheek and chuckles. "Oh, there will be sleeping too. You're the best, baby girl. Love you."

"You, too. Sweet dreams."

I consider heating a plate of breakfast casserole, then decide to stick with sugary carbs. Grabbing a large section of Gran's signature strudel, I take a bite.

OMG. Strawberry rhubarb…so good.

I take my large mug of tea and a wad of strudel as big as my head outside and find Gran, Kinu, and the wildlings on the back lawn petting deer. "Kinu, why don't you go take a nap? I sent

Aiden in to take another run at sleep, and he said you were up most of the night too. I have baby duty covered for a few hours."

My sister-in-law looks up at me, and yeah, the dark rings under her eyes don't suit her. "You don't mind?"

I finish chewing and lick my fingers. "Not at all. Go lay down. We've got you covered."

"Thanks, Fi." She sets Jackson on his feet and rises off the grass. "You guys will be good for Gran and Auntie Fi, won't you?"

Neither of them responds.

Hey, if you don't promise, you can't be held to anything.

I laugh and wave her away. "The deer are much more interesting than mommy's worrying. Go on. If you don't get there soon, he'll be unconscious, and you'll be outta luck on the adult segment of nap time."

Kinu chuckles and waves over her shoulder. "Honestly, I'm so tired I don't care."

When I sit with the kids, Meggie looks at me and starts to pout. Within moments, the pushed-out lip becomes tears. "What's the matter, Megs?"

"Why you gots that?" Jackson points at my arms.

I sigh and rub the bark bracers suckerfished to my arms. The tattoo of tree roots inks down my hands and fingers. The fretwork and vining are quite complex and dramatic.

Thankfully, she can't see that the bark pattern and branches also ink upward and cover my entire body. Like, all my parts. It's horrifying.

I knock my knuckles on my forearm and force a smile. "This is a not-so-fun game I'm playing. See, it's not scary, Meg. Auntie Fi is fine."

When the whimpered tears become full-blown crying, Gran pulls the baby to her chest. "Why don't ye join the boys at the rings, luv? Maybe ye'll be able to figure out what to do with those."

"I feel bad about leaving you alone with both kids. It was my idea to send Aiden and Kinu in for a rest."

She adjusts Meg onto her hip and takes Jackson's hand. "Och, don't feel bad. The three of us will have a grand time, won't we, wee ones? Do you want Gran to show you where the baby foxes live? If you're quiet, the mommy might come out and let you touch her tail."

The two of them glom onto Gran, and I'm officially dispensable. "Nice. So much for your favorite auntie."

Gran chuckles and brushes a finger across my cheek. "Off ye go. Figure out how to use those gauntlets. Lugh believes once ye do, they'll bond with ye fully. Then ye'll be the favorite auntie once again."

I hope so.

I watch them go, set my mug onto the stone half-wall, and stride off toward the back of the property.

The action in the rings is audible before I crest the rise. Calum, Dillan, and Emmet are down on the training floor and testing out their new skills. I stand there and watch them for a few minutes before I go down to join them.

"Hey, boys. Can I play, too?"

"Hey, Fi. Check it." Calum waves me over. He's standing in front of a wooden target board set sixty feet away. There are a dozen arrows lodged in the black bullseye area of the colored rings.

"Wow, that's awesome, Calum. You *are* Robin Hood."

"Now watch this." His grin is infectious as he steps in front of me. "How many arrows have I got left?"

I glance over at the feathered flights sticking up from the rim of the leather quiver. "Three."

He raises his bow arm, reaches back, and nocks an arrow. When he releases, it flies true to the bullseye.

"Hey, Fi, how many arrows have I got left?"

"Two."

"Are you sure?"

I look at the flights sticking out of his quiver and frown. "Okay, three."

He reaches back and shoots off one, two, three arrows in quick succession as if he's Legolas Greenleaf. "And now?"

I look again, and my mouth falls open. "What the hell?"

"*Right?* Still three arrows. It's a refilling quiver."

Da jogs down the last steppe of the rings while holding his new staff. He looks fresh from the shower and bright-eyed. "It's called an Eternalfull Quiver, and they're a blessing to an archer in battle. How's yer aim coming?"

Calum points at the target. "Whatever magical knowledge I downloaded included the skills to put these babies to good use. It's like they're a part of me."

"Well, ye accepted them as part of ye, so they are."

Calum chuckles. "Yeah, I guess that makes sense."

Da steps off and starts stretching. I've seen him work out in the basement of our house, and he jogs regularly, but I've never seen him stretch much before a workout.

It makes me wonder what we're in for.

"He's doing better, eh?" Calum says quietly beside me. "The drinking, I mean. I was worried about him and Granda getting into old squabbles and Da hitting the whiskey to escape. He's been a little shaky since Brenny, but seems better."

"Better, but not enough for us to stop paying attention. He's kissed me a couple of times, and I've smelled it on him when there hasn't been any around. Two nights ago when he came to find me in the forest, he said you boys were having beers, but he smelled strongly of whiskey."

Calum frowns. "No. He had beer with us."

"Did he grab any at the Duty-Free that you know of?"

"The airport chaos is a bit of a blur. I'll ask D. He went wandering with him when we arrived." Calum saunters off and heads over to where Dillan is practicing fighting forms with his daggers in hand. He still has his cloak on and his hood up, and I wonder if we'll ever get it off him.

I laugh at the thought. It's not the type of clothing that will blend in on the city streets of Toronto.

Distracted by my musings, I miss when Da begins his dance with the staff. I say dance, because the way he swings it forward and back, pinwheeling it in front of him and passing it behind his back as he twists and twirls is nothing short of a choreographic masterpiece.

The man has always been coordinated, but lawdy, lawdy, Miss Clawdy. With his heritage powers restored and his amp-up from the statue in the fortress, he's phenomenal. I can't help but stare. Gran said he was skilled with a staff, but I never expected this.

"Fi, you're gonna catch flies." Emmet closes ranks. "Your mouth is hanging open."

I point at Da, and his jaw drops.

"Holy geez, is that our old man? 'Cuz it looks like him, but I've never seen him do anything like *that* before."

The staff cuts through the air with such precision I can't wrap my head around it. When he slows, the four of us bow and lower our hands in praise. "We're not worthy."

Da chuckles and kisses the staff. "It's been a long time since I've fallen in love."

Dillan laughs. "Just take it slow, Da. She has a spear on one end and a club on the other. I can't see it working out for you if you rush her."

I roll my eyes and call for a family sparring match. "Hand-to-hand? I'm not a hundy percent sure I trust the skin as tough as bark theory of my new freaky bracers, and Emmet and I didn't get weapons last night."

Emmet scowls and throws up his palms. "Naked guy blasted me with a shit ton of knowledge, but I'm not sure what good that does me in a battle."

"Do ye remember what ye learned, Emmet?" Da asks.

"Nope. But it seems to come to me in waves when I need it. Watch this." He closes his eyes and opens his palms to the sky. A moment later, three squirrels bound over the crest of the top tier of the rings and scurry down to sit in front of him. The next thing I know, he's chattering and making squeak and click noises, and they're responding.

"Is he talking squirrel?"

Da has one eyebrow raised so high it disappears behind his russet hair. "That's bizarre. Even in the druid world of communicating with animals, that's bizarre."

Emmet looks at us, and the chattering continues.

I snort. "Whoa, Em. You're still talking squirrel, dude."

He pauses, then shakes his head. "Sorry. I said it's really weird, eh?"

"Yep. You win the prize for the most unique power. And hey, look at it this way. Now you can be the one to organize the squirrel army in our neighborhood."

Dillan barks out a laugh. "Emmet Cumhaill, the Pied Piper of Cabbagetown."

It's close to three when Aiden emerges from the back hall. He looks refreshed and rather pleased with himself. I don't want to know what that look is about. Lalalala. He grabs the last of the rhubarb strudel and pops it into his mouth. "Where are the monkeys?"

"Sleeping on the foam in the living room."

He almost chokes and pounds a fist against his chest. "You got them both to nap? At the same time?"

I giggle. "I can't take any credit. Gran's a druid superpower in her own right."

Finished chewing the strudel he wolfed down, he lifts the lid of the cookie jar and snags a handful. "What are you guys working on?"

I reach out, and he hands me a few. I frown at the mountain of musty parchment spread across the table in front of me as I lean back and bite into molasses heaven. "I'm trying to find a reference to safeguarding the fae from necromancy. Well, honestly, any reference to necromancy."

"And you're not getting anywhere?"

"Granda is so much better at reading ancient script, but he got called in by the Nine Families for a pow-wow. He took Da with him if you can believe that."

Aiden reaches down, picks up a piece of paper, and reads. "To you alone, 'tis given the heavenly deities To know or not know; secluded groves Your dwelling-place, and forests far remote."

I blink. "Is it me or does that make your head want to splatter against the wall?"

He drops the paper back into the pile. "It's not you. Here, have another cookie. You don't have to decipher a cookie."

I chuckle and accept the sugary diversion.

"What else did Granda and Sloan gather while we were in the fortress?"

I lean down and pick up the box on the floor beside my feet to look through the contents. "Loads of paperwork, a few cool wood and horn goblets, a couple of old gold coins, and this is cool."

I pull out a wide bone ring. "It's rough and asymmetrical and in no way fancy, but it speaks to me."

He takes possession of it to get a closer look and turns it in the band of light that streams in through the open ceiling. "And what is it saying to you?"

"First, it's not meant for us. As clearly as I felt the pull of the statues signifying the rightness of us claiming the gifts last night, I know this ring is meant for another."

"And second?"

"It wants to be claimed."

He hands it back. I'm still studying it when Sloan strides into the kitchen from outside.

Sloan nods at the two of us. "Good afternoon. Lara sent me in for the healing potion she made up for the Doyle grove. She said it was here in the kitchen."

I point at the water cooler jug sitting on the floor by the door. Next to it, there's a tube and spray nozzle that reminds me of Patty's Super Soaker. "It's that big jug and the pouch of herbs and mixed ingredients beside it."

I get up to help him and cross the kitchen floor. The closer I get, the more my hand tingles. Stopping right in front of him, I open my palm and look at the ring.

"What's that you say?" In truth, it doesn't say anything, but I get impressions, and the message is quite emphatic. "It appears you're the chosen one for this relic. The two of you must be meant to be, because it's quite insistent."

Sloan arches a brow. "Are ye makin' that up because ye think I was upset last night?"

"I *know* you were upset last night, but no. This has nothing to do with that. It's literally vibrating in my hand, eager to get to you. It didn't do that with Aiden or any of my other brothers I showed it to this afternoon."

He eyes the bone ring. "Ye think it's enchanted then?"

"I know it is."

"And what do ye think its enchantment entails?"

I chuckle. "Don't you dare give me the scaredy-cat routine. I got rushed to put on bark bracers and look at me. I'm a freak who should pose for the next cover of Inked Magazine."

"It's not that bad." Aiden frowns.

"And, ye've been a freak for as long as I've known ye, Cumhaill. I don't know why it would bother ye now."

His jab hits its mark. I take a step back and press a hand to my chest. "The kids wouldn't play with me today, and Meggie cried when she saw me."

Sloan matches my retreat and touches the bark on my arm. "I'm sorry. I was makin' fun, and it wasn't nice. If yer so unhappy with the inking, have ye tried to take them off?

I hold out my arms. "Seriously? You don't think I tried a million times? No. They are where they want to be. I think Granda is right. I need to get on board with them. Then they'll go internal like my brothers' ink."

"Technically, that's the opposite of what ours do."

I throw Aiden a glare. "Not helping."

He holds up his palms and makes a hasty exit, after grabbing another handful of cookies on his way out.

I take the beat of time while he makes his exit to get over my hurt and when I turn back to Sloan, I hold out the ring. "Okay, back to you. It wants you. I'm not making it up. It's not a consolation prize. It's determined that you're the one."

Sloan takes the ring from me and slips it onto his middle finger. The moment it settles into place, I feel the energy ease.

"Nice. It's happy."

Sloan flexes his fingers in and out and looks at the back of his hand, then flips it to look at his palm. "And you have no sense of what kind of enchantment the ring holds?"

"Nope. Just that it *luuurves* you, hot stuff. Do you feel any different? Any hints about what it does?"

He looks around the kitchen and shrugs. "Nothing yet."

I grab the pouch of mixed herbs and point for him to resume his task. "Then we await the big reveal. Consider me your shadow until the mystery is solved."

After rolling his eyes at me, he picks up the jug of grove remedy and holds his hand out for mine. "Yer ridiculous. Ye know that, don't ye?"

CHAPTER NINE

We materialize along the desiccated tree line of the Doyle grove. Iris Doyle and a couple of other people are busily working with the damaged trees. It's been two days now, and it doesn't look much better than it did that first day.

"We aren't staying long, are we?" I press my hand against my growling stomach. "I slept through breakfast and only had strudel and tea for lunch. After working out in the training rings all day, I'm getting hangry."

"Keep in mind, yer the one who tagged along on my errand. It hardly gives ye the rank to commandeer the schedule of my comings and goings."

I shrug. "Suit yourself. Consider yourself warned. You won't like hangry Fiona. She can be abrupt and a bit edgy."

He chuckles and shakes his head. "I'll watch for the swing in personality. Thanks for the warning."

"Sloan." Iris turns to greet us. "Thank you for coming, son. What have you there?"

Sloan sets the water jug down, then extends his hand to me for the herb mixture. "Lara asked me to bring this to you. She believes it will nourish the wizened and depleted plant cells and breathe a bit of life back into them."

I hand him the pouch, and he empties it into the jug. After dipping the tube in, he gives it a few swishes and screws on the lid. "If ye squeeze the handle here, it'll spray a fine mist. If ye cast a breeze to carry it—"

I follow his gaze, wondering what distracted him, but see nothing but dead and dying trees.

"Sloan?" Iris leans into his line of vision. "Are ye all right, son?"

"Apologies. I am. Where was I?"

"Spray the mixture and cast a breeze."

He nods. "Yes, spray the mixture and cast a breeze to spread it from roots to treetops. Lara believes it'll help a great deal, and ye'll see an improvement by morning."

Iris nods. "Kier, help me carry this to the center of the affected area. Lara has sent us a remedy."

As the water jug gets taken off our hands and the attention shifts deeper into the grove, I'm still watching Sloan. "What? Are you all right? You look like you've seen a ghost."

"Not a ghost," he whispers and turns his back on the grove. "Twenty feet along the tree line, at the base of the big fir. What do you see?"

I follow his directions and study the scene. "Nothing but a big tree. What did you see?"

Without turning his head, he casts a sideways glance. "Do ye see where the branches rest on the ground, fanned out like a lady's skirt?"

"Yeah."

"I see a wee fae female curled up as if she's ill, and she's holding tiny winged creatures that look even worse off."

"You can see the hidden folk?"

"Maybe, although I've never seen them before."

"Well, I don't see them, and I know I can if they want me to because they came to me the other night."

"So, ye think she wants me to see her now?"

I look back at the tree, and my instincts kick in big time. "It's the ring's power. For some reason, you're meant to see the unseen. The ring wanted you, and now you can see the fae. Are you supposed to help them? Maybe you need to take them to your father for healing?"

Sloan blinks at me. "And what does my father know about healing the fae?"

"I have no idea, but you can't just leave them there."

He looks over, and his frown deepens. "No. Yer right about that. Well, I suppose I should go introduce myself and see if I can help."

"Move slowly and make it clear you don't wish them any harm. They're skittish and leery of humans."

He chuckles. "I've studied them my entire life, and yer the expert after one late-night conversation?"

"I have more real-life experience than you, don't I?"

He dips his chin as we stroll toward the big fir. "I can't argue there. Ye definitely do."

We walk slowly, and I let him lead. If the ring chose him, there is a reason. When we're less than ten feet from where the skirt of the fir tree lays against the ground of the Doyle's back lawn, he stops and holds up his hands. "Don't be afraid. I won't hurt ye. No, no, don't try to move. I don't want ye to hurt yerself."

I watch and wait, and when he takes a step back, I do as well. "What's wrong?"

"Och, she's nervous. She doesn't seem hurt, but I don't want her to move until I'm sure."

I grip his forearm and magic rushes through me in a hot wave. My skin ignites, and I get a wave of goosebumps. The magic of his new fae sight extends to me. It flutters in my chest like a moth's wing, and the veil blocking human vision from the fae realm is gone.

"Hello there." I recognize her round globe eyes and bouncy antennae. She's not the same creature I saw in my grandparent's grove. That girl was minty green. This girl is more sage green, but she's the same species for sure.

"How can we help you?" Sloan asks.

Her mouth opens and a frantic flood of chatter ensues. I honestly think she's trying to communicate, but I have no clue what she's saying. "Did you get any of that?"

Sloan shakes his head. "Not a word. She nitters like a little woodland creature and I can't make sense of it."

Like a woodland creature... "I know what to do. I don't think it's your father we need. I think it's Emmet."

"Yer brother? Why?"

"You'll see when you bring him back. Go get him. I'll wait here. Last I saw him, he was at the training rings with Dillan and Calum."

"Do ye think it'll frighten her if I transport?"

"Maybe, although fae species are more magical than we are so maybe not. I don't know."

"Okay, I'll step away and be right back. Are ye sure yer all right to stay?"

"Are you worried about my safety or me causing trouble while you're gone?"

"Both, actually, but more the latter."

I nod and ease back a step before lowering myself to sit on my knees. "Does she look afraid of me sitting here?"

He looks from where the fae girl is to me and back again. "I don't think so."

"Then I won't move a muscle until you get back. I promise I won't cause any trouble."

"Okay, I'll be right back."

Once Sloan backs away and teleports, I sit quietly and smile at where I think the girl is. "It's okay. Sloan's a good guy. He'll figure out how to help you. He's good that way."

"Talking to yerself, Cumhaill?"

I don't turn to acknowledge Ciara. I've seen enough of her to last a lifetime and I don't want to spook the fae girl. I hope the ailing fae is accustomed to Ciara's venom. This is her family grove, after all.

"Ye know that's a sign of insanity in some circles."

"So is doing the same thing over and over again and expecting a different result. You haven't learned yet not to battle wills with me. You always end up with egg on yer face."

"If you think so."

I shrug. "I know so."

"Cumhaill. What a farce ye are. Do ye not realize yer the laughingstock of the Nine Families?"

I roll my eyes. "Yeah, yeah. Do you think I made it through grade school caring what every bully and loser thinks? Call me insane or a laughingstock, or my brothers call me the Queen of Amazeballs. You can call me that, if you like."

She steps around to loom over me and her eyes widen. "What the fuck have ye done to yerself?"

I sigh and tug down the sleeves of my sweatshirt. The whole bark arms and tats thing is getting old. "I'm trying out a new look. I'm going for urban druid biker. What do you think? Too cutting edge?"

"Yer seriously delusional. Ye've got half the breeding and none of the talent the rest of the heirs have, and ye still think yer something special. He's going to tire of yer strange and unusual act, ye know?"

I giggle, the dawning of her venom becoming so clear. "Seriously? Is that what this is about? You think I'm stealing your sunshine with Sloan? Oh, honey, you overestimate your appeal. Sloan's a free agent. If he wants you for another go-around, there's nothing cock-blocking him. I told you before. We're friends."

"And I told ye before ye don't fool me."

I chuckle. "Okeedokee then. I guess you've figured me out. Now, if you don't mind… I don't know for sure—because I can't see behind the faery glass of the hidden folk—but I'm pretty sure you're scaring the natives. You should deprive me of your company and go."

"Go? This is *my* house. Yer the one who should go."

I shrug. "Can't. I promised Sloan I wouldn't move before he *poofed* away. He'll be back though. Are you sure you want to be here when he arrives? Your hair's a bit wind-blown, and you have something in your teeth."

Ciara launches at me the same moment Emmet and Sloan materialize beside her. Sloan grabs her wrist and yanks her back from her assault.

He physically lifts her off her feet to keep her from coming at me and scowls at me. "And ye wonder why I thought ye'd get into trouble."

"She started it. And hey, I didn't move a muscle."

Sloan rolls his eyes and sets Ciara down to point at the house. "Yer dismissed."

"Fuck off, Sloan." When she notices my brother, her entire demeanor changes. She smiles and bats those long chestnut lashes. "Och, hello, Emmet. What's the craic? What have ye been up to on yer holiday?"

Emmet blinks at the mercurial transition. "Not much. I touched a naked man last night, and now I'm juiced up and super smart. What's up with you?"

She shakes her head. "I came to invite Sloan and yer bitch sister to the heir's event tomorrow night for Mabon. It's a tradition for the autumn equinox that we assist the elders with the rituals during the day and go out for rounds after. Yer as much an heir as she is and much more interesting. Care for a night out with yer peers?"

"You call my sister a bitch and in the same breath ask me if I want to spend time with you? That would be a big fat no." He steps around Ciara and smiles at me. "Hey Fi, making friends? I can't take you anywhere, can I?"

I chuckle. "Ciara's green-eyed monster escaped. She thinks Sloan wants to hakuna-my-tatas and I'm the only thing keeping the two of them from the big reunion scene at the end of their enemies to lovers romance."

Emmet snorts. "And in other news, shouldn't we focus on the little fae girl Sloan saw?"

"What fae girl?" Ciara asks.

"Remember when I asked you to leave because you were scaring the natives? Who did you think I was talking about?"

Ciara runs her French-manicured fingers through her silky brown hair and scowls. "I never know what the feck yer talking about. Yer insane and spew asinine nonsense."

I ignore the jibe and check in with Sloan. "Is she still there? Is she okay?"

Sloan nods. "Seems so. I did what ye asked and fetched Emmet. How do ye think he and I can help her?"

"After witnessing Emmet speak squirrel this afternoon, I'm betting he also speaks woodland fae. Go ahead. Hold his hand so he can see and hear her too. She seemed quite intent on telling us something. I'd bet it's important."

Sloan holds out his hand, and Emmet sucks in a gasp. "First I touch a nakey man, and now the tall, dark, and dangerous Sloan Mackenzie wants to hold my hand. Ireland is making me reevaluate things I thought I knew about myself."

I snort. "Emmet, focus."

"Family meeting," I call as Sloan, Emmet, and I portal into Gran's kitchen a half-hour later. "We have a news update, and it's time-sensitive. Gran, where is everyone?"

Gran turns from the stove and points her wooden spoon toward the living room. "They're in watching the football match on the telly."

I turn on my heel, and the three of us head into the sunken room with a giant tree growing up and through the thatched roof above. Everyone is lounging around watching the game, Meggie is climbing Calum, and Jackson is coloring pictures with Granda on the side table.

"News. Big bad news, everybody. We need an adult moment to discuss a few fae findings without the impressionable minds listening in."

Kinu gets up and grabs Meg from on top of Calum's curly mop of black hair. "We'll get our pajamas on."

"No supper?" Jackson looks stricken.

Da chuckles. "Och, ye can still have supper in yer pajamas, wee man. It'll be a fun holiday thing. Now, off ye go with yer mam for a bit."

When the room is clear, all eyes fall on us, and I start from the top: the bone ring wanting Sloan, delivering the remedy to the Doyle grove, Sloan seeing the little fae girl curled up on the fir, the woodland chatter, getting Emmet…

"And ye understood her?" Granda asks.

Emmet nods. "Yeah, I'm thinking of changing my name to Rosetta…Rosetta Stone. If I say it like Bond, do you think it will work for me?"

"Emmet." Da raises a hand toward Granda, who looks like he might need to take a breath. "Tell us about understanding the wee girl."

"Yeah, right. As soon as she opened her mouth, I could speak *brunaidh*."

"What's a *brunaidh?*" Calum asks.

"What ye'd know as a brownie," Da responds.

"You speak brownies? What does that mean?" Dillan's eyes pop wide, and he sits forward. "I bet I can speak milkshake. How'd you figure this out?"

"Not the brownies you eat, eejit." Da pinches the bridge of his nose and growls. "Brownies the wee folk."

Dillan sits up straighter. "That makes more sense but is far less interesting. Go on."

Emmet nods. "Pip is a sweet little thing, wide eyes, little antennae... Anyway, Sloan thought she was hurt, but she's sick and upset because her mate is one of the hidden folk taken by the Black Dog assholes at the Doyle grove."

"That's sad, but how is that big news?"

"Because mated brownies can share sight. Pip told me she sees a big cauldron set up outside with wood stacked beneath. The men who took her mate don't intend to imprison and siphon off their powers. They intend to boil the bodies of the fae to make a stock out of them. They plan to perform a Mabon ritual tomorrow night and consume them."

"Of all the chaotic evil horrors," Granda exclaims.

I agree, wholeheartedly. "It's disgusting. We have to assume they have all the fae folk from the Perry grove as well as those they were able to gather from the Doyle grove."

"We have to stop them," Emmet declares. "I promised Pip we'd find them before they kill her mate."

"Does she know where they are?" Da asks.

"I questioned her like any witness, sights, sounds, smells...the only thing she could say for sure is that it's a clearing in the woods with an open sky above."

Granda's brow pinches tight. "That's no help. If they have a wayfarer or a portal caster, that could be anywhere."

"Do mated brownies have a maximum distance for their shared sight?" Dillan asks. "Knowing their range might give us a search radius if there's a limit."

"I'll search for that." Granda heads off toward his office.

"What about other creatures in the forest?" Da asks. "If the brownie was willing to speak to you two, maybe there are others who might."

"You want us to go back, Da?" Emmet asks.

"I do. Grab something to fill yer bellies, then see what more ye can find out. In the meantime, we have twenty-four hours to pinpoint the location of the forest clearing. Dillan, pull up yer hood. We're going to check out the Perry grove. Maybe ye'll be able to sense something that can help."

Dillan bounds off the couch and has his hood up in a flash. "Ready when you are."

I laugh. Yeah, we're never getting that cloak off him.

CHAPTER TEN

As it turns out, even with all of Granda's texts, there is no recorded information on the distance at which mated brownies can still use their shared sight. When he asks around with the other elders, none of them know a range either. There's also nothing in either the Doyle grove or the Perry grove that any of my cop brothers or father can find that pinpoints where the ritual fae boiling might take place.

With energies raw and frustration high, we spend the morning hanging on the back lawn, working on hand-to-hand and brainstorming possible courses of action.

"What about Bruin doing an aerial search today?" Emmet asks. "Maybe he'd get lucky. I'm sure a huge cauldron set over a pyre in the middle of a forest clearing won't be hard to spot from above."

I sigh. "What if it's in Cork? Or Scotland? Or British Columbia? No. That exhausts one of our resources and sends him off when we might need him."

I'm more than a resource, Red.

I know you are, buddy. But you get my point, right?

I do. I'm just itchin' to do something. I want to get these bastards and stop them before they slaughter more fae.

You and me both, Bear.

"Druids are to remain neutral." Da swings his staff while muttering a rant. "The world is in balance when the life and death process is respected. It's harmonic. These men…these mythical Black Dog fuckers are a blight on nature. Abhorrent. Even when I left the Order behind, I never disrespected it. My beliefs were still rooted in my teachings."

Aiden and Dillan quit hand-to-hand and call their blades to face off against one another. Aiden's majestic curved blade against Dillan's two daggers. Since yesterday, the sparring has become more confident and the hits and swings truer to battle.

I'd worry more if I didn't know we downloaded a proficiency well beyond our experience. Some people study magic, some are given spells by their deities, some by an evil source, and some inherently know.

I don't know if Fionn mac Cumhaill can be considered a deity, but his magic certainly fast-tracked our little band of merry men into being a force to be reckoned with.

"Ha." Dillan laughs as his dagger clunks against Aiden's iron-wood buckler. "Your tiny saucer saved you there."

The round disc on Aiden's defensive arm isn't big enough to be used as a dinner plate, but it's supposed to keep him safe. "Supposed to" might be the wrong phrase since Aiden uses the guard like a pro and bats away Dillan's thrusts with his left as he swings with his right.

"You think you can beat me, little brother?" Aiden smiles as the two of them dance across the grass. "Prepare to be pwned."

When Sloan *poofs* in, I give up worrying about them and head over to say hello. "Tell me you've got good news. You didn't happen to spot a forest clearing genocide site on your way over, did you?"

Sloan shakes his head and waves for Emmet to join us. "No, but I had a thought."

"Hey, *whassup?*" Emmet holds up a fist and Sloan gives him a bump. The standard greeting of my brothers is becoming second nature with him now.

Oh, they grow up so fast.

"I was lyin' in bed this mornin', thinkin' about the wee brownie girl—"

"Dude, not cool," Emmet interrupts.

Sloan rolls his eyes. "Not like that, ye creeper. I was wonderin' how we might still figure out the maximum range for their shared sight."

"And how do we do that without knowing where her mate is?" I ask.

"Well, ye mentioned that ye'd seen a similar creature in the grove here the night the fae tree lady came to speak with ye. It got me to thinkin', what about another brownie couple helpin' us? Perhaps we can still narrow down the field. If Emmet can convince them, I can portal one of the mates to a great distance, then incrementally closer locations until we get an idea what we're dealin' with."

Emmet smiles. "I like it. It would be better if we repeat the experiment with two or three other couples, to rule out personal strengths and focus strictly on species ability."

"Agreed. So, will ye come with me into Lugh's and Lara's grove and see what we can find out?"

I squeeze Sloan's arm. "Good one, Mackenzie. If this works, you get an Oh! Henry bar."

I've walked through the trees of my grandparents' grove dozens of times over the past four months, but never saw the hidden splendor of what remained veiled from my mundane sight—until now. With Sloan's bone ring in place and Emmet and I holding his hands, the three of us are blessed to see the unseen behind the faery glass.

"Wow." I blink up at the little hummingbird people and the glittering silver and gold webs draping from tree to tree. There are rabbits with brilliant blue iridescent wings and kaleidoscope-patterned butterfly creatures with wide eyes and knowing smiles.

"*Sooo* cool. The fae realm smells like newly spun cotton candy." A memory flashes in my mind of being at the Markham Country Fair as a kid and Mam and Da getting us all a sugary treat for the hayride. The sun was warm on our faces, and I sat on one of the horses after to get my picture taken.

Emmet draws a long inhale and chuckles. "Your nose is broken, Fi. It smells exactly like Mam's freshly-baked cookies. *Mmm,* with lots of vanilla. I remember sitting on the kitchen floor with you in your bassinet and Mam baking. It smelled exactly like this."

Sloan lifts his chin and draws a deep breath. "I get warm apple cider with cinnamon." He doesn't share a memory triggered, but I'm pretty sure I already know what it is. He told me that the first time he met Gran, she made him warm apple cider and they had a tea party with the animals in her garden.

"So, I guess it's different for each of us because it's our innermost comfort smell?"

Emmet smiles at me. "I'll buy that."

Sloan nods. "Ye might be right."

Movement deeper into the woods brings us face-to-face with the wide-eyed antennae girl I met the other night. "Okay, Em. You're up, bro. Be your normal charming self."

Still holding Sloan's hand, Emmet settles on his knees on the ground. When he begins chattering, I soon give up trying to understand what he's saying and focus on the reaction of the fae folk he's speaking to.

I'm not the best at reading body language and facial expressions and when you complicate that by changing the person's species, I'm at a loss. If I am to guess, I'd say she doesn't want to. When she turns and walks into the forest, I'm sure.

Definitely no.

"She said yes. She's off to get her mate. Then we'll get started."

Ha! So much for my impressions. "That's great. I've been thinking. Sloan, take one of them somewhere far but not too far —somewhere you know the distance from here."

"I'll take him home to my place."

Huh. I've been to the Mackenzie's Stonecrest Castle, but Sloan *poofed* us there when I was unconscious. I don't actually know where it is. "How far is that?"

"Two and a half hours drive. We're up in Galway."

Wow. Farther than I thought. I guess if Sloan's family and mine weren't part of the Ancient Order of Druids, we never would've crossed paths.

"Why do you suddenly look so sad, Cumhaill? It's only a blink with my abilities."

"Sorry, my mind wandered. Yeah, take Mr. Brownie to your place, then phone me. Emmet can talk to Mrs. Brownie, and we can let you know if she sees anything."

When the mated couple returns, the tree lady I met is with them. She walks in long, measured steps and doesn't look pleased to see us. There's not much to be done about that. We need this to narrow our search.

"Hello again, milady." I bow my head as they approach. "I take it they told you about our problem?"

"Parted mates, shared sight, and gauging distance. To save others, we help this instance."

"That's all we ask. If we can narrow down where they took Pip's mate, we have a better chance at getting all the fae back before something awful happens."

"Too late for that, our lives are altered. The groves attacked; our faith has faltered."

The accusation in her tone isn't subtle. Neither is her anger. "That's understandable. Hopefully, we can earn back your faith. Druids are your champions evermore. I assure you, we'll do everything we can to make this right."

"In days of old, our true protectors. On this occasion, our tormentors. Druids noble or honor lost. Ties of past aren't worth the cost."

Wait… What the hell does that mean? Can the fae withdraw from the lives of druids? Can they rescind the gift of us having powers? These stupid Black Dog assholes are going to ruin it for everyone.

"We'll fix this." I'm impressed that I sound more confident than I am. "We'll find the ones responsible and bring them to justice."

"One chance you have, to right this wrong. Justice swift and punishment strong."

A woman after my own heart, Bear says in my mind. *Assure her Killer Clawbearer will see to the punishment. It'll be strong, all right.*

I bow my head. "Those responsible will pay for their treachery, milady. We won't rest until we stop these men."

Over the next hour, Sloan, Emmet, and I work with the brownie mated couple from Gran's grove. Then we find two mated couples in his home grove that agree to help as well. The data doesn't waver much between experiments. The range of shared sight seems to end once brownie mates are more than fifteen to twenty miles apart.

We find Granda in his study, poring over the scrolls.

"Och, that's great news, kids," he says when we report in. He pulls a large atlas off the credenza behind his desk and opens it to the page that shows Ireland's landscape. "That means that we're lookin' at an area no farther north than

Tralee or south of Kenmare. On the west, Glencar and the east Barraduff."

"That's still a large area," Sloan points out.

"But manageable." He grabs his phone, sends off a few texts, then lifts the cell to his ear. "We have a search area. I sent it to Dempsey, and he's takin' his wee plane up. Would ye ask yer boys to fly over the area of Glencar to Molls Gap and the Bridia Valley? We have the details of what we're lookin' for…that's right. And if they see anythin' they're wonderin' about… Perfect. Let me know."

He hangs up. "The Perry boys both have advanced Wildform Transfiguration and can shift into eagles. After what happened to their grove, they're burnin' to help."

I'll go too, Red. Let me out.

I release Bruin, and he takes form between the desk and the wall. There isn't enough space in the office for his hulking frame and the chair leg squeals as it scrapes along the floor. "Where can I look, Lugh?"

Granda points at the map. "Killarney National Park falls squarely in our search zone and is too big and dense for us to check on foot. Scour the area and see what ye find."

Bruin looks at the map, and his black nose twitches over the page. "I'm on it."

"Be careful, buddy." I wrap my arms around his thick neck. I kiss his ear and press my cheek to his head. He's warm and soft, and I love him so much. "Take care of you, Bear. These men are horrible."

Take care of yerself, Red. I love ye back.

When I straighten, Bruin disappears, and the room seems emptier than before. "And what should we do?"

Granda pulls up another contact on his phone. "Moira, it's Lugh. Could I entreat ye to do a favor for an oul friend? The druids are in a fix with the fae and need a win." He nods a few times and writes an address on a piece of paper. "I'm sendin' my grandkids over to fetch ye. I appreciate yer help."

When he hangs up the phone, he hands Sloan the address. "Moira Morrigan lives a block away from Trinity College across from the Regent House. She's expectin' ye, so quick there and straight back."

"And who is Moira Morrigan?" I ask.

"Lugh Cumhaill, ye didn't!" Gran is standing in the open doorway with her hands propped on her hips. She's scowling with more fire and fury than I realized she possesses. "Yer bringing that witch into our home after the way she carried on the last time she had ye alone in a room? Where's yer bloody head?"

Granda rubs a hand over his face. "Lara, that was forty years ago. She'll not be the same woman now she was then. There's no reason to get up in arms."

"Yer wrong about that, and ye'll not be alone with her a minute while she's here. Do ye hear me, man?"

Granda gives her a curt nod. "Och, I heard ye. The kids in the living room heard ye. I'm sure the O'Rourke's heard ye down the way, too."

I look at Sloan, and he finds this as baffling as I do. "I take it she's an old flame of yours, Granda?"

"Before yer Gran and I got together, I spent time courtin' the woman."

"And after ye were married, she took another run at ye. We had wee Niall runnin' around the house, and it didn't stop her. Shame on the woman."

"Nothing happened, Lara."

"Och, don't give me that. Do ye forget I walked in on her makin' her play?"

Granda winces. "All right, nothin' worth drudging up happened. How's that? I haven't spoken to her in over a decade."

"Ex's can be tricky," Sloan offers.

"She's a witch," Gran huffs. "A loose-bosomed, skirt-liftin', homewreckin' witch and ye invited her into our home. I'll not forgive that anytime soon."

Granda rounds the corner of his desk and moves to soothe Gran's pique. She won't have it. She turns on her heel and stomps off.

Granda sighs and blows out a long breath. "I best sort this out before ye get back. Maybe not straight home. Ye better give me twenty minutes."

The door to their bedroom slams down the hall, and it shakes the whole house. The vines growing on his office's living wall twine around his wrists and neck and pull at his clothes. He frowns and pulls himself free.

"Maybe make that half an hour."

Sloan portals us straight to Dublin, and we materialize in a shadowed back stoop of what I guess is one of the Trinity College buildings. I follow him off the steps, around the corner, and read the signpost for Grafton Street. With daylight still holding strong, I check out the interlocking brick walkways and the old buildings with iron rail fences and heavy wooden doors.

It feels like old Yonge Street back home.

I smile at the buzz of pedestrians, the double-decker buses, and the four-story buildings lining the street. It's funny, but although I've never been here, this is a world I can maneuver. As much as I enjoy Gran's and Granda's place, I'll never be anything but a city girl.

"This." I hold out my hands. "What's wrong with wanting to do what we do, be who we are, and live somewhere like this?"

Sloan shrugs. "Not a thing. If ye haven't figured it out by now, I'm solidly on Team Cumhaill. Keep in mind, though, Dublin is one-third the size of Toronto. The folks who make it work here don't face the same challenges."

"But it proves it can be done."

"With the ambient energy in the air and the ley lines pulsing in the ground beneath our feet, sure. I don't know that every druid could take on a city the size of yers, but I don't doubt that yer family will break the mold."

"Aww, that was super sweet. You better watch it, or I'll think you're going soft on me, surly."

He chuckles and steps aside as a cluster of university kids pass us. "Regent House is up here."

"You seem quite familiar. Did you go to school here?"

"I did. I took four years of Ancient and Medieval History and Culture."

"How'd you do?"

"Graduated at the top of my class."

"I'm not a bit surprised. And I bet you were a dream student, weren't you? Teacher's pet. Always bright-eyed and ready for classes."

"I enjoyed the learning, yes."

My stomach rumbles and I start searching the storefronts for someplace where I can fill my belly on the quick. There's a McDonald's down the way, but I don't feel like that. This is my first time in Dublin. I want something authentic.

"Hey, since we'll miss dinner, how about we grab a bite to eat while we give Granda a chance to settle Gran? This is your old stomping ground. Pick somewhere this girl can get a quality cheeseburger. Oh, and you're buying. I didn't bring my purse, and you owe me twenty-seven grand after convincing Bruin to order landscaping in my back yard."

He laughs and points the way. "I know the spot. We'll order to take out. We have a long night ahead of us."

"Villains to track, fae folk to save, yeah, I'm aware."

We order at O'Donaghue's Bar, and in fifteen minutes we're sitting on a bench pigging out. "Dayam, surly. This is good food."

He nods and licks barbeque sauce off his finger. "I don't know if the ethical debate of foods has entered the scope of yer thoughts yet, but O'Donaghue's only uses local organic, free-range, and ethically produced ingredients."

I look at my half-devoured burger. It's hot, juicy, and gloopy with cheese. I hadn't given it any more thought than that. "Is it wrong that I'm a druid and a total meatavore?"

"Not wrong. Make it a conscious decision though, and give thanks for the life that died to sustain you whether that's animal, vegetable, or mineral. We're part of the cycle of nature, and when we die, we'll be food and fertilizer for others as well. Just be aware."

"I buy local as much as I can."

He nods. "That's an important start. Less import means fewer food miles and lower pollution. It all matters."

I take another bite and decide my burger tastes even better, knowing it has the druid seal of approval. "Good call on O'Donaghue's."

"Yeah, me and my school buds used to meet up here after classes every day. Over the four years, I'd hate to guess how many hours we spent sitting in the front window. We called it 'the office,' so if anyone was lookin' and asked where we were, the answer was always, 'at the office.' Between the dart nights, the DJ's, the girls, and the food, the place never fails."

I swallow and wipe my mouth. "You'll have to bring me back one night when we can eat in and have a few pints of Guinness."

He gathers up our food wrappers. "We'll do that. If it's before ye leave this trip, yer brothers will enjoy it too. The live music draws a fun crowd."

I stand and wait while he tosses our trash in the bin. "What do you suppose happened when Granda and Moira were alone in a room that Gran labeled her a loose-bosomed witch?"

He shakes his head. “Not just that—a loose-bosomed, skirt-liftin’ witch. That paints quite a picture, don’t ye think?”

“It does, but Granda is devoted to Gran. I can’t see him getting swept away by an old love. Maybe it was a costume malfunction, and some girl parts spilled out.”

He waves his hands. “I don’t want to know.”

“How could you not want to know?”

When the light turns green, we cross, and he takes the address out of his pocket. “Because in five minutes, we’re going to introduce ourselves to the woman. I don’t want to have images of her flashin’ her tits to Lugh in my head while I’m shakin’ her hand.”

I laugh. “Okay, I’ll give you that. Awkward.”

Sloan points at the historic brick buildings that run the length of the block, and we find the unit we’re looking for. It’s a three-story rowhouse with arched windows and neoclassical lines and architecture. “Why do you suppose Granda wants her help? Is she a druid, do you think?”

Sloan squints at me like I’m daft. “She’s a witch.”

“How are you so sure?”

“Because Lara told ye as much. In fact, she said it more than once.”

I think back to Gran’s rant. “*Ohhh*, yeah no, I didn’t get that. I thought she meant Moira was a witch—like a hubby-stealing wench—but she meant a genuine Wiccan woman with powers.”

“Now you’re suckin’ diesel.” He lifts his knuckles to knock, and I catch his arm and pull out my phone.

“One sec.” I call up our family WhatsApp group.

Bringing an ex-flame of Granda’s home to help. She’s a witch...like, a real Professor McGonagall witch. No one step in it. Gran’s already furious and hurt.

Sloan reads what I wrote and chuckles. “Wise choice. Yer family tends to speak what’s on their mind whether it’s advisable or not.”

"It's part of our charm. At least you never have to guess what we're thinking."

"True enough." He knocks on the door and pegs me with a sober look. "Now, take yer own advice and don't step in it."

"Me? Seriously? I'm the reigning Queen of Amazeballs."

CHAPTER ELEVEN

As much as I hope Granda's old flame has aged poorly on Gran's behalf, Moira Morrigan is a traffic-stopping elegant blonde beauty with long legs, an hourglass figure, and a come-hither smile that could warm even the coldest of hearts.

Damn. In no scenario do I see this ending well.

"Ms. Morrigan?" Sloan asks without missing a beat. "Lugh Cumhaill sent us to fetch ye."

"I'm ready. Will ye be so kind, young man?" She steps onto the covered porch and holds out a large carpet bag. Sloan takes the weight of it and slips the long handles over his shoulder. "There now, let me lock up, and we'll be off."

The key *snicks* into the lock and she twists her wrist.

The action is more for show than anything because as the metal tumbler clicks into place, a rush of magic surges forward. I blink at the power of her wards as they go up. Either she's super protective of her space or she has some powerful enemies and wants to ensure she doesn't come home to any unpleasant surprises.

In a flash, she's finished. She straightens, drops her keys in her pocket, and smiles. "All set. Where's yer car?"

"I'm a wayfarer," Sloan says.

"Oh, that's fine. We're good to portal out from here. My front step is spelled for privacy. Shall we?"

Sloan *poofs* us onto the front doorstep of my grandparents' quaint little thatched-roof home, and I understand his reluctance. He doesn't want to offer her entrance into Gran's space. She's here for a visit only, so should come in like any other stranger.

Sloan gets a point in the win column for that.

"Shall I pull up a chair or will we go in soon?" Moira casts a knowing glance between Sloan and me.

"Oh, sorry." I shake the cobwebs free and grab the handle of the door. "Come on in."

It's only been half an hour since I left the house, but I blink at the condition of things when we step inside. The heap of shoes at the front door is gone. Every surface is polished, and every nook is tidied.

Yay team! Oh, how I love my boys.

No doubt they got my text and knew a glowing impression of our life would make Gran proud. It's not over the top. When we step into the sunken living room where everyone's hanging out, no one is putting on airs, but they're all well put-together.

"Moira." Granda strides over to welcome his guest. "Thank ye for coming. I wouldn't have bothered ye if it weren't a true case of life and death."

Moira leans forward and does the European double kiss greeting. Granda's smart enough to step back as soon as that finishes. "Of course, Lugh. I'll always come when you need me. Whose life or death are we talking about? Are you and yours in danger?"

"Och, not directly us. We're well. Thank ye for askin'."

Gran enters the living room from the kitchen entrance, and I give her credit. If I knew my nemesis female was coming to see my man, I would've dolled up and shown off.

Gran's wearing the same cotton dress she had on earlier, her hair's the same, and she's carrying two plates of warm pastries for the family. "Fresh from the oven, my darlin's."

When everyone launches up to claim their prize, Gran exchanges the plates for Meg and makes her way over. "Hello, Moira. It's good of you to come to help the Order."

"Hello, Lara. You're lookin' well."

She is. Gran might not put on a show of looking snazzy, but she's a beautiful woman. And as far as I'm concerned, every gray hair and laugh line she possesses was well earned in a long, happy life with Granda. "I *am* well. *Slainte.*"

She brushes a stray lock of Meggie's hair out of her face and smiles. "Now, it'll be dark in a few hours, so time is of the essence. I'll take Kinu and the great-grandbabies outside while you all talk. Good luck."

When she turns, her spine is straight, and her head is held high. Good one, Gran.

"Come." Granda gestures to the room. "I'll introduce you to my kids, and we'll get to business. Lara's right. We haven't time for pleasantries tonight."

"Necromancy is a nasty business," Moira says after Granda explains everything to her. "I can see why the fae races are upset with ye. To have their druid protectors turn on them and use them as batteries to power up is vile, to say the least."

"It is," Da agrees. "Which is why we hope you can help us ward the sacred groves. These men are druids. They can theoretically undo any wards or spells we cast to protect the groves from a future attack."

"So, you want magic with a different set of rules and parameters to help foil future harvesting?"

"That's right," Granda concurs. "Nine sites protected from ill intent. Something along the lines of a Narithmore Shield but without restricting the passage of those who mean no harm and belong there."

"And when do you want these wards put into place?"

"Immediately," Granda says. "When we find the ritual site, we'll move in hard. If all goes as planned, we'll find these bastards before they can utilize the powers of the fae they've taken. If they lose that source, we don't want them able to simply go back and take others."

"But the sacred groves of the elders of the Order aren't the only place where fae dwell, Lugh. What stops these men from finding another way behind the faery glass to continue their evil? This is a temporary solution at best."

Granda drops his chin. "It may well be, but one of our groves provides the home for hundreds of members of dozens of species. These men know how to access them. We'll not stop our hunt to take them down. Warding the groves is only one protective step."

Moira considers that for a moment. "Very well, I'll speak to my coven and we'll discuss terms."

Granda's brow tightens. "Ye want to negotiate payouts when the well-being of nature's creatures are in peril?"

Moira laughs, and the sound rings through the air like chimes of an enchanted bell. I sit up straighter, my back tingling and starting to itch. "Still the same oul bleedin' heart, Lugh. The world we live in isn't about right and wrong, my darlin' man. It's about leverage and need. The druids need a favor. That gives my coven the leverage to make demands. It's simply business."

From where I'm sitting on the arm of the club chair, I see Da's expression darken. He doesn't like the sound of this. Neither does Sloan. The two of them share the same worried scowls. What's the witch up to? What does she want? And why is my Fianna shield reacting to what she's saying?

Moira steps outside to use her phone, and Da shakes his head when several of us open our mouths to speak. Not now. Got it. Before someone fills in the silence, I need to get my point out. So far my shield has protected me from poisonings and hexes, but maybe something Granda's ex said is triggering it now.

"Funny thing," I say matter-of-factly. "The tattoo on my back got super itchy just now. I think something I've recently been exposed to might be irritating it."

Granda frowns. "When did that start, *mo chroi*?"

"When we were being taught the finer points of good business. Strange, huh?"

"Strange, indeed," Da agrees.

Granda runs a hand over the back of his neck and exhales. "Let me know if it gets any worse. If so, maybe ye'll need to excuse yerself to put a balm on it or something."

Granda's phone rings and he checks the ID of the caller. "Tell me they found something." When his lips tighten into a fine line, we know they haven't. "Och, well, keep them searchin'. Ye got the parameters I sent? Good. Dempsey hasn't gotten back to me, but—"

Bruin materializes in the middle of the living room. "I found it."

"Hold on, Malcolm. We've got something."

Da launches off the couch and to his feet. "Where? Is there a landmark or town nearby ye can direct us to, Bear?"

"Och, no need. Ye'll know where, I'm sure."

"You were searching at Killarney National Park, right?" I hurry over to the atlas page where we've marked out the radius of our search range. "Was it in there?"

"Almost." Bear lumbers forward and rises to set his front paws on the table. "On the north end of the park, above the body of water, there's a stone tower of a fifteenth-century fortress. Do ye know it?"

Sloan runs his finger over that section of the map and stops. "That has to be Ross Castle. It's right where yer describing, Bear."

"Have you been there?" I hope beyond hope he has. Sloan can't *poof* anywhere willy-nilly. He has to have been someplace before to be able to set his internal navigation GPS to get him back there.

"I have. A couple of school trips in my younger years. There's the castle proper and a great deal of forested area surrounding it."

"There's a jut of land that goes out into the water. It's away from the castle but still close. The fae clearing is there."

Da nods, and my brothers all jump up and run to get their boots on. "How many of us can ye take at once, son?"

Sloan looks at us. "Seven grown adults on one go isn't great—"

"Six," Granda says. "I can't leave with Moira here thinkin' she's gonna put the screws to the druids. We can't afford to vex her, and Lara won't take it well either."

"Take Da and the boys, then come back for Granda and me. I have to pee, and my Spidey-senses are telling me I need to be here for the witch negotiations."

Sloan nods. "Five is doable. I'll take them, get situated, and be back for you two in a flash."

Granda nods. "Go. I'll spread the word to the Perry boys and Dempsey Flanagan. Assess the opposing force and let me know if we need more bodies for the fight. It's the Autumn Equinox, but I'll try to connect with the others if I can."

"Will do."

After everything had moved painfully slow over the past twenty-four hours, Bruin finding the ritual site throws all of us into fast-forward. I run to the loo, and on my way back to the living room, I grab my casting stones out of my bag.

When Moira steps back inside, she's wearing a Cheshire grin and takes a seat in the sage green club chair I was in earlier. "Where did everyone go? Was it something I said?"

I ignore the coy seductive tone in her voice, mesmerized by something far more interesting. The closer I study her, the blurrier she becomes. Weird.

"I spoke with my sisters," she says. "Like me, they are happy to be of service."

"And you mentioned a cost?" Granda snaps.

"Och, don't be like that, Lugh. We have history. I want to help—honestly, I do—but it's not only me who weighs in on the magic contracts we accept. I'm in a coven. There is a process."

I rub my fingers over my eyes and stand. My back feels like ants are crawling under my flesh.

It's making me squirmy.

"All right, Fi?" Granda casts me a concerned gaze.

"It's my itchy back. It's getting very uncomfortable. Where are the healing stones?"

"Here, luv." Gran joins us. "Yer back's botherin' ye, is it?"

"Uh-huh. Remember that time Sloan and I went to Ardfert Cathedral, and I got that bad rash? It feels similar to that."

Gran looks at me, and I'm thankful she's such a quick wit because she doesn't miss a beat. "Och, like that, is it? Well, then, let's see what we can do to address the problem."

"Sorry about this," I say to Moira. "You two go about your business. Don't mind us."

Gran pulls a woven basket off the shelf by the television and takes it to the table where Jackson and Granda worked on coloring earlier. She also sets a pen and paper down beside my hand. "Now, take the amethyst. We'll start ye off with that for healing."

I pick up the pen and write. *There's something freaky about her. An illusion or spell I can almost see through. My shield is going crazy.*

Gran nods and passes her hand over the page, rendering it

blank once more. "Keep the amethyst, and I'll give ye a few more that I want ye to concentrate on."

I hold my palm open, and Gran adds hematite, black tourmaline, a beautiful multicolored fluorite, and smokey quartz. If I'm not mistaken, these are the stones you'd find in an empath starter kit.

Cutting negativity, mind clarity, seeing beyond the illusion. Yeah, I see what she's doing here.

"Now, luv, take a seat and focus. If ye have the peridot that yer friend Patty gave ye, it wouldn't be bad to hold that one as well for luck and a bit of extra oomph."

Sloan flashes back into the living room and looks from Granda and Moira talking to Gran and me. "What did I miss?"

"I'm glad you're here." I reach forward. "Can you please hold my hand? I don't feel well."

Sloan reaches to meet my outstretched hand but isn't as quick to pick up my meaning as Gran was. His first instinct goes straight to being alarmed for me. Sweet. I run my thumb over his bone ring—the ring that allows him to see the unseen.

"Focus, surly." I tap the ring on his middle finger. "I need your insight as to what's bothering me."

Sloan laces his fingers with mine, and I see the dawning as his confusion clears. I close my free hand around the gemstones and let the negativity and deception melt away.

I feel Sloan's energy as he casts a spell. Like a curtain lifting, our vision is no longer clouded by the illusion Moira is projecting.

The mirage of her endless beauty drains away, and we're in the presence of an average-looking woman with thinning hair and a dark and haunted aura.

She hasn't noticed that her lies have been stripped away, so we can hear the persuasion spell working its magic on Granda when she speaks.

She wants an ancient chalice called the Narstina Cup from the shrine of the Order—hammered gold, bejeweled, and with a wide foot with Celtic engravings carved into it. A historical trinket, she calls it, but it's much more than that to the witches. Her longing for the chalice is ugly and dark and makes me want to push her away from Granda.

Sloan must feel the same way because he steps forward, grabs the carpetbag and the woman, and flashes away. A moment later, he flashes back looking furious.

"What the hell is this?" Granda snaps.

"That witch was ensnarin' ye, Lugh. That's what was settin' off Fi's mark. The witches want a chalice from the shrine, but not as a token payment for their services. The woman has foul and dark plans for the thing and was goin' to turn the groves' wards to her advantage."

"Yer sure of this?" Granda asks.

I nod and set Gran's gemstones back in the basket, keeping only my peridot. "We're sure. Gran's help with the gemstones, my shield's warning, and Sloan's enchanted fae ring merged to show us the truth. That woman is all kinds of nasty, Granda."

Granda nods and looks sad. "Well, I told ye this afternoon, Lara, that she wouldn't be the same woman she was forty years ago, and I guess I proved myself right. Too bad, though. I wanted to protect the other groves."

Gran walks into Granda's open arms and kisses his cheek. "Yer idea to utilize another sect of magic is a good one. We'll revisit that and look for a better choice than Moira Morrigan and her duplicitous coven."

"What did ye do with her, son?" Granda asks.

"Och, I dumped her on her front stoop and told her we saw through her deceptions. I don't think she'll be contacting you again anytime soon."

With Moira gone, Granda and Sloan do a quick magical sweep from the front door into the living room in case the witch left any kind of hex bags, tracking spells, or listening devices. The area is clean.

"She likely didn't think she'd need anything beyond her beguiling spell." Gran picks up the empty pastry plates. "Good one, Fiona. Ye saw through the oul hag."

As much as I don't like the idea that Granda was being manipulated, I'm glad Gran is vindicated in her mistrust of the woman and that Granda won't trust his old flame any time soon—if ever.

"Be careful, Fi." Kinu comes out from putting the monkeys to bed. "Safe home to you all."

I nod and put my hand out to connect with Sloan and Granda. "Hopefully, this won't take long, and we'll have the fae safe home to their mates as well."

Sloan waits until both Granda and I nod, then he flashes us to join up with the others.

CHAPTER TWELVE

The gray skies of night are encroaching on the horizon by the time Sloan, Granda, and I sneak into position behind the ritual site. Da has my brothers, the Perry boys, and Bruin far enough away that they won't be detected, but close enough that we can see and hear the conversations of the cloaked minions of the Barghest, a.k.a. the Black Dog.

"It sounds like there are a lot of them." I look at Da. "Like, a *lot*. How outnumbered are we?"

Da frowns. "Very. Any chance ye can call in a backup team? I figure there's close to forty men out there. Bruin's worth at least five in a fight, but that still leaves us heavily outnumbered."

Granda looks at the nine of us and frowns. "It's the Autumn Equinox. I reached out, but most of the Nine Families have private celebrations and don't have cell phones or technology with them for their hours of offerings."

"That's okay." Dillan shrugs and adjusts the hood of his cloak. "We've got this. If Bruin's worth five warriors, that means we're fifteen against forty. With our Fianna upgrades, I think we're good."

I blink at him. "And this is why you failed math. Fifteen against forty is *not* good."

The murmur of male voices in the distance falls to a hush, and a single voice breaks through the strengthening darkness.

Goddess of Flame, of hearth and ember,
God of Fire, of blazing timber,
Crackle of hazel, ash, and lime,
Heat the cauldron to boil. It's time.

"They're lighting the fire," Emmet says. "I don't suppose it's customary to enjoy a couple of rounds of S'mores before ritual killings, is it?"

Da frowns. "Afraid not. We're out of time."

Sloan looks at his watch. "I can get us another seven or so. Be right back."

I realize I'm touching his arm too late. I'm portaled with him into a pub. No one gives us a glance when we appear in the center of a busy establishment, so I guess it's a magic people pub.

"What the fuck did ye do, Cumhaill?" Sloan turns on me while looking green. "Have ye any idea how dangerous it is to tag a ride if I don't know yer comin'? I could've lost ye in transit or dropped ye somewhere. Dammit, I could've killed ye."

If I couldn't see how upset he is, I'd know it anyway by his accent's thickness. Da's like that too. His tendencies get much more pronounced when he's losing his mind.

"First off," I lean in and lower my voice, "don't yell at me in public. Second, I didn't mean to do it. I didn't realize I was touching you. Third, you didn't kill me—yay for that—so focus. I'm sorry you're upset, but we have more important things going on right now."

He takes my hand and squeezes it. "Not more important than yer life. By the goddess, my heart is racin'. What would I have done if I lost ye?"

"Easy. You'd come find me."

"Not funny."

"A lover's quarrel already?" Ciara stops beside us with a round of drinks in hand. "I can't say I'm surprised. The two of ye are like oil and cat piss. Ye don't go together and gross, who'd want that?"

I stick out my tongue. "Oh, Ciara. Good, your shirt's still on. I'm glad we caught you before you started exposing your boobs to some unwitting sucker in the back room. We've got druid problems. Where are the others?"

"Over there." Sloan places a hand at the small of my back to get me moving. We join a group of seven people, some of whom I remember from the night they attacked me in the alley.

The heirs of the Nine Families.

"Mackenzie, color me surprised." A slick frat boy sits up straighter at the back of the table. "Ye decided to share yer pet and join us. Pull up a chair and introduce us properly."

I recognized that one. It's the other wayfarer of the group, Tad McNiff. And Ciara's co-ringleader in arranging my hazing during the Tralee Festival.

Sloan flashes Tad a middle-fingered salute and leans in. "We've got trouble, buds. It's line of duty time. There's a rogue bunch of druid necromancers about to slaughter the fae captured from the Perry and Doyle groves. Lugh's and Fiona's family are outnumbered, and it's going down now. Are ye game to fight?"

"Are ye shittin' us?" Tad's gaze narrows. "Is this payback for past transgressions? Do ye think ye can get the better of me, Mackenzie?"

I frown. "Hubba-wha? How did what he said get flipped to be about you?"

Sloan sighs. "Tad thinks everything in life is about him."

"No. It's for real," a guy to my right says. "The twins were in the air looking for a clearing all day. Da said it was a favor for Lugh."

I recognize him. It's the guy Bruin almost killed in the alley. He flung him against a dumpster and broke his insides.

Sloan meets my gaze. "That's Jarrod Perry."

I nod. "Yeah, your brothers are already there and about to fight alongside my brothers. FYI, if we don't make this right and save the fae, there is talk of them pulling their favor from druids altogether. No more magic powers."

The group stands, looking alarmed.

"Can they do that?"

I shrug. "I don't see why not. Our powers are a gift of connection. If the fae sever it..."

"First things first." Sloan takes a firm grasp on my wrist. "Those willing to fight to save the fae, link up and I'll take ye there. McNiff, ye'll have to lend me some wayfarer juice to get us all there safely."

"A real battle," another guy says. He meets my gaze and nods. "Eric Flanagan. It's nice to meet ye properly, Fiona. I'm ever so sorry for our first encounter."

Everyone grabs hold of one another, and even Ciara abandons the drinks to take Sloan's other hand. "Don't look so surprised, Cumhaill. Some of the fae they plan on killing came from my family grove. Of course, I want them to pay."

I shrug. "I guess we'll see how you handle yourself when you're not skulking in the shadows, gang-attacking innocents. This will be new for you."

Sloan meets Tad's gaze and nods. "Ready?"

Tad nods. "Take it away, Mackenzie."

We materialize back where we'd been in the woods by Ross Castle. The original group has spread out since we left. I crouch low and crawl in behind Da. I touch his shoulder to let him know we've returned. "Hey. Where do you want us?"

"Yer brothers are circling the site. There's no sign of the fae, so we assume they have them caged and cloaked somewhere close by. The boys went to find the perspective from where Pip saw things. Once the water boils, Barghest will release them from their prison, and we'll move in. When they have eyes on the fae, Emmet will signal us."

"What's the signal?"

"With Emmet involved, there's no tellin'."

I smile, kinda jazzed to see what he comes up with. He's been awarded more than a few Oh! Henry bars for his pranks. Emmet has a creative and slightly off-kilter mind. "So, we're not at the boil and bubble, toil and trouble stage of the evening yet?"

"Close to it, I expect. The fire's been ragin' for ten minutes, and I'm sure they're boostin' it with their powers. It's full dark now. If I were them, I'd be anxious to get started."

My shield tingles, and I pull off my hoodie. I'll need freedom of movement to fight, and my ugly bark arms and tattoos might work in my favor and gross out the Black Dog members.

I shuffle back to the cluster of druid heirs and ignore the wide-eyed stares when everyone takes in my Frankenstein impression. "The others left to encircle the clearing. When they locate the fae, they'll signal, and we all move in to fight. Sloan and Tad, your primary job is to rescue the fae and *poof* them to the Doyle grove. We'll sort them out later. For now, we need them safe. We need to restore faith in the fae and prove to them that we're still their protectors."

"I want to fight," Tad says.

"You will, but the fae are the priority."

Tad runs a finger over the bark gauntlets attached to my bare forearms. "A spell gone wrong, beautiful? If ye want to swing by my place sometime after all this is over, I'll help ye reverse it."

"Keep it in yer pants, McNiff." Sloan pulls a dagger from where it's sheathed against his thigh. He points the business end at Tad and scowls. "Ye have no business pretendin' to know what those bracers are about, and she'll not succumb to yer smile and fall into yer bed like some chippie."

Sloan's use of the word amuses me to no end. I accused him once of wanting to make me his new world chippie. It's fun to know he does pay attention.

The steady beat of a bodhran brings the chanter from earlier back into the center of the clearing to begin the ritual.

Day to night, and life to death.
Dark Mothers in every breath.
Demeter, Nemesis, Hecate,
Kali, Morrighan, Tiamat,
Bringers of destruction, ye who embody the Crone,
We offer these fae lives, power in blood and bone.

I search the darkness at the far side of the clearing for Emmet's signal. "Come on, Em. It's gotta be happening."

The redneck lyrics of a country song blaring at top volume break the pregnant silence. The Black Dog druids freeze. The sound of a fiddle picks up in the clearing and a strobe of disco lights start flashing up into the night sky.

"He didn't," Da says.

I snort and grab a branch from the ground. "Oh, he *did*."

Cotton-Eyed Joe blares through the air, and the sound-activated strobe machine picks up on the frenetic beat. Colored lights explode into the sky and create one helluva laser light-show diversion.

"He gets this from yer mam." Da produces his staff and launches into the fray.

I follow behind while raising my hands and calling my gift. "Nice try, old man."

There's a moment when the clearing is solid chaos, and I wonder how we'll know who's on what team. Then I see all the black cloaks. It's nice that the enemy wore a uniform so those of us who don't know the faces of all the players can keep things straight.

Bruin, Aiden, Emmet, and the Perry twins flood in from the opposite side of the clearing. I hear Eric Flanagan's whimper on my right flank and understand his terror. Bruin in a full raging run is a terrifying sight to behold.

"He only attacked you because you attacked me. Your fault. Don't do it again and you'll be fine." A bolt of energy streams at us, and I wind up and connect with it using my branch. It's a line drive up the middle but leaves me holding splinters.

I think about my enchanted spear and regret leaving her at home in Toronto. "Gawd, I miss you, Birga. I wish you were here right now."

The moment I call her, she appears in my hand. The enchanted spear that belonged to my ancestor, Fionn mac Cumhaill, is a thing of wonder.

Her spear is a wickedly sharp chunk of green Connemara marble latched onto the end of a gnarled ironwood stick with an enchanted creature's sinew. I haven't learned what creature yet, but I sense that it was rare and powerful.

"I missed you, girlfriend." Birga is old, raw, and rough.

Although she's not pretty, she ebbs with power—and together, we are a force. We cut a swath through the enemy and make our way closer to where my brothers fight.

Da is a phenom. I could watch him spinning his staff forever and never tire. He's a natural. Brutal and swift, he uses the blade at one end and the club at the other.

Aiden is a beast with his sword and strength. I know Kinu worries, but she's never seen him like this. Maybe that's a good thing. Perhaps it's best that she knows him only as her loveable protector.

Calum must be perched in a tree at the end of the clearing because volleying rounds of arrows arc at us, and although no one is standing still or staying in one place, he's only picking off the Black Dog.

He truly is our Robin Hood.

Dillan has his hood up—big surprise there—and wields his dual daggers as he minces, stabs, and slices his way through black-cloaked men.

Then there's Emmet. My nutty, sweet, goofball of a brother is… "What *is* he doing?"

"He's a buffer." Sloan spins off an attacker and turns so we stand back-to-back. "The naked man in the fortress must've been Fionn's buffer."

Emmet's dancing around, raising his hands, casting, and deflecting…he's not so much fighting but cavorting.

Cotton-Eyed Joe must be on a loop because we're on our second time through. Emmet looks as amused as he was the first time around. "What does a buffer mean?"

"He's a power booster to the party."

Oh, that's interesting. His hands are up, and he's casting like a fiend, with a wide smile, so whatever is happening, he's having fun with it. He's good, and he's safe.

That's all that matters.

"Oh shit." The ground beneath my feet rumbles and crumbles. Sloan grabs me around the waist and flings me clear. I'm flying. I'm falling. Part of my mind stalls out from being catapulted in the air. The other part searches my trajectory for what I'm going to hit.

Tree.

I crash into the wide trunk of an ancient ash. When I hit, I have my arms up to protect my head. I expect to break at least one of my forearms, but I barely feel the impact.

I crumple to the base of the tree and roll to my knees. With solid ground under my feet, I spin in time to see Sloan swallowed by the gaping earth.

"Sloan!"

I run and dive at the closing hole. There's no way for me to get there in time. The ground seals and the ache of losing another person hits me so hard, my legs fail. My knees hit the ground, and the jolt causes me to bite my tongue.

"Pull yerself together, Cumhaill. It'll take more than an Earthquake spell to take me down. I portaled out."

I launch up and punch him in the gut. "Don't do that. You scared the crap outta me."

He buckles at the waist and gasps. "I can tell."

I hold out my hand and call Birga. The moment she's firmly in my grip, I feel our connection and turn back to the fight. "Come on, Mackenzie. Now's not the time to lally-gag. Villains to kill and fae folk to save."

He lets out a coughing laugh and straightens. "Apologies. My mistake."

Surrounded as they are, and dropping like splatted flies, it's easy to read when the Black Dog members realize the tides have turned and there's no escape. Some drop to their knees and lace their fingers behind the backs of their heads in surrender. Most of them choose to fight to the death.

I feel exactly how excited Birga is at the prospect.

Four months ago, the concept of lethal force was reserved for only the most heinous of criminals. I never would've taken a life myself but understood that my father and brothers might be put in that position.

Now, I see the world from an altered perspective.

Things are different in the fae world.

Three men rush in from my right and I duck the blade of a sword and swing Birga to keep them at a distance. A creeping vine wraps around my left foot, but I'm too busy defending to untangle from it. When the first man rushes, I sink Birga's spearhead into his stomach and swipe left.

I stumble to one knee as the vine pulls tight and tugs my ankle out from underneath me. I try to counter the Creeping Vine but don't affect the spell. My other two attackers take advantage and launch forward.

Rolling to my back, I brace for impact.

I grip Birga in both hands and use her to keep the men off me. I grunt at the weight of two grown men landing on me. One has a dagger and is banging the blade's point against my side. He's getting nowhere.

As much as I hope someone will see I'm in trouble and help me, Da's words ring in my head.

Yer always responsible for saving yourself. Always.

The world spins as the vine around my leg pulls harder and drags me toward the woods. I'm skidding over the uneven ground. With my shirt rucked up, each rock sticking up from the soil should be scraping and scoring my flesh. They aren't.

One of the men kicks me in the ribs.

I expect the air to rush from my lungs with violent force, but I barely feel the impact.

I see the beauty of Fionn's bracers. Honestly, in this instance, I don't hate having skin as tough as bark.

The guy who kicked me might've thought I'd reel from the strike and be dizzy and gasping, but I'm not. When he comes at me with a follow-up attack, I use his moment of confusion to my advantage.

I release Birga with one hand and grip his face. *Frostbite.*

He screams in rage as the skin of his face freezes beneath my touch. When he pulls back, he rips and cracks his brittle flesh. His buddy curses when he sees bits of his friend's face stuck to my hand.

I flick the chunks of cheek into the grass. "Did you want a facial, too? Two for one, tonight only—Equinox special."

When he lunges, I'm ready.

I prop Birga up, and her green marble spearhead buries deep. The man's blood bursts free of his chest. He falls forward, and I'm coated in a fountain of scarlet fluid.

It's *soooo* gross, but I don't have time to worry about looking like an extra in a *Saw* movie. I'm at the edge of the clearing and about to lose sight of my family.

Rolling to the side, I brace my feet against a tree's trunk and refuse to let myself get dragged into the shadows.

This vine is determined to take me.

I *can* save myself.

I register the shifting shadows and swing my vision, trying to see who or what is approaching. The vine around my ankle is wound up to my crotch and is obsessed with pulling me into the trees.

Using Birga, I work on cutting myself loose. She's super sharp, and I want to avoid slicing my leg off. The Tough as Bark might keep my skin free from damage against regular offenses, but what about against enchanted blades?

I'm not willing to bet my leg on it.

The shuffle of footsteps closes in, and I spin onto my knees. I'm getting nowhere on the vine, and I'm losing my hold on the tree.

Warning tingles across the back of my neck, but I can't see who's coming. Someone is watching me, and it doesn't feel like a Black Dog minion about to attack.

It feels more sinister than that.

I grip Birga and strain to see into the darkness.

Bruin. I need help. Someone spelled a vine to drag me into the forest. I can't break the spell and can't cut loose. I feel him waiting for me. Watching.

The roar of my bear explodes in the clearing behind me. There's a violent threat in the timbre of it, and I know it's for the fear he feels across our bond.

A moment later, he's there. He swipes the vine pulling at me, swings his head, and roars.

"I've got her, buddy." Dillan drops to his knees beside me.

Sloan's there too, and he casts an illumination spell so we can see. Bruin turns and charges off into the woods.

"Have ye got her?" Da runs to join us. "Christ, Fi, where have ye been?"

I blink at my father, and when Aiden, Calum, and Emmet arrive, they're wearing the same worried looks on their faces.

"I got kidnapped by a crazy-determined Creeping Vine spell. I couldn't break it."

"That's a lot of blood." Emmet points at my top.

"Not mine. I took out three during my drop-and-drag trip to the woods."

Da helps me to my feet and wraps an arm around my hips while Dillan and Emmet cut the vine and untangle it from my leg.

"So, a vine drags ye away," Sloan says. "And ye still managed to take down three men?"

I brush at the death I'm coated in, but there's no helping it. I'm a disaster. "Uh, yeah, but then I got here and knew I couldn't break free. I panicked. I felt someone or something in the trees. He wanted me—was waiting for me. That's when I freaked out and called Bruin for help."

"And thank the Powers ye did." Da presses his hand to the side of my head and kisses my temple. "We lost track of ye, Fi. I don't know how, but ye dropped off the map."

Sloan curses. "One minute ye were in front of me, and the next ye were gone. Ye gotta stop doin' that to me, Cumhaill. It's hard on my nerves. I thought Baba Yaga took ye again."

I wave that one away. "It wasn't her. Honestly, I doubt I'll hear from her again."

"I may know how we lost track of you." Dillan stands, holding a section of the vine. He lifts the twining green rope to his nose and sniffs. "This plant has a quality of invisibility to it. I'd guess the more of a hold it got on you, the more unlikely it was that we'd find you."

I frown. “How do you know what invisible smells like?”

Dillan shrugs. “With my hood up, I know lots of things I don’t know I know. You know?”

My brain hurts.

“Are ye hurt at all, *mo chroi*?” Granda joins us.

“No. The bracers kept me safe. They’re amazing.”

“They also kept ye from bein’ poisoned.” Sloan eyes the thorns on the chopped vine segments. “I bet there’s paralysis as well as invisibility at play here. If these had punctured yer skin, ye wouldn’t have been able to fight and call for yer bear.”

Granda scowls and moves to see what Sloan’s talking about. “Who’s after ye now, Fiona?”

I shrug. “Maybe no one. Maybe the vine just picked me out of the crowd.”

No one seems convinced.

Da kisses the side of my head again and hugs me. “Or maybe, once again, the Fianna target on yer back has drawn attention.”

I sigh. Yeah, that’s most likely it. “Lucky me.”

CHAPTER THIRTEEN

Bruin's back within five minutes, and he's one ornery bear. He stomps through the woods, crushes plants, and swipes his claws through the scrub while letting out loud bellows of fury. *Whoever it was left a very distinct scent, but he's gone. I'm sorry, Red.*

I press my face into the warmth of his fur and breathe in the wilds of the outdoors. "Not your fault, buddy. You're my hero, you know? You got the girl. That's most important."

The rumble of his amusement does a lot to ease the tensions of the night away. *Yer hero bar is low.*

"Nonsense. You found me, and you kept me from getting dragged into the woods. I'd hate to think of myself like one of those pathetic girls in every slasher movie ever."

I'll always find ye. Or at least, never stop tryin'.

"Like I said. My hero."

Dillan and Granda are examining the scraps of the vine and the thorns attached. They're wondering out loud what kind of poison my bracers saved me from. If I had been paralyzed and dragged away, unable to defend myself, things would've ended very differently tonight.

I turn away.

I saw the live show. I don't need a replay.

Truly thankful for the bizarre gauntlets for the first time, I close my eyes and accept the gift that they are. The rush of magic that warms my skin washes me with a sense of rightness. Fionn considered them part of his treasured armor, and I will too. I open my eyes, ready to accept them for the eyesore they are but so incredibly happy to see that Granda and Sloan were right.

My arms are as pasty pale and smooth as ever.

"Thank you, baby Groot."

With that in mind, I hold my hand out and call Birga. She appears in my grip, and I repeat the gratefulness process, absorbing her into me as well.

Da looks down at me rubbing the spear tattoo lining the inside of my right forearm and nods. "Ye did well tonight, Fi. Ye should be proud."

I surveil the warzone and smile at Emmet's strobe machine. "*Cotton-Eyed Joe* will be tough to beat as a diversion."

"Right?" Emmet nods and waggles his dark eyebrows. "Touching the nakey guy may have taught me lots of new things to use in battle, but sometimes you gotta fall back on what you know."

I chuckle and look at Sloan. "Did you and Tad get all the fae evacuated?"

"We did. Tad and Ciara are there now and will protect them for tonight. Emmet and I thought you'd like to come with us tomorrow to check on Pip and her mate."

"Absolutely. And what about everyone on the rescue squad? Is everyone whole?"

"A few close calls, but nothing Da can't handle. I flashed Flanagan and one of the Perry twins home for him to tend to. The rest suffered only cuts and some magic burns. They can heal up at home tonight."

I nod, suddenly exhausted. "Then, if it's all right with everyone, I'd like to go home, have a shower, and burn my clothes. I've had enough for one night."

"Good thinking, baby girl." Aiden takes Da's place at my side and hugs me. "Sloan, would you mind taking a few of us back? I think Da, Granda, and Dillan are still busy, but Emmet, Calum, and I are ready, aren't we?"

My brothers nod. "Hells to the yeah," Emmet says and reaches over to grasp Sloan's arm. "Home, James."

One of the nice things about Gran and Granda being nature lovers is that they have an outdoor shower at the side of the house. It's surrounded by the perennial garden and hidden by a vine-covered lattice. It's nice for them because they can have a lovely summer shower while basking in the sunlight and smelling the season's blooms. It's lovely for me because I can step under the water flow, rinse off the blood, and not track death through their house.

The only drawback is that it's the third week in September and nighttime. It's past the time of year where this is a warm and pleasant experience.

"And everyone's all right?" Gran stands outside the little lattice stall with a towel ready to wrap me up. Yes, I know I'm a grown woman, but I'll take getting snuggled by my grandma after nearly getting kidnapped.

"That's what I was told." I rinse my hair under the spray of water. "I know for sure our clan is good. I saw all of them and spoke with them when it was over. The others, I can't say for sure, but Sloan and Granda said so."

"Good," Gran says. "And the fae are safely returned, that's most important."

I run my hands up and over my face and shut off the water. "I don't understand how anyone could think to harm them like that in the first place. It's sickening. I'm thankful Bruin found the clearing in time to stop it."

I shake off and wring out my hair. Gran hands me the thick towel, and I tuck it under my arm and wrap it around me a few times before I step out of the shower.

Emmet and Aiden are lounging a way off on the lawn, and I call, "Next!"

Aiden rolls to his feet and walks toward us. Then his footing falters, and he stops. He has a weird look on his face as he stares past me, and I sense the presence behind me before she speaks.

"A human of honor, a rare trait today. You promised results, that the offenders would pay."

I turn and meet the gaunt lady with branches and leaves growing out of her arms and head. "Most of them died trying to hurt others tonight. I believe all the fae survived."

"Your matron is correct. It's good no fae were lost. Let this happen again, and you won't like the cost."

Okaaay. It rankles me a little that we put our lives on the line and she's threatening us, but whatevs. She's obvi still pissed that the fae were targeted in the first place.

"The Ancient Order of Druids regrets this incident," Gran says. "Our commitment to safeguarding the fae is unwavering. We will be vigilant in tracking down those involved and protecting the groves more ardently in the future so nothing like this happens again. To that end, we've already contacted a local wizard who says he'll be able to ensure no necromancer comes at you again."

The tree lady bows and the leaves sticking out of her brain-branches flutter. "Matron Cumhaill, it is a pleasure. Your devotion is a known treasure." When she straightens, she casts one last glance over us. "Fionn's heirs, young and green, prove yourselves brave and keen. With fresh blood, noble and true, rebuild the Fianna to what we knew. Traditions are vital but time gives sway. To thrive in this world, there's more than one way."

I hear what she's saying and am surer than ever that I'm on the right path. Druids need to break free of the past to thrive in the future. I bow my head. "Namaste."

"Namaste." Tree Lady steps back and dissolves into the shadows of the grove.

I look at Gran, Aiden, and Emmet.

Emmet makes a face. "Well, that was ominous."

The next morning, Emmet and I are dressed, have had our breakfast, and are out on the back lawn playing with Bruin and the kids when Sloan *poofs* in.

He takes one look at Meg and Jackson climbing on my bear and scowls at me. "Small humans are usin' yer mythical spirit warrior as a climbing gym."

I chuckle. "I'm aware. Meg and Jackson love Bruin, and he loves them right back, don't you buddy?"

"They are pure heart and raw energy. How could I not?"

"See? S'all good."

Sloan shakes his head. "There's no talkin' to ye about stayin' in yer lane, is there?"

Emmet bursts out laughing. "Why would she do that when it's so much more interesting to weave all over the road? Grannies keep it in the slow lane, bro. Does Fi look like a granny to you?"

Sloan eyes me up, and his glance lingers. "No. I can't say she does."

"Well, good. I'm too young to be in granny territory."

I wave to Kinu that we're leaving, and she and Aiden rise from the café table at the side of the house to assume kid duty. "We're off to the Doyle grove to check in on the recovering fae. We'll be back."

Aiden nods. "Is Bruin going with you or staying here?"

I look back at my bear and giggle. Hopefully, the kids don't start telling people they play on Auntie Fi's grizzly bear. "Are you staying here or coming with?"

"Stayin'. Gran's cleanin' out the fridge. She told me there's leftover breakfast casserole with my name on it."

"Perfect. Enjoy. Everybody play nice. We'll be back." Emmet and I clasp palms with Sloan, and he transports us to the Doyle grove. "Wow, it looks so much better."

Iris Doyle strides out of the trees and greets us with a warm smile. "Top o' the mornin', young druids. What brings ye by?"

Sloan releases our hands and gestures at the trees. "We wanted to check in on the fae rescued last night and see that they have what they need to put this all behind them. I see Lara's tincture is workin'."

Iris nods and smiles at Emmet and me. "Yer gran has a gift unequaled in our world. She's truly goddess-blessed in her natural abilities."

Emmet nods. "And she's a rocking-good cook too."

Sloan straightens and holds out his hands once more. "We have an audience, folks. Shall we make our rounds?"

"Please do." Iris steps back to give us a clear path. "And wish everyone welcome from us. The Perry grove isn't recovering as well as ours yet, but I'll be sure to make everyone welcome until those fae can return to their home."

Emmet and I accept Sloan's offered hands and the moment we make contact, the hidden beauty of life behind the fae veil is revealed once again. With Sloan's bone ring in place, the secret world of the unseen is no longer a secret.

I blink at the splendor. It's like the sun is streaming golden radiance and the air shimmers with color and life and magic. One of the rabbit creatures flies past us, his brilliant purple wings iridescent as they reflect the light.

I breathe in the sugary warmth of cotton candy and smile. "It's amazing, isn't it?"

"It is," Sloan and Emmet agree in unison.

"Do either of you see Pip?"

Emmet nods. "Yep. She's climbing down from that tree."

I watch as first she, then her mate climb down from their perch behind the lush leaves. He seems a little reluctant, but Pip strokes his arm and encourages him.

I don't blame him or take it personally.

He's had a rough week at the hands of druids.

When they get close, Emmet gets down on his knees to speak to them. Pip climbs up onto his legs and hugs him before starting to chatter.

Even without understanding the woodland brownie talk, I can tell that she introduces her mate and she's happy and grateful for his return.

They're a sweet couple, and I'm glad it worked out for him. Having never met the male before, I can't say for sure that he's still traumatized over the whole thing, but he's not at ease. He still looks quite afraid.

Whatever Emmet's discussing with them, Pip seems quite insistent. She keeps nodding and gesturing at her mate. We're also gathering the attention of the other creatures.

"What was that about?" I ask when Emmet stands.

"They want to come with us. Nilm thinks he owes us a debt of life and he wants to come live in our grove."

My mouth drops open. "That's sweet, but their lives are their own. They should live free with their friends here in their home. It's thanks enough to know they're safe."

"I told them as much."

"Besides, our grove is in its infancy. We have nine trees and a couple of bushes. They won't be happy there."

"I told them that too."

"Next to yer house is a great wooded area," Sloan says.

That's true. We live in the last house on the street, and over the dirt laneway, we have access to the Don River Valley Park.

The wild area runs along the river and connects the Toronto urban areas with a vast and wild green space.

In hindsight, I suppose that's why Da settled there.

Pip says something more and her eyes glass up.

"She's begging us. It's a point of pride to tend to our grove. Brownies serve to earn honor, and they want to serve us. To turn them down would be dishonoring them after they've already suffered the indignity of him getting kidnapped and nearly eaten."

I can't stand to see her tears.

Sinking onto my knees, I keep one hand linked to Sloan and hug Pip and Nilm with my other arm. "Tell them we'd be honored to have them but make it clear that if they change their minds or can't make a home for themselves in the city, that we hold them to no obligation. They come as our friends and are free to choose when to come and go without any fear of dishonor."

Emmet chatters to them for a bit, then nods. "Sloan, are you able to transport them home? We can't take them on the plane, and they're anxious to go."

I sigh and offer Sloan an apologetic smile. "Sorry you're getting dragged into Cumhaill chaos again. I know you have things in your life to tend to as well. Can you get away and spend a few days with us?"

Sloan dips his chin. "Happy to help."

Emmet finishes chattering, and the brownies straighten, looking excited. When they nod, their antennae bob and bounce. Hand-in-hand, they rush off and scale a different tree, chattering the entire way.

Many of the other creatures are buzzing and bustling too. I wave at one of the winged rabbits wriggling its nose at me. "We seem to have caused quite a stir."

"By my experience, ye usually do, Cumhaill."

I chuckle, and Sloan pulls my hand to help me get back on my feet. "You know what they say. 'A well-behaved woman rarely makes history.'"

"They also say, 'The one who is crazy enough to think she can change the world is the one who will.'"

Emmet chuckles. "That sounds about right. I told Pip and Nilm we'll come back tonight, and that Sloan will transport us straight home."

"And miss the airport chaos tomorrow?" I say.

"Exactly. And sleep in beds."

I groan. "Best idea *evah*."

CHAPTER FOURTEEN

After a huge family dinner and more than a couple of toasts, Emmet slings his duffle over his shoulder, and I zip up my trusty red suitcase, ready to roll.

"Och, do ye need to leave so soon?" Gran gives me a pitiful look.

"I'm only missing the sleeping and leaving part of the visit, Gran. We were leaving in the morning anyway. Besides, it'll make things a little less chaotic on the airport ride if there are two fewer bodies. And Sloan's truck will be available."

"Speaking of which." Sloan holds the keys out to Granda. "I'll collect it when I get back."

Granda accepts the keys and slides them into his pocket. "*Slainte mhath.* Come again soon. Yer gran will miss ye and will whine and carry on somethin' awful 'til ye get back to visit."

Gran gives him a look. "And yer any different?"

Granda's cheeks pink up with his blush. "Och, I suppose I like havin' ye here almost as much."

I chuckle and hug them both. "Thank you for everything. I love you. And we'll video chat soon."

Gran gives me an extra squeeze and kisses my cheek. "And

take good care of yer *brunaidh.* They're a lovely, hard-working species of faery. Remember, all faery love lights and color and music. Ye may not see them there, but leave out some spirits for them from time to time and talk to them often. Let them know what needs to be done in the garden and thank them when it's finished."

"I'll remember."

"Of course, ye will. Yer a fine woman and ye'll build a fine grove." She lets go of me and moves to Emmet. "Och, my sweet boy. Ye must call me soon. I miss yer crazy notions already. Be good to yer new wee friends and watch over yer sister. She's a bit of a magnet for disaster."

Emmet laughs and lifts Gran off her feet to swing her in his embrace. "You're being kind, Gran. Fi's a hot mess when it comes to disaster, but yeah, I'll take care of her and so will Bruin, won't you, buddy?"

"I do so swear." My bear wraps his massive paw around Gran's back as she hugs him goodbye.

"Ye did us proud this week, Killer Clawbearer," Granda says. "Without yer help, we wouldn't have found the fae in time. The Ancient Order of Druids owes ye a debt, son."

Bruin lowers his round head, and Granda scrubs his ears.

"Until the next time, Bear." Gran kisses him. "I'll send Fi the recipe for the breakfast casserole ye like so much."

"*Slainte mhath,* Gran."

She nods and tears up. "Off with ye now. Ye don't want to miss yer ride."

Bruin dissolves into his spirit form and bonds within me, settling in my chest. With the big goodbyes behind us, I kiss the kids and wish everyone luck on their journey home in the morning. "Safe home, everyone. See you tomorrow."

The Doyle grove is strung with solar lanterns swinging from branches and is empty of Doyles for the night. "Oh, shoot. It looks like we won't get to say goodbye to Ciara. Are you sad, Emmet? How about you, Sloan? She's still got it bad for you. You know that, right?"

Sloan arches a brow and pegs me with a dirty look. "The only thing either of us ever had for each other was an itch. Trust me, that was scratched and forgotten. That you think she's jealous of you because of me is ludicrous. She's jealous of you because of you. Next to you, she pales as a druid, an independent woman, and someone to inspire."

"Yeah, baby." Emmet raises his fist for a bump of approval with Sloan. "You're the 'real deal,' sista. She's 'fake it 'till you make it.'"

"Wow. You boys are full of compliments today."

Emmet snorts. "We're full of something, for sure."

I chuckle and follow them into the trees.

The moment Emmet and I join hands with Sloan, the grove comes to life before us. Pip and Nilm are front and center, looking even more excited than they did this afternoon. other fae creatures surround them, some we'd seen before, others we hadn't.

I release the handle of my suitcase and wave to all the excited faces. "Wow, it's quite a going away party. Are they sure, Emmet? I don't want them to be lonely."

Emmet takes a knee and speaks to them in woodland chatter, and they hug him and nod. "They're sure. They also say the fae have a gift for us for saving them from the evil men in cloaks."

"We don't need a gift. That they're safe is enough."

"I said that, but they're an insistent bunch."

One of the bunny creatures with wings lands in front of Sloan's feet and wriggles his nose up at us. He's a big boy with patchy fur and a fluffy, double chin. He thumps his big back foot a couple of times, then goes very still. The creatures of the grove move closer and bend to see.

Big boy bunny looks like he's concentrating on something consuming, his nose wriggling, his ears twitching.

No one makes a sound, and there's a sense of awed reverence in the air. I bite my tongue and watch. After a long moment, the bunny hops to the side, and the crowd breaks into a rush of excited chatter.

"And voila, our gift." Emmet looks up at us and sweeps his hand toward the ground. "A heap of psychedelic rabbit poop."

I stare at the clustered pile of droppings and tilt my head so I can't see Emmet. If I do, both of us are going to crack up.

"Thank you." I bite the inside of my cheek to sober. I meet the gaze of the bunny who bestowed the colorful offering and drop my gaze. "We are honored by your thoughtful gift."

"Pick a good one," someone in the peanut gallery shouts.

I look at Sloan, hoping he knows what's going on. He seems as baffled and bewildered as I feel. "Ladies first."

Nice. I lower myself to the ground to take a better look. The rabbit droppings are amazingly round and swirled with color like fancy marbles. The cluster is a bit stuck together, and it takes a moment for me to break one loose. With everyone's expectant gazes burning into me, I eye a navy, bronze, and teal globe and pick up the fae raisinet.

"Oh, and it's still soft and warm too. Lucky me. That's…awesome."

Emmet follows my lead and picks a gold and green one. "Yep. Never a dull moment with you, Fi. That's for sure."

We both look at Sloan, and he shrugs. "If I let go of you two, you won't be able to interact. Looks like I'm outta luck."

"Nonsense." The exclamation comes from a lithe, muscled guy with long silver hair and pointed ears. He's sitting in a tree off to my left, and his leg swings freely in the air below. He's dressed in form-fitting hide pants and is bare-chested.

My mind stalls out.

He's an elf. I'm sure of it.

"If them seeing behind the faery glass is what's stopping you, I can fix that." The elf drops twenty feet from the tree and stalks closer. He's got swagger in his hips, and his gait reminds me of a panther on the prowl.

He stops in front of me, and I'm wondering what he's going to do when—Oh, kissing me...

Okay, *wow.*

The elf is quite the kisser and brazen with his tongue.

As quickly as he advanced, he retreats, and he steps back unaffected. When he steps over to Emmet, my brother drops his duffle and holds out a hells-no hand. "Simmer down, Legolas. I'd rather not have your tongue in my mouth if it's all the same with you."

"Suit yourself." He takes Emmet's hand from Sloan and sticks his thumb into his mouth.

"Ow, fuck," Emmet snaps while pulling back. "Why'd you bite me? Are you rabid?"

The elf chuckles. "You didn't want my tongue, but you wanted to see us, didn't you?"

I realize then that yeah, I'm no longer holding onto Sloan, but I see everything I could a moment ago. "Your saliva has magical properties."

He winks and bows. "Fayolorn, at your service. Now, Mr. Dark and Stormy Nights over there can choose his favor."

Sloan's glare is more heated than usual, and I'm not sure which offense of Fayolorn's has pissed him off most—there's so many to choose from. Still, he seems to swallow his ire and reaches down to select a swirly green and purple poop.

"I am humbled by the gift and the thoughtful intentions behind it." He nods to the winged bunny. "Blessed be."

"Blessed be," Emmet and I repeat.

I slip my rabbit raisin into my pocket and collect my suitcase.

It came a bit undone when I dropped it, so I zip everything back up and grab the handle.

Emmet picks up his duffle and lifts Pip into his arms.

Sloan reclaims his bag and lifts Nilm.

When the connection between the five of us is established, Sloan gives us a last look and flashes us home.

Magic never fails to awe me. One moment we're standing in a grove in Ireland, and in the next second, we're continents away and standing in our back yard. Emmet and Sloan kneel to set Pip and Nilm on the grass. Nine o'clock at night in Ireland is four o'clock in the afternoon in Toronto. A moment ago, we were in full dark. Now we have a couple of hours to show our brownies around before we lose the last rays of sunlight.

"It's not much yet." I know they don't understand me, but I feel it needs to be said. "The whole urban druid concept is new. We're on the cutting edge of starting a trend. Lucky you. You're in on the ground level."

Sloan chuckles. "Who are ye trying to convince?"

I shrug. "I wish we had more for them."

"Cumhaill, they're here for yer family not for yer trees."

"But they have to live in my trees. They need a home." I sigh and look at the old Victorian where I grew up. "Homes are important."

I'm still glancing up at my house when movement in one of the upper windows catches my attention. The hair on my arms stands on end until I recognize the slim build and blond hair of the guy in Calum's bedroom.

"Why don't you and Emmet take them across the lane and show them the forest? I'll take the bags inside." I reach down to grab the handles and—"*Hubba wha?*"

I jump back and squeal as Sloan's bag wriggles.

"Something you want to tell me, surly? Are you smuggling weirdness into my house?"

He unzips his bag and chuckles as two large, pointy-legged fuzzy spiders scramble into the grass and two bunny creatures hop out and fly into the top branches of the cherry tree. "We have stowaways."

"Let's hope they didn't gift you with more psychedelic turds en route. After a week away, I've got my own laundry to do." I remember my bag being unzipped back at the grove and undo my suitcase. "Oh, hello there."

Five of the tiny hummingbird people fly out of my suitcase and hover while looking around.

"Emmet, ye better check yer bag." Sloan's amusement is thick in his deep voice. "It seems Pip and Nilm weren't the only ones who wanted to move to the big city."

Emmet blinks at the small crowd we've smuggled into Toronto. When he unzips his duffle, a horned stag lifts his head and rises out of the nylon bag one-third of his body size. When he steps out, a doe follows close behind. Emmet covers his mouth, laughing. "How did I miss that? You'd think carrying two deer would've been heavy."

I wiggle my fingers at him. "Magic."

Emmet turns to listen to something Nilm is saying, then shakes his head. "They're afraid we're mad that their friends wanted to join them in starting a new grove. Pip's worried we'll send them back."

"No, no. Assure them it's fine. I'm only worried about them finding what they need here to live happily."

Emmet relays my message, and Pip rushes to hug me.

"It's okay, sweet girl. I'm not mad." Her big globe eyes are far too watery. I hug her, remember Kevin inside, and point at the side gate. "Em, why don't you and Sloan introduce them to the trees here and take them across the lane? I'm going to take the bags inside and freshen up for a sec."

I drop Sloan's bag at the top of the basement stairs and take Emmet's and mine up to the bedrooms. When I creak on the stairs, and Kevin doesn't say anything, I realize he's probably wondering who's in the house. We weren't expected to arrive home until tomorrow night.

"It's me, Kev. All's well."

Kevin pokes his head out of Calum's and Brendan's room, and he looks like hell. "Is he here? Did you catch an early flight? Did something happen?"

I drop my suitcase and rush to hug him. "No, only me and Emmet. What's wrong? What happened?"

Kevin is a Hollywood hottie blond with perfect hair and genuine goodness in his heart. He and Calum were buddies growing up long before they were a couple. He's been in my life since around the third grade, and I love him. To feel him hurt, hurts me. When he doesn't say anything, I hug tighter and wait. He'll get there.

"You know I love him, right?"

What? "Of course. He loves you too."

He draws a deep breath and heads back into the bedroom. Crossing the room, he picks up a note from Calum's pillow and holds it out to me.

"What's this?"

"I'm breaking it off."

"What? Why?"

He sinks onto the bed and runs his hands over his face. "He's lying to me, Fi. He's keeping things from me and has been for months. Even before Brenny was shot. I've asked him…I've begged him to let me in, but he says he can't. He says we're good and I need to trust him. I've tried, but this week I've been doing a lot of thinking. As much as I love him, I can't be on the outside. It's killing me."

"Oh, gawd." I drop to the bed beside him and my stomach knots. "I know Calum's had a hard time. I'm sorry, Kev. This is all my fault."

"Your fault? I doubt that."

I pull the elastic out of my hair and try to ease the tension in my skull. "No, seriously. This is all on me. I'm sorry."

The hurt in his gaze melts me. "Did I do something that upset you, Fi? Is Calum mad at me for something specific? He's fiercely protective of you, so if I offended you—"

"No, no, it's nothing like that." I stand up and pace to the dresser. When I rebound back, I see the disillusionment in his eyes. Gawd, it must be gutting Calum. "Okay, I'll tell you everything. Then you'll be on the inside. You won't believe me, but I'll prove it once I finish. Okay? You gotta stay with me."

"Okaaaay."

"It started the night I was attacked in the alley behind Shenanigans." I turn and pull my shirt off, giving him my back. "This tattoo appeared the next morning."

"What do you mean appeared?"

"I mean one minute it's not there, and five hours later it has risen from beneath my skin and is there in full detail. I asked Da, and he balked and acted like he knew nothing..."

I tell Kev about my first trip to Ireland and finding out we're druids, then about Baba Yaga, the Queen of Wyrm Dragons, and Patty.

"Then, a few weeks ago, we ran into a ring of dark druids living here in Toronto." I tell him about the bodies the cops found in the Don, and meeting Fionn and our quest to go back to the Fianna fortress.

"And so, you all trucked off to Ireland to reclaim your warrior heritage and the magic your family holds?"

"Right. And we weren't allowed to tell anyone. Da didn't want anyone else hurt."

"But Aiden told Kinu."

"Only a couple of days before the trip. She's going to start seeing the kids do things. She had to know."

He rubs his chest. "Christ, Fi, this hurts. I thought I was family. Liam knows. Shannon knows. Hell, I was the one drawing the picture of the guy who attacked you, and I still couldn't know?"

"Da was unwavering. He said it put you in direct danger to be part of it, and Calum didn't want you hurt."

"But I *am* hurt."

"*Fi!* I need you," Emmet yells from downstairs.

"In a minute."

"No, seriously, we need you outside." Emmet comes bounding up the steps and stops when he sees Kevin. "Oh, shit. Hey, Kev. Uh... Fi, can I talk to you downstairs for a quick sec?"

"He knows." I meet Emmet at the door to Calum's bedroom. "I told him everything. Kevin's part of the inner circle."

Emmet relaxes. "Have you shown him Bruin?"

"No. I haven't gotten to the fine details yet."

"Have you told him Calum's a badass archer?"

"Not yet."

"What about bringing home fae to spruce up our grove?"

"Nope. Hadn't got there either."

"Okay, well, we need to get to that part PDQ because big things are happening in the backyard and you're gonna want to see them. Come down. And bring your swirly rabbit poop."

CHAPTER FIFTEEN

"What. The. Hell?" I'm stunned as I hop off the back steps and stare at the yard. "This is still our backyard, isn't it?" I glance over my shoulder at the house, then at the mass of trees filling the fifty-by-seventy-foot rear lot. "What did I miss?"

Emmet chuckles beside me. "I guess our fae guests don't only live in a grove; they bring it to life."

"Magic," Kevin says beside me.

I take his hand and pull him across the little patch of back lawn we have left. It's a postage stamp area off the deck big enough for a couple of chairs or a sun lounger, then a straight shot past trees to the cars parked in the lane. That's it.

"Magic, you say? You ain't seen nothing yet." We stop next to Sloan, who's standing ten feet into the treed area observing. "Would you mind holding Kevin's hand for a little?"

Kevin looks from Sloan to me. "Are you trying to get me in trouble with your brother?"

"Nope. You'll see."

"Are ye sure about this, Fi?" Sloan's brow pinches. "Yer da won't be happy."

I shrug. "It's too late for that. It's a lot easier to let the cat out of the bag than to force him back in. Kevin gets to know everything. I made the call, and I'll take the heat."

Kevin kisses my cheek. "I owe you big for that, Fi."

"No. I owe you and Calum a huge apology. I'm sorry the druid stuff left you on the outside. Not anymore."

Sloan shrugs and takes Kevin's hand.

I'm not a hundy percent sure the magic of Sloan's ring will allow Kevin to see behind the faery glass, but it's obvious the second the wonder takes hold.

Kevin tenses and his jaw falls slack. "That's amazing."

"What do you smell?" I ask.

"Your brother." He looks around. "At the end of the day when there's only a hint of his cologne left on his skin, and he's a bit musky...how do I smell that now?"

Aww. And just like that, I love Kevin even more. "Because that smell is your warm and fuzzy happy place."

Nilm trundles out of the trees and starts talking. He seems so much more relaxed than he was, his antennae bobbing as he chitters on.

"He wants to know if you like it," Emmet translates, "and if there is anything specific you want in our grove?"

"I love it." I bend down and hug him. "Tell him it's amazing, and anything they think we need will be perfect."

Emmet relays the message, and Nilm tugs on my hand to pull me with him. He leads me deeper beneath the canopy and points at the buds and blooms still forming.

"Happiness?" One of the little hummingbird people asks. She's tiny and mostly purple with lacy, white wings. A Spriggan. The recognition of her species downloads and I'm at a loss, once again, at the magic of this world.

"It's perfect. You've all done us an amazing honor."

"Take out your poop," Emmet's excitement spills over.

I reach into my pocket, careful not to squish my fingers into the round rabbit raisin I chose in the Doyle grove an hour ago.

When my fingers close around it, I'm confused. I take it out and look at it. It's still teal, bronze, and navy blue, but it's not warm or squishy.

It's as hard as stone, shiny, and tingles in my fingers.

"It holds power now." I roll it in my palm while assessing its contained fae energy.

"It's a charm stone," Emmet says. "Jinji was telling me that the rabbit dude that pooped that out for us is the original Ostara hare. Very old. Very rare."

"What is an Ostara hare?"

"The goddess Ostara's rabbit companion. The myth says the goddess of spring transformed a bird into a rabbit and in the spring it laid eggs for her festival celebration. It's the foundation of the Easter egg tradition."

"I thought that was the Hershey's commercial with the clucking bunnies."

Emmet chuckles. "Oh, I love that one…but nope."

"So, this is real?" Kevin waves a weak finger toward our surroundings. "I'm not hallucinating this because I'm messed up about Calum? You didn't slip me a mickey?"

"Nope. This is real. Trippy, isn't it?"

"And you haven't even met Bruin," Emmet says.

"Hold onto your hat, Kev." I check that my bear is ready to come out and play, then take a step back. "This one's going to blow your mind. Just remember, you're safe."

Sloan takes a stronger hold on Kevin's hand and nods. "Take it away, Cumhaill."

I release my bear, and if Sloan weren't holding him, Kevin would've ass-planted in the trees ten feet back. "Holy shit."

"Kevin, this is Bruin."

Bruin bows his front half and holds up his massive paw. "Tell him I'm pleased to meet him and that Calum has told me much about him."

I relay that, and his shock increases. "He talks, then?"

"You can't hear him because you're not a druid, but we all can."

Kevin pulls up his big boy pants, straightens, and uses both his hands to shake Bruin's paw. "Kevin is friend—not food."

I laugh. "He knows you're family and he's here to protect us as a family, you included."

"Hopefully he won't need to protect ye from much," Sloan adds. "That was the point of keepin' ye out of the know. It's dangerous for ye now that Fi involved ye in our world."

Kevin waves that off. "No. I'm glad she did. Calum and I would never have made it if she hadn't."

Bruin raises his nose and sniffs. A low growl rumbles from his chest and Kevin takes a step back.

"What's wrong, buddy?"

"Thought I caught somethin' on the breeze. I'll sniff around on my way to find my lady friends. Don't wait up."

"Treat them well, big guy. Safe home."

Sloan snorts. "Treat them well? Ye weigh in on yer bear rutting in the wild?"

"Sure, bears are people too."

He rolls his eyes at me. "No, they aren't. They are bears. It's right there in the name. Yer ridiculous."

Kevin looks at his and Sloan's joined hands. "And you're a druid too?"

"I am."

"Of the stuffy, stick up his ass variety," I add.

Kevin ignores me. "And the last time you were here...when I saw those pictures on the kitchen table of the crumpled car… when Fi had her accident…"

I wince at the memory of being t-boned and rolled through the intersection. "It wasn't an accident. The group of evil druids I mentioned attacked me. It's an organization called Barghest, which translates to Black Dog. I'm sure you'll hear us talking about them sooner or later. They have roots in Toronto, Ireland, and who knows where else."

"And they plowed into your car?"

"Rude, right? And that was before they kidnapped me and tried to sacrifice me on an altar to use my blood to power themselves up."

Kevin pales. "Shit like that actually happens?"

"It's cray-cray, I know. Druids never ventured off the Emerald Isle that we knew of. When I declared my intention to be a druid in Toronto, it ruffled a few feathers. I upset the applecart and dragged the whole family into hot water."

"Totally wasn't your fault." Emmet is holding one of our Ostara bunnies and stroking his ears. "And besides, being a druid is the coolest thing ever. You should see the shit we can do when we're properly juiced up. It's more difficult here, but we'll get there."

I explain to Kevin how Ireland's ambient magic feeds a druid's cells and how the ley lines and other fae creatures help keep our magic fully charged. "We don't have that here."

"Yet," Sloan adds, "but with the improvements in yer grove and the fae who decided to live here, that will change."

I smile at Pip and Nilm, and at the Spriggans flying from tree to tree, the Ostara hares, the deer, and even the pointy spiders draping silver and gold webbing in glittery swags from tree to tree. "It's pretty incredible."

Emmet grins and points at my hand. "Take a tip from Elvis. A little less conversation, a little more action, please."

"What kind of action am I doing?"

"Try out your Ostara charm stone."

"How? What does it do?"

He shrugs and releases the bunny to fly away. "No idea. Pip says they adapt depending on intention and need. Focus and project its power. We'll soon see."

I hold up the multi-colored rabbit turd between my thumb

and index finger and focus on releasing its power. The last of the day's light catches the bronze streaks and refracts out into the trees' growing shadows.

Intention and need.

As we stand there, the depth and width of the treed area expand, stretching beyond our backyard's physical boundaries exponentially without spilling out onto our neighbor's property.

"Cool." Emmet steps into the new section of the grove. "Sloan's stone added trees, mine added ambient magic in the air, and yours multiplied all of it."

My heart races as I step deeper into the woods. "It's like a Star Trek holodeck or something. It feels so real—like the grove's depth is real."

"Is real, silliness," the purple Spriggan with the lacy white wings says. "Is magic."

Pip raises her hands, and I pick her up and sit her on my hip like I do Jackson and Meg when I carry them. She places both of her tiny hands gently on my cheek and chitters.

I look at Emmet to translate.

"She says that supporting a grove fit to power the heirs of Fionn mac Cumhaill is a worthy and honorable task. They are so pleased to be part of our successes."

I draw a deep breath. "Tell her it's us who are honored to have all of them. Any success we achieve will be because we make a great team."

It's late the next morning by the time I get up and get dressed. Sleeping in my bed is a luxury after a week on a foam mattress on the floor, and I laze about in my sheets longer than I likely should. By tonight, everyone else will be home, and the house will be full and busy again. This morning though, it's a lazy daisy kinda moment.

"Morning." Emmet smiles up at me when I shuffle into the kitchen. He pushes the carton of almond milk across the table for me to use. "You headed into the bookstore today?"

I grab a bowl from the cupboard and float my cereal. "Yep. I'm taking Sloan in to say hello to Myra. He wanted to talk to her about some ancient Aztec healing ritual book Wallace is looking for."

"Cool. Did Kevin stay over?"

"No. We talked into the wee hours. Then he went home. Calum is supposed to head over to his place tonight when they get home. I asked him not to say anything to Calum until I've had a chance to tell everyone that he knows the whole story. I also told him we'd call with flight updates if there are any."

Emmet finishes his breakfast and heads to the sink. After rinsing his bowl, he stacks it in the drying rack. "I was thinking about what Gran said about the fae liking light and music in the grove. I thought I'd head over to Lowes or Walmart and grab a couple of dozen solar lanterns and a mile of string lights to hang from the trees. You know, like Iris Doyle had in her grove."

"That's a great idea."

"It is, at that." Sloan joins us in the kitchen. He sets his spellbook on the table and reaches into the pocket of his swanky vest to pull out his slim-line wallet. He makes a selection and hands Emmet a credit card. "Get anything you think might make yer grove homier for yer fae. My treat. No spending limit."

I wave my spoon. "You don't have to do that."

"Like ye mentioned when we were in Dublin. I owe ye twenty-seven grand for tellin' yer bear to order trees. I suppose I should start payin' ye back somehow."

I finish with my cereal and dump the milk into the empty sink. "I was razzing you. Of course, you don't owe me that."

"No, I do. I'm embarrassed to say I don't think about money the way most do. I'm accustomed to picking up what I want when I want it. It was thoughtless not to realize that not everyone lives that way."

"Not thoughtless." I wash up. "Naïve, maybe."

"Semantics. Whatever the word, I've put ye in a spot, and I'll make it right. I could use magic to wipe the debt clean."

I laugh and toss him a smile over my shoulder. "No. Don't do that. The landscaping company provided a great service, and I'm thankful for their efforts. The way I look at it, I lost on the debt to Calum, but I gained on my Hellcat SUV, so I'll consider it a car payment. I've had those before, and I'm good with that. You really shouldn't worry about it."

"Buuut," Emmet says, a glimmer of mischief in his bright green eyes, "if Fi doesn't want you as her sugar daddy, I'm willing to put out for a new audio system."

I toss a tea towel at my brother's head. "You're a nut."

A thump and rustle noise at the table draws our attention to Sloan's spellbook. It's flapping its cover and getting antsy.

Sloan looks at me and shrugs. "He misses Beauty. Do ye think she'd welcome a visit?"

I smile. "Aww, of course. She's in my bedroom, dude. On the side table by the window. Go on up."

I've barely got the words out before the brown leather book flaps its covers and flies like a bird out of the room and up the stairs.

Emmet snorts. "Damn, Fi, both your bear and your spellbook are getting more horizontal hijinx than me. Have I lost my game? Did that Ciara chick hex me?"

I laugh at the impossibility of that. "Go check on the grove. I'll help you string the lanterns around four. Until then, you have the house to yourself. I don't care what you do or who you do it with, but stay out of my room."

He holds up his hands and laughs. "One time. You gotta let that die its last death."

I meet Sloan's curious gaze and give in. "I came home from a concert night sleepover and found this numbnut and one of my classmates sprawled and asleep in my bed."

Emmet's grin is so unrepentant it's hilarious. "Calum wouldn't give us the room. What can I say? I was a horny and impulsive teenager."

I laugh. "And what's your excuse now?"

After breakfast and checking in on the grove, Sloan and I head out in my beautiful new Dodge Hellcat SUV. When we defeated the Black Dog brigade a few weeks ago in the druid circle—killed them is more accurate—they left behind half a dozen vehicles.

After magically altering the paperwork, I claimed this one. Calum and Emmet chose a sexy new Lexus, and the rest we either returned to a significant other or donated to a good cause that needed a car.

"How are ye likin' yer new job?" Sloan asks as I park on Queen Street in front of Myra's Mystical Emporium.

"I love it. Myra is great, and she's been incredibly good to me." I open the back door and pick up the box Gran sent for her. "She lets me set my schedule and decide what days I come in and for how long. It makes it super easy to coordinate with Shannon when she needs help at Shenanigans."

"So, yer still working at the pub, too?"

"On occasion. I suppose I'll always pick up the slack at the pub. Shenanigans is part of our family."

Sloan's usual scowl is firmly in place as he pulls the door open for me. The brass bell over the door announces our arrival, and I breathe in the magic that is Myra's Mystical Emporium. Home sweet home.

"Why does me working at the pub bother you?"

"It doesn't."

"Uh-huh. I don't have to be an empath to know your pants are on fire."

He chuffs. "Ye needn't worry about the fire in my pants."

Okay, that's just wrong. I'm not sure if it's a language thing or he doesn't understand the idiom or what but I'm not touching that with a ten-foot staff. Shaking my head, I head to the back. "Myra! We're home!"

"Fiona!" Myra waves from the third-story bookshelf. "I'll be right down. Handsome, come help me, would you?"

Sloan strides over to stand at the base of the rolling metal ladder. "What can I help ye wi—*oh*—"

Myra leans back into the open air and drops over the rail.

"Slow Descent." Sloan raises his arms, and my eccentric, meliae boss falls the two stories into his open arms. I imagine that was much the same scenario as when he caught me in the fortress, except I flailed and flattened him.

Myra relaxes in Sloan's arms and pats his cheek. "Thank you, hotness. You don't disappoint."

I laugh and set the gift on the old, antique display counter. "My gran sent you this for your home tree."

"Lovely. What is it?" Myra, like most fair folk, has the soft, magical features humans find attractive: an enthralling smile, a melodic voice, and a slim, willowy frame. What makes her stand out though—and is most assuredly hidden behind illusion when she leaves the bookstore—are her vertically slit eyes, her funky electric-blue hair, and her silver skin, which if you look closely, is cracked with darker tones beneath like bark.

The effect is stunning and cool.

"It's nectar for his roots, I think. She said the tree that comes through the center of her house sometimes gets cranky because of how little direct interaction it has with the outdoors. She concocted this elixir a few years ago, and her tree has been happier since. There are instructions, and if your tree likes it as much as hers, Sloan can bring more when he comes to visit."

Myra's smile brightens the entire bookshop. "How thoughtful. Let's see what he thinks."

Sloan and I follow Myra through the side entranceway into the reading area. The stained-glass domed ceiling lets in the warm, autumn sun and the leaves on her home tree reach almost to the glass. "Does your tree turn color and shed his leaves in the winter?"

"No. He gets cranky and lethargic in the fall, but doesn't fully embrace the winter."

"Who in their right mind really does?"

"Exactly." She approaches the wide trunk.

The tree sits in the center of the area with three floors of bookshelves reaching up to the glass ceiling. Myra bought the land and had the building built around the tree rather than see it cut for the oncoming construction. "Look what we have here my love, a gift from Fiona's gran for you."

Myra sits on one of the leather couches beneath the lush umbrella of the tree's canopy to open the box. With it propped on her lap, she takes out a mason jar of clear liquid with herbs and essential oils floating in it and the instructions included within. "According to your gran, I pour this in a withershins ring around the trunk, and it will feed his roots and give him new life and vigor."

"If Gran says it will, I wouldn't dream of doubting her. She's incredible with nature magic."

"Lara is a wonder." Sloan beams. "While Fi was in Ireland this week, there was an attack on a few sacred groves. Lara has them well on their way back from complete desiccation."

"Desiccation?" Myra gasps. "Who on earth would do something so horrifying?"

I explain to Myra about the Barghest being in attendance for the Mabon ritual and kidnapping the fae from the groves.

"Thank the goddess you were there to stop them."

I couldn't agree more. "Speaking of the fae in the groves.

When we returned, a selection of them came with us. They want to help our family establish our grove here. Could you help me with their care regimen until I learn what they need? Maybe you could meet them and see what they've done."

"What have they done?" she asks.

"Honestly, a lot. They went straight to work and filled in our grove with a hundred trees. The growth is astounding, and we can already breathe in ten times more ambient power than we could before they got to work."

"And did their work, by chance, get underway last night around five-fifty in the evening?"

I think about that. We arrived home around five, gave Pip and Nilm the tour, discovered the stowaways, and I chatted with Kevin. "Yeah, it would've been right around six. Why? How'd you know that?"

Myra frowned. "Because that's when I noticed the ambient magic dip dramatically here. There's only a finite amount of natural magic in the city, Fiona. I think your little helpers are taking more than your fair share to fuel your new grove."

Oh, no. "I'm sure it's unintentional. They're used to the ambient power being practically unlimited in Ireland."

Myra nods. "Likely so, but that's not the case here. In Toronto, like any of the major North American cities, there is only so much magic to go around. It doesn't matter whether it's fae magic, Wiccan, blood magic, or archaic, there's a limit to what we can draw on before affecting the others."

Sloan purses his lips and looks more dour than usual. "And when these other sects discover it's Fi's grove drinking up all the power, what do you suppose they'll do?"

Myra frowns. "I don't expect they'll thank you."

"Well, no." I try to think of what to do, but I've got nothing. "It was an honest mistake. Our fae didn't know any better. They certainly shouldn't be put on the hot seat for being thoughtful and trying to help."

Myra doesn't look so sure. "Look at it this way, Fi. I know you and believe what you're saying, but I'm no less concerned about my home tree. I won't let him suffer so that you can have your sacred grove."

I hear the undercurrent of threat in Myra's voice and understand. Her tree is her soul. Lines of friendship pale in importance next to that.

"And yer not the only one who will feel that way." Sloan meets her gaze, and I can tell he picked up on the same warning vibe. "There will be powerful folks from different sects that use their magic to sustain their lifestyles and their control over others. They won't appreciate being downgraded by the noob druids."

I sigh. "Especially when they didn't want us here in the first place."

Myra swirls the herb mixture in the mason jar elixir and sighs. "You were determined to find a source of magic before you left for Ireland. I'd advise you to continue with that and do it quickly. You're about to have a lot of angry magically empowered folk beating down your door."

I stare up at the beautiful glass ceiling. "Why can't anything be easy? Every time I think we're moving forward, we get punched in the gut."

Sloan chuckles. "Speaking from a person on the receiving end of more than one sucker punch to the gut lately. Sometimes it means ye gotta pull up yer big-boy pants and work harder."

Myra frowns. "If you're lucky, maybe we can find a way to keep you from becoming enemy number one in the magic world by the end of the week."

"That would be nice. But it's not like this is totally our fault. Surely, we can't be the only people who think the city has more potential for magical energy. Haven't some of the other sects looked into it?"

"Sure. That's why the Wiccans have their Sabbat rituals, and your Barghest people are slaughtering innocents on the altar and draining them of blood. They're making do in different ways."

"Well, the necromancer ways suck. We need more power, Captain." I hold up my hands and do my best Scotty impression. Neither of them gets me. If my brothers were here, they would've got that. "Okay, so where do we start?"

Myra raises her hand and gestures at the hundreds, possibly thousands, of books on the shelves surrounding us. "Dig in, pumpkin. If the answers aren't here, I'm sure there will at least be a thread that leads you to an idea."

"So, I have to figure out a magical shortage problem no one has figured out in centuries, and do it before every super-powered being within an eighty-kilometer radius bangs on my door demanding my head?"

"Sounds about right. Pitter patter, best get atter."

"Awesome." I blew out a breath and look up at all the spines rising around us. *"Living the dream."*

CHAPTER SIXTEEN

Sloan and I search the bookstore and read everything we can on ambient magic, direct and indirect power sources, magical creatures that create energy fields, and naturally occurring ley lines. There are no cut and dry answers. Still, we need to find something because I'm not going to let angry witches hurt my fae or kill my family.

The only witch I've ever met was Granda's ex, Moira. I admit that I'm biased about not liking her, but I get the feeling that witches and I aren't going to get along. I'll take the Queen of Wyrms over cozying up to people like her again.

"As much as there is on ley lines in Europe," Sloan flops back in the leather couch looking beat, "there's almost nothing about them in North America and even less about Canada. Look." He points at a rudimentary sketch of the naturally occurring rivers of power beneath the Earth's crust. "Why is there nothing at all above here? The magical energy just stops."

I study the map and shrug. "Well, it's not a nature problem. Canada is the second-largest country in the world after Russia and has the third most forest on the planet. If ley lines and fae magic like nature, we have a shit ton of it."

"Maybe it's because most of yer country is buried under a sheet of snow?"

I laugh. "Are you serious? Do you know anything about Canada?"

Sloan shrugs. "Yer allegedly overtly polite—although that has not been my experience—ye end half yer sentences with, eh?—I'll vouch for that one—ye eat a great deal of maple syrup, and yer people live in igloos."

I roll my eyes. "You're staying at my house. It's a century-old Victorian. My neighbors have a pool. Have you seen any sign of snow?"

"No, but I've seen the pictures."

The text notification on my Fitbit buzzes against my wrist, and I read what Emmet's saying. "Oh, shit, it's four-thirty. I said we'd help him with the lanterns in the grove before everyone gets back. Bring the books of interest with us, and we'll go through them at home."

Sloan and I put back the books we're finished with, pack up, and say goodbye to Myra. "I'll bring these back tomorrow. Is that okay?"

Myra waves her hand in the air. "If they help you restore the city's ambient magic, take as long as you like. In the meantime, watch your back, Fi. There aren't as many dark magic users as there are light, but they make up for it by being brutal and vile."

"Warning received. Thanks."

"Oh, and thank your gran for thinking about my home tree. That was super thoughtful."

"I'll let her know you appreciated it. And you'll have to tell me if you notice any difference."

"Will do."

"Sorry, Emmet." I rush in from the back lane and beeline it into the trees of the grove. "We got waylaid by research rabbit holes at the shop. Where do you want me?"

He points at the bags and bags of lanterns leaning against the trunk of the cherry tree. "I ran the fairy lights around the line of the fence and plugged them in. I'm stringing some of the lanterns up on twine and hooking others on branches. Jump in wherever you want. Where's Sloan? We'll need to stretch for the higher branches."

"He's taking a stack of books into the house. He'll be right out to help." I look around the grove, amazed at how much it's filling out. It's growing so quickly—too quickly.

Last night when I saw the growth, I was excited.

Now I'm nervous.

As much as I want to tell Emmet about the ambient drain and the new target we now have on our heads, I don't want our little fae family to hear it and feel bad or be scared.

I decide to keep that to myself until later.

"Where do ye want me?" Sloan joins me at the base of the cherry tree.

"Emmet voted you in for hooking these up on some of the higher branches. You likely have a better idea of what works than we do. Is your grove lit?"

"It is." He grabs three lanterns and a few 'S' hooks and gets started. "But our grove is lit by tiny faery bugs called winnots. They sleep during the day and light up at night. The next time I come, I'll see if any of them fancy the idea of relocating to the new world."

"Thanks. That would be awesome."

Emmet grins. "By the time they get here, this will be a full-fledged sacred grove. Can you feel the magic in the air?"

Sloan raises a brow at me, but no, I'm still not getting into it in front of our fae. They meant well. I'll figure this out before danger darkens our doorstep—I hope.

"Sure do." I send Sloan a look to stay quiet. "I feel it. It's amazing what having a real grove can do."

We work for an hour, hanging lanterns and spending time with the creatures who immigrated to our backyard last night. Pip and Nilm are happily chittering with Emmet, pointing out good spots, and eager to help.

The Ostara rabbits are hopping and flying around, quite content to spread their magical poop.

The Spriggans—the little hummingbird people—are busy flying back and forth into the Don Valley forest beside our house to find materials to build their nests. I worried about that at first, but then I remembered that regular Torontonians wouldn't be able to see them.

The pointy-legged spider things are busy spinning gold and silver webs and running sparkly swags of webbing from tree to tree.

And the stag and doe have claimed an area in the back corner by the koi pond and are working on creating a lean-to of leaves and sticks. How they're doing that without opposable thumbs, I have no idea. Must be magic, I suppose.

Busy, busy.

"What do ye think?" Sloan hangs the last lantern and takes an assessing look.

I step into the center of the trees and turn in a slow spin, checking out our beautiful grove. "It's perfect."

Emmet smiles at something Nilm says and nods, their attention on me. "You're right, she does."

"I do what?"

"Standing there with your arms out and the rays of the sunset coming in from behind, you look like a Celtic goddess. Or at least like my sister infused with the grace and power of a Celtic goddess."

I chuckle and wag my finger at him and Nilm. "We have another charmer in our midst, do we? Pip's a lucky lady."

Emmet repeats my comment for them, and Pip giggles and covers her mouth with her little hands, her antennae bobbing as she nods.

"Hello, the house," Da calls.

We hurry out of the trees and into the yard as he and Dillan drop their bags inside the fence. "By the grace of the goddess, what have we here?"

"Come see what you've missed." I wave them forward. "It's the grand beginnings of the Cumhaill family grove. What do you think?"

Da looks at me, and his brows are arched high on his forehead. "Well, I think it's grand indeed. How did ye ever do it?"

Sloan holds out his hand, and Da meets him palm-to-palm without questioning why. When the sight kicks in, Da's grin grows wide. "Well, hello there. Welcome to ye, one and all. I'm honored to have fae folk in our lives. Namaste."

I order four large pizzas around seven o'clock, and after Aiden gets Kinu and the kids settled at home, he joins us for the family druid meeting I called. "Okay, since last night, we've got good news, bad news, and update news. Where would you like to start?"

"Och." Da scrubs a rough hand over his face. "Why must there always be bad news when ye call us together, Fi?"

I shrug. "Just keeping things interesting, Da. Okay, let's start with good news then. Our grove is up and running, we have thirteen Fae folk of five species living in it, and we're now putting out a ton of juice and enough to keep us powered up for the foreseeable future."

Da sighs. "And the bad news?"

"We're siphoning the ambient magic from everyone else in the city. Myra figures we have two or three days before the drain on magic gets traced back to us, and we have every evil druid, pissed-off warlock, and demented were-shifter on our door demanding payback."

"Fucking hell." Dillan pauses mid-reach while going for his fourth slice. "You never go halfway, do you, Fi?"

"Sorry, boys. I'm an all or nothing kinda girl."

Da swallows a good portion of his beer and pinches the bridge of his nose. "And the update news?"

"I told Kevin everything."

Calum stands, looking shocked. "I was with him an hour ago, and he didn't say a thing."

"I asked him to let me be the one to fill you all in. I found him here in Calum's room last night, and he was a wreck. Whether he let on or not, he's been struggling with the secrets, and it was coming to an untenable head."

"Ye shouldn't have interfered in yer brother's business," Da says.

"Maybe. But I won't let my decision to open the door to the druid world ruin their relationship. I told him everything. He understands the risks and why we kept silent, but he's hurt and disillusioned that Liam, Shannon, and Kinu knew and we didn't consider him 'family' enough. We have making up to do with him on that front."

"Well, fuck." Calum grabs his keys off the coffee table and rushes toward the hall. "Thanks for the fucking heads up on this one, Fi."

The back door slams and the rumble vibrates in my chest. I meet the anger in Da's gaze and shake my head. "You can be mad. I get that you are, but it's done, and I refuse to regret it."

"This wasn't solely yer decision."

"Maybe not, but what I didn't say in front of Calum, and what none of you will ever mention, is that when I found him in Calum's room last night, he was leaving him a letter explaining why they were done."

"Shit." Dillan grabs his pizza after all.

"Yeah, shit. I won't have them break up over this, Da. Calum and Kevin are as much in love and have as much right to the future in front of them as Aiden and Kinu. He deserved to know."

"Moot point now, isn't it?" Da snaps. "Are ye done droppin' bombs on us so we can get back to it?"

"I am. Now, I'm heading into the dining room for the brainstorming part of this disaster. You can all be mad at me later. Our fae didn't realize the magic in the city is finite. I won't have them killed for their kindness or regretting their help. We need to figure out another power source, and we need to do it quickly."

Da's jaw flexes as he clenches his teeth. "Fine. Ye heard yer sister, boys. Unpacking has to wait. We need to dig ourselves out from under yet another massive hape of shite."

I grab a can of ginger ale from the table and raise it to the room. "Oh, and welcome home."

It's close to ten that night when Calum returns. I leave the others in the dining room and rush out to meet him. "Is everything okay?"

He meets my gaze and dips his chin. "It will be. Thanks, Fi. I'm sorry I jumped down your throat. I know ye wouldn't have made such an important decision unless you were forced into it. He didn't say as much, but I know Kev was at the end of his tether."

I hug him and hold on tight. "I couldn't let my impulsiveness ruin you two. I need my brothers to be happy and healthy. You're my touchstones."

He kisses my head and squeezes me back. "Same."

I ease back. "He loves you so much."

Calum nods. "It's mutual. He's my one."

"And you patched things up?"

"It was shaky for a bit, but then he said Emmet mentioned me being a badass archer and he wanted to see what that looked like. When I called my bow from my tattoo, and he got a load of me like that, the tides turned."

I burst out laughing. "You mean he got hot seeing you like that, and you made your transgressions up to him by showing him your new athletic prowess."

He flashes me his teeth and waggles his brows. "Something like that."

I hug him again. "Good. I'm so relieved to hear that. It'll fuel me through the mind-numbing task of sussing out a sustainable magic power source in the next forty-eight hours."

I loop my arm around Calum's elbow, and we make our way back to the dining room. He takes one look at all of us poring over textbooks and laptops and tosses his keys at the basket in the hall. "Okay, where are we and where do you need me?"

Da leans back and looks wiped. "Honestly, I don't know anymore. I can't see straight. If this were Ireland maybe we could find an untapped ley line and draw on it, but this is Canada. We don't have them here."

Sloan leans back in his chair and cracks his knuckles. "I asked Fiona about that earlier. Why is that? Why would ley lines be there and not here? Why in some parts of Canada but only pockets out west?"

"I suppose if we could answer that, we might have an answer." Da pushes back from the table and heads out the front door for some fresh air.

Sloan stares up at the ceiling. "It seems to me that if ley lines are magical rivers veining the Earth's surface, they wouldn't only be in selected pockets. Rivers flow—even magical ones."

Dillan stands, stretches, and pulls up his hood. "Could they be here but blocked or strangled somehow?"

I plunk back into my chair and frown. "You think someone's

blocking them? Could a powerful warlock or coven be holding the magic hostage for their private use?"

"I don't think so." Sloan sits up and rolls his shoulders. "If it were a person, I don't think he or she would be able to contain the entire country under their power for centuries. It makes more sense that it is something about Canada itself that blocks the flow."

Emmet chuffs. "Well, if that's the case, two or three days from now it's gonna suck to be us."

Sloan glances over the texts stacked on the table. "Who has the geographical map that shows the ley lines?"

Dillan pushes the book toward him. "I've been studying them for an hour. There are lines of energy across Europe and Africa, and even in parts of Australia and South America. Then, in North America, they are there in the States but with a noticeable reduction from the southern states up to the Canadian border. It's pretty much exactly by the border."

I shift on my seat to get a better look. "And almost no detectable levels of magical flow in central or eastern Canada. Why?"

Emmet rubs his eyes and yawns. "So, unless we relocate to B.C, Alberta, Saskatchewan, or the Northwest Territories, we're shit outta luck."

"But why?" Sloan asks again. "Nature doesn't pick and choose that way. As I said, ley lines are magical rivers veining beneath the Earth's surface. Something's either stopping the flow or masking the magic. It makes no sense to assume it simply isn't here."

"Okay." Emmet shakes out his fingers over the keyboard. "So, what has the power to block or suppress the magic of ley lines?"

Sloan shrugs. "That's the question we need to answer."

CHAPTER SEVENTEEN

The house is dark when I wake with a start. With bleary eyes, I roll to the side of my pillow, wake my cell, and groan at the time. Four-thirty-seven in the morning. Seriously?

"Bruin? Is that you, buddy?"

While my bear does come and go at all hours of the night and day, being able to travel in spirit form, he doesn't usually jolt me out of a dead sleep. I blink and focus on his pallet beside my bed. No giant grizzly.

I'm not surprised. We were a week in Ireland, and with bears extinct there, he was eager to get home to his regular "bears with benefits" routine.

A clunk down the hall brings a round of hushed shushing and whispered laughter.

Good gawd. Who's drunk and still up?

There's a scuffle and shuffle of things against my bedroom wall, and I sigh. That's the closet in Calum's and Brendan's room. When the shushing morphs into drunken snickering, I throw back my quilt and force my feet to carry me down the hall.

Calum's and Brendan's room is bigger than mine, but with two beds, two dressers, and a desk, it has always felt smaller.

What is definitely smaller is their shared closet. I don't mind having a smaller room because my closet space more than makes up for it.

"What are you nimrods doing?" I whisper-hiss at them. "It's *waaay* too early to be fooling around in the closet."

Calum straightens, and I'm surprised when it's not Kevin rustling around in there with him. It's Sloan.

It takes my sleepy hamster brain a minute to get back in his wheel on that one. "What's going on? I thought Calum and Kevin were rocking cocks in the closet, but I take it that is not what's happening."

Calum laughs. "Sloan *is* drool-worthy—"

Sloan grins wide. "Nice of ye to notice."

"—but Irish don't swing that way, do you?"

"Nope."

Calum shakes his head. "Didn't think so. Anyway, that's not what this is."

Sloan tries to straighten, but he's too tall and off-balance. He ends up cracking his head on the bottom of the shelf and almost knocking himself out.

Calum snorts and uses the frame of the closet door to keep from falling on top of him.

"What exactly are you two goons doing?" I step into the room fully and close the door. After flipping on the desk lamp, I point from Calum to his bed. When he obeys my unspoken order, I grip Sloan's wrist and get him up on his feet.

Once he has some momentum, I shove him toward Brendan's bed and let the chips fall where they may.

"First," Calum says, "I thought Sloan would be comfier on Brenny's bed than on the pull-out in the basement, so I invited him up to be my roomie."

"And we brought a bottle of liquid with us," Sloan adds.

"Two, actually." Calum holds up fingers to punctuate his point. "Well, we brought one, then had to go get the second."

"Cuz Georgie boy got lonely." Sloan points.

Calum giggles while looking at the two empty bottles on Brendan's dresser. There's a Post-It cutout with what I guess is supposed to be a circle on each of them. "So, we got him a friend and polished him off too."

"And whose idea was it to give them sad faces?"

"Mine," Sloan says. "Yer brother had something far cruder in mind."

Calum devolves into a fit of giggles. "Cruder but much funnier. Your boy here needs to learn to let loose a little."

Sloan is not "my boy" but Calum's right. Sloan is far too tightly wound. Ignoring that, I try to stay on track.

"And where does wrestling in the closet enter this drunk and disorderly tale?"

Calum's eyes brighten as if he forgot all about that. "I had a thought. You know how you're trying to think of something, and it's at the edge of your memory and you can't quite grasp it, then you're doing something else entirely and it whacks you right in the balls?"

"I'm with you until the balls part, but yeah, I'll take your word for it. I know what you're saying."

"Grade seven geography." Calum points at the closet as if that explains everything.

"Once more from the top? Your recollection whacked you in the sack and… How'd we get from there to you in Mr. Vallin's geography portable?"

He shakes his head. "You and Emmet had Vallin. I had Miss Robinson." He looks at Sloan. "That's when I was sure I was gay. All the guys in my class were in love with Miss Robinson's boobs, and I couldn't wait for the gym class change room. Kevin was in that class."

Sloan nods. "It's sweet you two have history. I love history. I majored in history at university. Did ye know that?"

I roll my eyes. "We're not talking about history right now.

We're talking about geography. Calum, why are you two up at this unholy hour wrestling in your closet talking about grade seven geography?"

"The Canadian Shield." He flips his hands in the air with an uncoordinated flourish. "Ta-da, I remembered."

"Awesome. Now, tell me what the Canadian Shield has to do with—" It strikes me like a bolt of lightning out of the blue sky. "*Dayam,* Calum. You might be on to something."

Calum flashes Sloan a shit-eating grin. "Told ya! Bam, drop the mic!"

"Shh." I head to the closet. "You did your science project on the shield, didn't you?"

"Yep. Miss Robinson gave me an A+ and took my picture for the achiever's board."

I'm only half-listening now, abandoning my path toward the closet for his laptop on the desk. Why they thought they'd find more answers from a grade seven science project than on the internet is beyond me—or beyond the reason of two bottles of Redbreast Whiskey.

As soon as I type in my search parameters, I know that Calum *is* on to something. When the map comes up, it exactly mirrors where we saw the ley lines die off.

I laugh and shake my head. "We wondered what was shielding this part of the country from nature's magical bounties and it's an actual freaking shield—three million square miles of solid crystalline rock exposed during the glacial shift two billion years ago. It covers more than half the country."

"Problem solved." Calum curses while fighting with his button fly, then kicks his feet to free his legs from his pants. "You're welcome."

The kicking gets frantic, and I abandon the computer search before he hurts himself. I grab his pantlegs and free his feet. After folding his jeans, I set them on the dresser and go back to staring at the image on the screen. "We know the problem. Now we have to figure out how to fix it."

"What the fuck are you brewing, Fi?" Kevin steps into the kitchen with his hand cupped over his nose. He quickly grabs a dishtowel and fortifies his defenses. "That smells like festering maggots. Tell me you don't intend to eat that."

I stir the pot simmering on low on the back burner of the stove. "Not me. It's Gran's never-fail hangover cure. I asked her to send it first thing this morning."

"Oh, and who do you hope to poison with it?"

"Your better half and Sloan were up brainstorming until almost five this morning." I pull two mugs down from the cupboard and divvy up the mixture so each of them gets a couple of inches at the bottom. Then I grab the coffee pot and fill the mugs to half. After giving it the sniff test, I smile. "They won't even know about the festering maggots part."

Kevin takes a guarded sniff, then flashes me a grin. "Sneaky. So, druids do potions and stuff like witches? I haven't thought it all through, but that's cool."

"Some things overlap. I don't know much about the other magical groups yet, but yeah, White Wicca follows the same practices. Respect nature, nurture and grow, and the power of healing found in essences, herbs, and crystals."

We carry our offering up to the bedroom, and Kevin gets the door. He takes one look at Calum half-dead in his boxers and Sloan still in his usual GQ fashion, lying face-first on the floor and drooling. "And a good time was had by all."

"By them, maybe. Not so much for the girl who got woken up while they rummaged in the closet at four-thirty looking for Calum's grade seven science project."

Kevin smiles and stares off into the distance. "Ah, Miss Robinson. She had the nicest, big, round…eyes."

I laugh. "Calum said boobs."

"Oh? Really? I hadn't noticed." He laughs harder when I peg him with a look. "Hey, I'm gay, not blind. Those were confusing times."

I hand him one of the mugs. "You take Robin Hood, and I'll take McDreamy Drooler over here."

Kevin checks out Sloan and grins. "Aw, look how sweet he is snuggling one of Calum's Vans. You should get a picture of that for later use."

"I like the way you think."

Kevin moves on to revive Calum and sits on the edge of the bed. "And why exactly was Calum looking for his science project in the early-dawn hours?"

I set my mug on Brendan's dresser and take out my phone. After I snap a few quick pictures for posterity, I roll Sloan over. No change. Man, he's out cold. "Well, despite the drunken delivery of brilliance, they get full points for solving Canada's magic problem. They are the heroes of the hour."

Kevin looks from Calum to Sloan and laughs. "I don't think they're up for accepting their medals just yet."

Between the two of us, Kevin and I revive our little hungover heaps, get them to drink their potions, then leave them to die another death. It'll be interesting to see how quickly Gran's miracle of hangover recovery takes effect.

Until then, we head down to the dining room to continue where we left off last night.

"So, you think it's the stone of the Canadian Shield blocking the flow of ley line magic?" Dillan looks at Da, who's in his suit and ready to leave for work. "What do you think, Da?"

He's leaning over my shoulder and reading the science pages I have pulled up on my laptop. "It's possible. I'd even say probable. It says here the shield is a solid sheet of Precambrian igneous and high-grade metamorphic rock, and that it covers the area we know has no access to ambient magic."

"Damn. The area it covers is huge," Dillan says.

I zoom out so they can see the map. "Three million square miles from Michigan and New York up to the Arctic and Greenland."

Da straightens and checks his watch. "All right. Call yer Gran and Granda and talk to them about how we might create access to the magic beneath, assuming there is magic beneath."

"Oh, I believe there is."

Da kisses the top of my head. "Always my optimist."

"Or crazy dreamer." Dillan winks across the table. "And if there is magic below the stone, we have to figure out a way to unblock it, go out and get it done, and have the city powered back up by tomorrow or the next day before every angry preternatural being in a city of three million ends up on our doorstep to destroy us, our grove, and our fae who stole from them."

"Busy, busy," I say.

Da checks his watch again and frowns. "Calum and Sloan get another twenty minutes to pull their shit together, then sic Emmet on them. They're the men of the hour, but we don't have time for them to rest on their laurels right now."

Emmet snorts and rubs his hands together. "Is it all right if I hope they don't get up?"

I laugh. "Do you have something devious planned for them already?"

His grin is too funny. "Who, *moi?*"

"Yer out of luck this time around Emmet," Sloan says while jogging down the steps to join us. "We're both alive and well and reporting for duty."

"Well damn." Emmet grabs his coffee mug and stomps toward the kitchen. "That's really freaking disappointing."

"I'm off." Da grabs his sack lunch off the table and waves at us. "Keep me posted. I'll see Aiden at the station later. I'll fill him in and have him check in after his shift. It's all hands today, boys and girl."

"Safe home, Da." I give the dining room table a hard rap with my knuckles.

"Safe home," is repeated by one and all.

I check my phone and calculate the time change between Toronto and Ireland before sending the text requesting a video chat with Gran and Granda. The response comes almost immediately. Then the invitation pops up on my screen.

"Good morning, you two." I smile at my grandparents' foreheads. They haven't gotten the gist of where the camera is on their computer yet, so they never look in the right place. That's half the fun.

"Hello, the house," Granda says.

After everyone finishes with the pleasantries, I explain our ambient magic dilemma and our theory about the Canadian Shield being the problem. "So, what we need to know is one, if we're on the right path, and two, how do we penetrate the shield and release the magic mojo?"

"And three," Dillan adds, "how do we do that before warlocks and werewolves come to rip out our throats?"

"Have ye got a werewolf problem?" Granda scowls. "A nasty bunch, them."

I shrug. "We have no idea who's out there yet."

"Other than Black Dog bastards," Calum says.

"Yeah, other than them. So, the stone… Gran, you're our nature expert. How do we get around this?"

Gran is staring at the maps and frowns. "Technically, Toronto isn't built above the shield. Lugh, correct me if I'm wrong, but if I'm reading these maps right, the stone ends at the top of Lake

Huron and runs east to the top of Lake Ontario. Toronto is nestled between three lakes and pocketed. I'd say the shield is cutting you off from the ley lines but the city itself isn't shielded."

Calum unfolds an insert and expands the map. "Okay, I'll buy that, Gran. So, if we're below the bottom edge of the stone and the rock is cutting off the flow of magic before it gets to us, how do we free it to flow here?"

"I'd say use the lakes."

I look from Gran to the map and back again. "How so?"

"Water is a conductor, and three of the five Great Lakes surround you. Use that to your advantage. If there are veins of magic suppressed under the stone of more than half yer country, it'll have filled all the cracks of all the passageways as close as it could flow to the surface. My guess is if you find one or two large ley tributaries and connect them to the waterways, the magic could flow straight to ye."

"Does anyone have a map of the water table?" Sloan asks. "Or maybe a flow diagram of where the tributaries of the lakes are near enough to the surface that we might be able to free magic to seep into it?"

"Oh, this is good." I look at the maps. "You're right, Gran. If ley lines run under Canada the same way they do in other places of the world—"

"And there's no reason to suggest they wouldn't, luv."

"Agreed. Then if we find spots above us on the map where we can free magic into lakes and streams, it stands to reason the magic would flow right to us."

"I like the sound of that," Calum says. "Flowing right to us sounds easy."

I snort. "When has anything we've done been easy?"

"Hey, Negative Nancy, there's always a first time."

"My advice to ye," Granda leans toward the screen, "is that ye trek out in different directions and stop at intervals along rivers, streams, and inland lakes. Use a Rock to Water spell to drill down and see if ye sense any magic."

"How deep will we have to cast down into the stone?" Emmet asks.

I skim the text on page after page of information. "It looks like anywhere up to five miles."

"Shit, that's deep."

I nod. "Do we have the juice to do that?"

Granda frowns. "Hopefully, if ye hit a vein of power along the way, it'll give ye the strength to drill the next site. And so on. And so on."

"And if we don't?" Emmet asks.

"Och, well, then the experiment will be over before it starts, and ye'll be preparing for unwanted guests."

Gran smacks Granda in the shoulder. "It'll work. Positive energy. Take yer casting stones and branch out. Druids are the protectors of nature. Anything within that realm falls within our domain. I have faith in this and all of ye there doin' the work of the goddess."

I study the faces around the table and draw a deep breath. "Thanks, Gran. It looks like you're the only one who does."

CHAPTER EIGHTEEN

We're in the back lane, getting ready for our nature excursion when a breeze picks up and swirls around me. I catch a chunk of hair as it flips up and into my face. *Red, I need to talk to all of ye before ye go. Meet me in the grove.*

I close my car door and relock my truck. "Momentary delay, boys. Bruin needs us in the grove before we go."

"Has he got news?" Dillan asks.

"Do bears shit in the woods?" Emmet asks.

"Wouldn't that be shitting in our backyard?" Calum asks. "You're never supposed to shit in your backyard."

"I thought it was don't shit where you eat."

"Well, we eat in our backyard."

"But we'd never eat shit."

"No. I prefer to eat humble pie."

"I'd eat crow."

"I've seen you eat your heart out."

"Can't have your cake and eat it too."

Sloan stops and stares at my brothers.

I grab his wrist and tug him along with me. "Don't stare or

you'll get sucked into the vortex of nonsense. They get like this when they're anxious."

"It's incredible," Sloan says. "They don't miss a beat."

"Years of practice," I say.

"Practice makes perfect," Emmet says.

"No. Perfect practice makes perfect," Dillan says.

"Practice what you preach," Calum says.

"Practice is the best master."

"Master your fear before it masters you."

"Eternity is a master. Time is its disciple."

When we arrive beneath the leafy canopy, I scrub a hand over Bruin's ear and hold up my other hand to silence the insanity. "Thank you for that whirlwind of proverbs, quotes, and senseless sayings, boys. Bruin, you now have the forest floor. Take it away."

Bruin lifts his black nose and sniffs the air. "Last night when we were out here, I thought I smelled a familiar scent. It was similar to the one intent on draggin' Fi into the woods at the battle to reclaim the fae at Ross Castle."

I shiver while remembering the dark yearning I felt coming from the shadowed darkness. "Similar to? What do you mean, buddy? It wasn't the same guy?"

Bruin shakes his head. "It was, and at the same time, it wasn't. It was a transferred scent. The person I smelled wasn't the same male but he'd come in contact with him—and recently by the scent's strength."

"Was it a member of the Black Dog scoping out the house?" Sloan asks.

"I can't say. I tracked his scent to a subway station and deep into the tunnel where the tracks disappear, but once I got down there, I couldn't track it any further."

"Ye lost the scent?"

"No. The scent of his kind floods the entire place—the man who was here, not the one I smelled from Ireland."

"And he went to the subway?"

"He did. There is a maze of tunnels down there, and I got turned around more than once. With all the air smellin' like that species, I found it disorientin'."

"But you didn't recognize the species?"

"I didn't. I'm sorry."

I wave that away. "Don't worry about that. It still tells us that whoever was skulking around lives down in the subway tunnels and is in cahoots with the creepy Creeping Vine guy from Ross Castle."

"And that he knows where we live," Dillan adds.

Sloan frowns. "Vampires then, or maybe trolls, or goblins. Mound dwellers or crypt, I'd guess."

"What do they want with Fi?" Calum asks.

"I can't say." Bear's words are more growl than voice. "So far they've been movin' outside the periphery of her life, but that could either be curiosity or gathering intel. Until we know for certain, we need to keep our guard up."

"Thanks, Bruin." Calum pats my bear's muscled shoulder. "And you have my vote to go Killer Clawbearer on anyone who comes at Fi."

"Mine too," Dillan says.

Emmet nods. "Mine too. Slice and dice and we'll pick up the pieces later."

"I appreciate all the testosterone in the air, but let's not borrow trouble." I hug my bear and kiss his ear. "Like you said, maybe these tunnel-dwellers are simply curious about the weird new girl on the preternatural block."

Sloan's scowl is firmly locked in place. "Still, I say we take the time now and boost the wards around the property before we leave."

I huff. "That's overkill, Mackenzie. The day is already getting away from us. We should focus on our waterway work today and circle back to this in a day or two."

"How long will a power-up on the wards take?" Calum asks Sloan.

"If you boys help, an hour tops."

Dillan nods and raises his hand. "I'm with Sloan. Fi's creepy stalker needs to keep his distance."

Emmet raises his hand. "He has my vote, too."

Calum nods and raises his hand. "Sloan for the win."

I open my mouth to argue and Dillan cups his hand over my lips. "Look at it this way, Fi. If we strike out on the waterway work, our home will already be warded before the big bad wolves come to huff and puff and blow our house down."

It's obvious that I lost this one before I began.

"All right, Sloan. Tell us what you need and let's get it done ASAP."

With the wards up, the enchantments secured, and the entire property charmed to only let in us, Sloan, and humans we invite onto the property, Sloan and the boys finally give me the thumbs-up to get back to the immediate problem at hand.

Mission: Penetrate the Shield is a go.

The convoy sets off an hour and twenty-five minutes later. Sloan goes with Calum and Dillan to help them with their spells, and Emmet comes with Bruin and me with the hope that his buffer abilities will amp me up and give us the power we need to get things done.

Bruin is on edge and coming as my guardian bear more than a magic helper, but Sloan and my brothers feel better that he's sticking with me, so I don't argue.

Our plan is simple. Pick the strongest, most encompassing waterways, and go as far as we can making as many stops as we can.

Emmet and I are headed straight north to the Oak Ridges

Moraine, the Rouge River System, Lake Simcoe, and Lake Scugog. Then we'll make our way farther east to Rice Lake, the Trent-Severn Waterway, and the Bay of Quinte.

Team Two is going the other direction and tackling the Don River, the Sixteen Mile Creek, Humber River, Credit River, and ending up at the Niagara Escarpment.

"Surely, between their list and ours, we'll be able to get something happening."

"It's too bad we don't have time to get all the way out to the Laurentian River Systems." Emmet thumbs through data on his phone. "That river predates the recent ice ages and is filled with glacial debris. I bet we could find a way to drill down through the stone of the shield. It deposits more water into the system than any other waterway in Canada."

"Looks like we're taking a family trip to Quebec. Maybe we'll retrace the migration route of the French settlers."

"We're kind of settlers. Trend settlers." He snorts.

"Druid settlers…breaking new ground and lighting the way for all those who gave up before us."

He enlarges the text on his screen. "Check it. The underground source of the Laurentian's aquifer is Georgian Bay, and it says here that it reaches to High Park."

I blink at him. "High Park? Seriously? That's five miles from our house."

"Crazy, right? Who knew all this was going on underneath our feet?"

"Who knew, indeed." We travel along for a while, and I keep an eye on the GPS screen. "What do you think our chances are?"

Emmet leans back in the shotgun seat and shrugs. "I have no idea. Can we penetrate five miles of prehistoric stone? Will there be magic under there? If there is, will it be pocketed or accessible? There are a lot of ifs."

I hit my indicator and take the highway onramp to the 400. "I love that Gran thought of freeing the magic into the water table. If it flows naturally, it is better for everyone."

"And it beats us blasting through the earth's core every hundred feet to try to build our own ley line rivers. I looked into how we could shift the tectonic plates of the shield thinking that might work, but it's seriously one huge-ass sheet of stone—no faults, no wiggle room."

When the highway expands to four lanes in both directions, I press down on the accelerator and get us moving. We have a long day ahead of us and a short time to get it done.

To avoid getting caught in Toronto traffic, we decide to skip the Rouge River System as our first stop and go straight north out of the city and up to Lake Simcoe. It's a two-hour trip to get there. Then we can use country roads to move east and come down once we get past the Greater Toronto Area.

Emmet is lost in a geological rabbit hole of information. "Lake Simcoe is a remnant of a much bigger, prehistoric lake known as Lake Algonquin."

I chuckle. "You're going to use up all your data researching fun facts. You should save some."

He closes his search and drops his cell into his lap. "More importantly, I don't want my phone dead if we need to call for backup from the middle of nowhere."

"There's that too." I turn up the radio, and the two of us ride in companionable silence. Emmet's good like that. He's all jabber and goof when life is chaotic, but he doesn't have to fill every quiet space with the sound of his thoughts.

"This whole thing blows my mind," he says later.

"Which whole thing?"

"Tectonic plates, glaciers, pocketed magic... Think about it. We're talking about releasing magical mojo that's been trapped for millennia. Does age make it powerful old magic? Does magic go stale?"

"Like a day-old donut?"

"Just spitballing. There's so much we don't know."

"Preach. I think about that every day."

He stares out the window as the factories lining the highway thin out and we pass longer stretches of natural land. "Think about it. We may have all the magic we need trapped just beyond our fingertips. It's cool."

"Cool, yes. Convenient, no."

I follow the 400 until the GPS lady tells me to get off the highway. "What's our Plan B in case this fails?"

Emmet looks over. "No idea. We hope it doesn't fail?"

"That's what I was afraid of."

We arrive at Lake Simcoe's shore, and I follow the instructions until we're driving with a large body of water on our right-hand side. "Okay, where are the beaches we can use to gain access to the water?"

Emmet looks into that and calls up another search. "It looks like there are six close by to choose from…oh, and one of those is a nude beach."

"So, there are *five* to choose from."

Emmet snorts. "Where's your sense of adventure?"

"Nowhere near going to a nude beach with my *brother*."

"Oh, good point. I hadn't got there yet. Yeah, hard pass on Bare Oaks. How about Innisfil Park? It's close, people won't be nakey, and it looks like it's less populated than some of the others."

"Good, we'll start there."

Emmet navigates the way, and after I park in an empty public lot with about fifteen spots, he hops out and looks at the parking kiosk. "How long are we staying?"

"An hour? I have no idea."

He slips his bank card into the machine and comes back with

a receipt. “It’s three dollars an hour. I bought two. Put that on the dash.”

I place the receipt face-up and pull the keys from the ignition. “That should be plenty of time to figure things out. Any idea where we’re going?”

“There’s a path and info board over there.”

I follow Emmet to the board and trace my finger over the shellacked map that marks the bike and walking paths, and water access. “Okay, so we’ll take the dirt path straight to the water and see how things look from there.”

“Cooleroo.”

“Bruin, do you want to come out and play?”

Sure do. I want to secure the area.

I smile at the flutter in my chest and the build-up of pressure that precedes my bear’s release. He bursts from me with a gentle pop of pressure in my lungs and a swirl of a breeze around my body. “You do you, buddy. Have fun. You should be fine in bear form, but if you run into any trouble, spirit out and find us.”

Stay locked and loaded, Red.

Such a worrier.

CHAPTER NINETEEN

Emmet and I tromp along, and although we're here with a purpose, the pristine, natural surroundings make our mission a pleasure. Autumn is an amazing time of year in Ontario. It's after the thirty-eight-degree Celsius heatwaves of July and August, and before the minus thirty-two-degree winter freeze of January and February. With Thanksgiving and changing leaves and Halloween, it's awesome.

Since connecting with our druid heritage, the natural world has grown on me more than I ever expected. "We should start family nature walks on the weekends. Maybe give Kinu a break and take the kids with us."

Emmet smiles up at the autumn sun breaking through the canopy of leaves. The dappled light covers him in patches of sun and shadow. "Sounds good to me."

"Keeereee."

The shrill cry has me searching the break in the trees ahead and focusing on an enormous bird plunging its talons toward the surface of the massive body of water. In an almost uninterrupted descent and ascent, it flaps its mighty wings and pulls back into the air with a fish wildly thrashing in its clutched talons.

"Respect." Emmet fists his hand over his chest. "Is that an eagle?"

"Osprey." I'm not sure how I know.

We watch him carry his prey up to a massive twig nest at the top of a tall tree. "Lunchtime."

My stomach growls and I search the forested shoreline for a good spot to venture out. There isn't one, which is likely why there aren't any other people here. "I could use some food too, but it looks like we're out of luck here."

"Agreed. Our next stops, Johnson's Beach and Centennial Beach are ten minutes up the road and look much more heavily used by the public. I bet there will be a food truck or vendor there."

"Okay, let's do what we came to do and move on." I stare out at the body of water and wonder how we're going to get out there. "You didn't happen to bring a canoe did you?"

"Damn. Sorry, I left it in the pocket of my other jeans."

"Unfortunate." I search the shore, wondering where to start. "It's late to ask, but how do we figure out where the magic is?"

Emmet snorts. "*Now* you think of that?"

The two of us stand there glancing around, feeling a little daft. I send a quick text to Sloan and look around. "Come on, Emmet, buffer me. I need to find magic. Our lives depend on it. Access your naked man magic and tell me how."

He laughs. "Maybe my naked man magic would've been stronger with the Bare Oaks naturalists."

"Still a hard pass." I wave that away and pull my phone out of my pocket when it vibrates. I read the text from Sloan and smack my forehead. "Divining rod. Okay, that makes so much sense."

"Do we know how to do that?"

I turn my cell for him to see. "Sloan sent us a spell."

"Yay, Sloan! That boy is clenched tighter than a camel's ass in a sandstorm, but he has know-how."

"True story." I skim through the spell and read what we need.

"Okay, this looks doable. We need a forked branch from an oak or ash tree or a yew shrub."

Emmet's bright green eyes widen. "I can do oak. Do you have any idea what ash or yew look like?"

"No. Yew?"

Emmet snorts. "I see what yew did there. Yew so funny."

"Oaky doaky, let's get serious."

"Oh, yew are such an ash."

I look around. "Thankfully, there is no one here to hear us murdering humor."

Emmet laughs. "Isn't there a saying about cracking jokes like no one is watching?"

"That's dancing."

"Oh, then I've got nothing because I rock the dance floor. People should always watch me."

I spot a forked branch in the scrub and bend—

The blur of a projectile whips past my face. The whistle makes me duck, and I drop as it *thwacks* into the trunk of the tree. "Incoming!"

The forest spins as I roll to my knees and scan the trees in the attack direction. "Emmet? You good?"

"Fine." He runs low to the ground and slides in beside me behind the oak tree. "Did you see who's shooting at us?"

"No. You?"

"No."

I close my eyes and reach out to Bruin using the shared mental frequency we use without words. *We have a hostile in the woods. Intel would be nice.*

On my way to you.

"Bruin's coming." I lean forward, glance up the tree, and look at the feathered flight on the projectile that buzzed my ear. "It's a dart."

"Poisoned dart? Tranquilizer dart? Pub dart?"

"I can't tell. No dartboard though, so not a pub dart."

The rush of evergreen and outdoors breezes past me, and my heart rate eases a little. "Bruin's here."

A moment later, there's a roar in the trees fifty yards away, then the crack of wood splitting. Another roar and Bruin tumbles out of the trees and rolls into view with creatures wildly attacking him.

"What the hell are those things attacking my bear?"

Emmet makes a face like he's concentrating, then smiles. "River otters. *Lontra canadensis.* Carnivorous, semiaquatic mammals known to be an aggressive member of the weasel family."

"Hey, Google, stop."

As quickly as Bruin bats one away, two more climb him. I focus on his health and throw him some curative energy. *"Cure Wounds."*

"What's with the psycho attack otters?"

"No idea."

"Stop," someone yells while running from the trees. It's a tall man, lean and ropey. While he looks dressed as a park worker, I see through his guise immediately. He's man-pretty, like the elf who kissed me in the Doyle grove. He has long, sea-green hair and pale blue skin and is scantily clad in a seaweed skirt. "Don't hurt my girls. Please."

I'm about to stand when the tingle at the nape of my neck goes mental and my shield burns. "It's a trick."

I grab Emmet's shoulder and roll him with me as I dive to the side. The air fills with the hollow *clunk* of a spiked net falling to the ground behind us. I press my hands to the soil and call upon the stone shield. *"Wall of Stone."*

I raise my hand, and a protective blind grows out of the ground to shield my brother. *"Detect Magic."*

I'm flooded by the awareness of magic all around us. And not just any magic… "That's fae magic."

Emmet grabs my wrist and raises his palm toward our attacker. "*Siphon.*"

The influx of energy is intoxicating, and I'm quite sure I am now heavily under the drunken influence of an inadvisable amount of fae power. "Birga, do you feel like coming out to play, girlfriend?"

I flex my wrist, and she's firmly in my palm. I call on my gauntlets, and my skin alters with the effects of the bark protection. Standing tall, I round the stone wall and march at the scrawny man.

Birga spins in my palms and cuts the air with a whistle that sings to my soul. "Call off your pets, or they die."

The man pales when his sight locks on my natural armor. Yeah, I have a feeling my Tough as Bark will always get that kind of response. "Who are you?" His eyes are dark and rage-filled.

"Call them off."

"*What* are you?"

I raise my hand toward my bear, tighten my fist in the air, and swing my grip. My magical hold on the whirling dervishes attacking my bear sends his otters flying.

The man screams.

He raises his palms toward the flying furballs, but after Emmet's siphon, he doesn't have the juice to soften their landing. They collide with trees and hit the ground hard.

I reach out with my instincts and pinpoint what he is. "Naiad, why did you attack us?"

He looks from me to Bruin to his otters. "You attack us."

"No. You attacked us first. Your dart almost pegged me in the head, your rabid rodents went apeshit on my bear, and your felled net wasn't a welcome mat."

"You came to take our power. You project your intentions. You came to take what is ours. You attack us."

Emmet joins me and frowns at the crazy man. "Okay, I give. What's a Naiad?"

"Where Dryads are tree fae, Naiads are the energy of the rivers and streams. Gnomes live in the hills and mountains and under the earth. Sylphs float in the air. Faeries live in plants, herbs, and flowers. They all live behind the faery glass but have gateways to take on our material form to coexist with humans."

Emmet swings his finger through the air, taking in Bruin, the downed net, and the flailing otters. "I wouldn't exactly consider this coexisting."

I chuff. "No kidding."

"You have no right," the Naiad snaps. "Our home. Our magic pond."

Emmet's brow arches and he smiles. "Magic pond, you say? And where might this magic pond be?"

Red, Bruin says. *Some faeries are as likely to eat ye as help ye, but for them to assist humans, they must be asked. Some of the dim ones delight in attention. The more ye flatter, the more helpful they become.*

Seriously? You want me to placate this turd after he tried to kill us?

Ye don't have to, but ye want to learn about his magic pond and how to access the magic beneath the water. Seems to me that a water fae might be the one with aid to give.

I roll my eyes and sigh. "All right, let's start on better terms, shall we? I am Fiona Cumhaill, a druid of the Ancient Order of Druids. I'm also a Fianna warrior. And you are?"

"Iridan."

I turn to Emmet and point at the three furry and groaning mop heads lying stunned and mostly broken across the way. "Emmet, please heal Iridan's girls."

Emmet looks from them to the blood on my bear and makes a face. "And when they try to eat me?"

"They won't." I pierce the Naiad with a glare. "Will they, Iridan?"

He meets my glare with equal hostility. "You swear he'll not hurt them more?"

"Not unless he's defending himself. My brother is a gifted

healer in the druid order. It would be his greatest honor to restore your beloveds to full health by way of an apology. We didn't realize a fae such as yourself lived along the shore of this lake. Had we known, we would have brought you an offering befitting someone of your obvious standing."

He smiles and lifts his chin. "Yes, well, it was quite rude of you to show up unannounced."

"Our bad." I bite my tongue. "Now, if I tell my bear to stand down, do I have your word that there will be no further assaults? I'd hate for our first meeting to end in tragedy. Especially with the exciting news we have for you and the gift we came to deliver."

"A gift? What gift?"

Yeah, not the brightest bulb. "We came to realign the ley lines in the area. It is our quest to free the magic beneath the stone. That was our intention, not to take it, but to release it."

The man looks at me and wipes a hand over his face. "Truth?"

"Truth. And since you are familiar with these woods, perhaps you could help us find a forked branch of oak or ash we could use to divine where the ley lines lay."

"Give me my powers back and I will."

"Within the hour. You have my word."

But not yet. I'm giddy with the amount of power coursing through my veins. If I'm to drill down five miles into solid rock, this is exactly the kind of power boost that will help me getter done.

Iridan glares, but in the end, he turns to where he shot the dart from. A moment later, he returns with a strong branch with a definite 'y' at one end. "Will this do?"

I nod, having no idea. "Perfectly. You did well."

I take the stick from him and he stares. I can't remember the spell and don't want to blow my cover by letting it slip that I'm a novice who has to read it. To get him to stop staring at me, I point toward Emmet. "Go check on your girls. I'm sure they'll be comforted by your presence."

He seems to like that idea and shuffles off.

Layin' it on a little thick, aren't ye, Red?

I have no idea. He's only going to be honored by my attention if he thinks I'm something special.

So, prove to him that yer something special.

I call up Sloan's text, reach into my pocket to grip my casting stones, and read out the spell.

"Hold onto it, Emmet!" I chase my brother as he is dragged through the woods on his belly like a criminal behind a horse in an old western. He has a death grip on the divining rod and to say it's working would be the understatement of the century. His jeans are riding dangerously low considering the likelihood of poison ivy, and I'm already carrying the shoe he lost when he got air flying over a log.

"I hate you right now."

I don't blame him. As he bumps and bangs off the forest floor, he looks a little like a rag doll. He's making really good time though, getting to wherever we're going.

I dodge the patch of prickly scrub the divining rod pulls him through and wince. Yeah, I'm not going to be popular for a while over this one. "You're doing great, Em! Love you."

Bruin is in his spirit form, and I feel his presence on the wind that encircles us as we run. He's no doubt monitoring the surroundings as we push through, making sure we're not going to be attacked by any more maniacal otters.

"I may have put too much *oomph* into the spell. My bad." Note to self: with Iridan's magic still within me, I didn't judge my juice properly.

Well, at least we know the divining rod has enough power to

take us where we need to go. Hopefully, that also means we have enough to drill down through the shield when we get to wherever it takes us.

I'm still contemplating that when Emmet launches over the bank of a stream. He hangs in the air for a good long time before he splashes into the water and disappears.

I stop at the stream's edge and search the rippled surface. "Emmet? Emmet, where are you?"

A few racing heartbeats later, Emmet breaks the surface coughing and sputtering. A moment after that, he regains his footing and stands in the center of the stream.

"Are you okay?"

He's doubled over, hacking up water, and gives me a wave of assurance. When the cough and sputter stops, he runs a rough hand over his hair and blinks away the water in his eyes. "So, being in charge of the divining rod... Not as much fun as I expected."

"I am genuinely sorry about that. I'll make it up to you, I promise."

He wipes his hand over his face and shakes his head, throwing off excess water like a Golden Retriever. "Okay. I'm here now. What next?"

"I guess I join you in the middle of the stream."

Emmet's grin widens. "Well, good. Come on in, the water's fine."

I take off my shoes and socks and wade in the first couple of feet. "Frickety-frack, Emmet! Fine, my ass. It's freaking freezing."

Emmet snorts. "Mid-September. What did you expect?"

Still grumbling, I join him in the center of the stream and slip my hand into the pocket of my khakis. I close my hand around my peridot's natural shape, the smooth round surface of my Ostara turd stone, and the hematite I bought at the crystal shop with Sloan. While focusing on where my feet connect to the silt at the bottom of the stream, I sink deeper and draw power.

I close my eyes and send the command straight down from where we stand. "*Stone to water.*"

I sense as my intention morphs the previously impenetrable stone into a shaft of water. Testing the funnel, I figure I made it about three or four miles down. I draw a deep breath and send down another wave of power. "*Stone to water.*"

Come on, magic...bubble up to us.

We wait, standing there covered in goosebumps. Emmet's lips are purple, and I take his hand in mine.

"*Internal Warmth.*" I sigh as a rush of heat suffuses my body and chases away the chill. "Better?"

"Much better. Thanks, Fi."

I keep his hand in mine and close my eyes again. It's easier to focus on things now that my teeth aren't chattering and my muscles aren't locked in a hypothermic spasm. *Come on, magic. Where are you?*

"*Stone to water.*" As I cast the spell for the third time, I sense the last of the shield's stone breaking away. The fae magic holds a warm, swirly purply-pink energy, at least in my mind's eye. I see it mixing with the water now, filling the funnel down almost seven miles.

"It's coming." I'm relieved. "Close your eyes and call it, Emmet. Can you feel it?"

"No, but you're a much stronger caster than I am."

"For right now, maybe, but not for long. You guys are gaining on me."

We stay silent for a little, and I focus on the approaching magic. After millennia of being dormant, it's slow and listless, mixing with the stream water in a half-daze.

I plant my feet deeper into the silt and call it again. Once it knows how to find freedom, I believe it will find its way into the stream, flow into Lake Simcoe, and begin its journey through the waterways toward Lake Ontario.

"Damn, Fi. If it's taking this long to get to the surface, how long will it take before it gets to the disgruntled magic users of Toronto?"

I don't want to think about that. Too long, I expect.

When I sense it's nearing the surface, I look down by our feet and wait. I draw the first deep breath I've managed in two days and call to the energy.

"That's it. Come to Mama."

I now understand how the Wyrm Queen felt waiting for her eggs to hatch—watching and waiting. Knowing it's coming, but not fast enough.

"This is a little anticlimactic."

Emmet chuckles and squeezes my hand. "It's always an adventure with you, Fi. There's no one I'd rather stand balls-deep in a freezing stream with."

My smile grows as the water around us swirls purply-pink. "We have our first win. Yay team."

"Off to the next beach, or do you want to check out the Naiad's magic pond?"

"I suppose I have to give him his powers back."

Emmet sighs. "I suppose. But if he morphs into a duplicitous dick and attacks us again, we take them and keep them."

"Agreed. Done deal."

It's close to three in the morning when I pull into my parking spot in the back lane. Calum's and Emmet's new Lexus is in its place, so the others must have finished quicker than us. I slide out of the passenger's side and drag my lead legs beneath me as Emmet and I trudge into the back yard.

"Long day?" Da asks. He's sitting in one of the wooden Adirondack chairs on the edge of the grove.

"Yeah." I flop onto the ground beside him and look up at the stars. I used magic to dry off, but being cold and wet so many times today has left me achy and with a bit of a chill.

"Night." Emmet doesn't stop to chat. He drags himself up the back steps and into the house.

"Night," Da and I both say back.

"How did Calum and his group do?"

"They seem confident the first phase of the mission was a success. Now we wait."

I yawn and smile when the doe from the grove steps cautiously out of the trees and lays in the grass beside me. She sets her long neck onto my chest, and I stroke her velvety ears.

"Yep. Now we wait."

CHAPTER TWENTY

I wake in my bed with no memory of how I got here, but thankful that someone scooped the unconscious girl off the grass and brought me inside. One thing I love about a century-old home is that it talks to you if you take the time to listen. This morning, I'm too wiped out to do much more than lay there and listen. Someone's in the shower, a couple of people are puttering around in the kitchen, and someone is—

My eyes pop open, and I find Liam sitting in my reading chair beside the window. "Hey, trouble."

I relax back into my pillow and exhale. "Geez, you scared me."

"Sorry. I have the day off, and we haven't spent any time together since you guys got home from your big quest. I thought we could hang out and you could tell me all about your magical adventure."

I roll onto my side and stretch. "And here I lay, sleeping your day away."

"Nah, you're good. Your dad and Calum told me about your big day yesterday. He said you were physically and magically wiped out by the time you got home."

"True story." I sit up, flip back my quilt, and head to my dresser. After grabbing some clothes, I open my bedroom door wider so I'm first into the bathroom when whoever's in there now finishes.

Growing up in a family with five older brothers, you had to be strategic to get bathroom time. "So, what do you want to do today?"

He shrugs. "What were you planning on doing?"

"Honestly, more of the same. Yesterday we hit a dozen spots where we thought we could release ley line magic from beneath the stone. We've only scratched the surface on that and need to continue."

"Is there a lot more to do?"

"I think so. It's running a lot slower than I imagined, and there are going to be a lot of empowered people annoyed with us unless we restore the magical balance."

Liam's ice-blue gaze sparks with adventure. "I'm game. Hiking. Swimming. And watching you do your thing. Sounds like a perfect day off."

"Thanks. I can't take my foot off the gas just yet."

"Because of the warlocks and vampires who will end you for stealing their magic?"

I roll my eyes. "My, my, someone has been chatty."

"So, it's true, then. You're in the crosshairs again?"

"Again? When haven't I been?"

The bathroom door opens, and Dillan comes out dressed in his uniform.

"You off to work?"

He nods. "No rest for the wicked."

"Same." I grab my clothes and head toward the cloud of humidity oozing from the shower. "Safe home. Love you."

"Same."

After a shower and breakfast, Liam and I meet up with Da in the grove. For a guy who gave up being a druid almost forty years ago, he seems to be gravitating to it now. "Howeyah, oul man." I lean in and kiss his cheek. "I figured you'd be at the station by now."

"I had court first thing, then came home to change." His gaze moves from me to Liam. "You two heading out?"

I pull out the list of places on today's waterway magic tour. "Yep. I figure if we rinse and repeat what we did yesterday, it'll help. Calum's with me, and Aiden and Sloan have already gone out. Do you feel anything yet?"

He shakes his head. "No. Nothing yet."

Me either. "Tough times never last. Tough people do."

"Right ye are, *mo chroi*. Right ye are."

By six-thirty, the sunlight has lost its luster. The golden warmth is gone and replaced by the cool, gray light of the promise of cooler days. Liam, Calum, and I have had a full and exhausting day, and are about ready to wrap up and pack it in for the night.

On the bank of yet another river, I watch and wait while Calum finds our next location. "With Samhain coming up, we should plan a celebration. Do you think your mom would consider a theme night or something fun at the pub?"

I unbutton my long, winter coat and step into the icy water where Calum stands with our divining rod pointed straight down.

A couple of lessons I learned yesterday were to wear water shoes today so I don't have to keep taking my shoes on and off, and to wrap myself in my floor-length winter coat to keep my seats dry and preserve my body heat between icy dips. Magic is great, but I don't have much to spare for body warmth by the end of the day.

I consider our second day a success. We made another six stops today along the Rouge River System, and while I can't feel the effect in the air yet, I can feel it tingling around my legs beneath the water.

"I think once we hit the Laurentian waterway and around Quebec and spend time branching out, we'll have transformed what magic looks like in Canada."

"Have you ever wondered about *not* transforming it?" Liam is sitting on a large rock on the bank, looking concerned. The day's enthusiasm has worn thin, and we're all tired and ready to go home.

Calum and I both stop what we're doing to look up.

"What do you mean by that?" Calum asks. "Not free the trapped magic?"

"I mean, Canada has gotten along fine with little or no fae or magic-fueled people. Sure, if you're releasing magic it's better for you and your grove creatures and your boss and her tree, but is it better overall? What will the evil druids and the warlocks and the vampires do with the boost in their power? Maybe the lack of ambient magic is the only thing holding the bad eggs at bay."

I have considered that but dismissed it as quickly as it entered my mind. The truth is, we need the influx of power to fuel the good guys. If that emboldens the bad guys, we'll deal with it as things come.

"I hear what you're saying. Honestly, I don't have an answer. The last thing we want to do is contribute to the opposing team, but right now, they're pulling power from blood sacrifice and torture. Is it better that they might be able to access ambient magic? The people who aren't bled out on the altar might think so."

Calum nods. "She's right. Evil is as evil does. If they're determined that the lessers rue their existence, whether the power comes easier doesn't change their intentions."

"Stone to Water." I send the command into the ground and get

this process started. Reaching down, I connect with the earth beneath me and sense that the stone isn't as thick here as it was in some of the places we've encountered over the past two days of doing this.

Mark a point in the win column.

I draw a deep breath and send down another wave of power. "*Stone to Water.*"

Calum takes my hand in his, and it's warm and strong. "*Internal Warmth.*" He sends a rush of heat into my system, and I breathe deep and groan at its decadence.

Fortified with warmth, I send another pulse down. "I think it's too early to hit the panic button. We don't know the players yet. Maybe the Black Dog is the worst of the worst and the rest of the Toronto preternatural and ethereal populations are benign and happy to live their lives without people bothering them."

Liam looks at me, his frown locked in place. It's obvious he disagrees, but it's too early in the game to take the ball and go home.

"We'll figure it out." I hope I sound surer than I feel.

"Maybe, but when? After magic freaks and killers overrun normal people? Who made you God, Fi? I know you mean well, but you're in way over your head."

I draw a deep breath, pulling oxygen against the sudden weight on my chest. "Thanks for the vote of confidence."

The ride home is silent and fraught with hostility. Somehow my day with Liam, one of my closest friends and a guy who means more to me than I can explain, turned ugly. He doesn't approve of us trying to free the ley lines, but his opinion is valid. What cleaves through my heart like Birga's blade is his shift in mindset. He drew lines in the sand, and somehow we ended up on opposite sides.

"Bad day?" Sloan asks as I blow past him.

I launch up the stairs, my wet socks slipping on the wooden steps. I stomp into the bathroom and peel off my clothes. After wringing out my socks and pants, I pull my shirt over my head and grab a towel off the shower rod. I snatch up my comb and pull it through my hair and curse when it gets stuck in the damp, tangled depths.

The *snap* of the handle brings tears burning behind my eyes. I can't stand seeing myself in the mirror and bolt across the hall and into my bedroom.

Sloan's there, and I shake my head and point at the door. "Don't. Go. I don't have the energy right now."

"What happened?" His voice is deep, his tone dangerous. "Are ye all right? Were ye attacked again?"

I swipe at the tears leaking down my cheeks and pull open my drawers. Emotionally, yes. Physically, no. "Look. I'm cold and tired. Nothing happened that involves you or anything druid. I need a moment to get dressed and regroup."

He reads my expression. I don't know what he sees, but he gives me his back and makes no move to leave. "Get dressed. Get warm. Then ye can tell me what the fool said that hurt ye so."

I drop my towel and pull on a fresh pair of yoga pants and a fleece hoody. With a balled-up pair of fuzzy socks in hand, I plunk down on the end of my bed.

"He said 'normal people.'" My voice chokes, and I can't breathe. The dam breaks and Sloan is there, pulling me tight to his chest. "He asked me what gives me the right to make choices that affect *normal* people living in Toronto. And what...I'm not normal anymore?"

I pull away from Sloan's comfort and start to pace.

As I cross the room, it dawns on me that I only have one sock on, and I sink to the floor. "When did I become *other* to him? That hurts. I never expected it. Not from him. I'm not *other*. Am I?"

Sloan takes a moment to consider his answer before he

speaks. "In a sense, maybe, but I've been *other* my whole life, and it's not so bad. I love my life and my gifts."

"I get that, but he accused me of playing God and endangering 'normal' people for my gain."

"Och, well, I doubt he believes that even if the words came out of his mouth. He's scared, Cumhaill. Yer changin' before his eyes. Yer in danger, and he can't help. Ye need things he can't give ye. Where yer lives have always been tightly knit, now yer branchin' off in a direction that not only doesn't he understand, but he'll never be able to follow."

I accept the box of tissues when he holds them out. After a few steadying breaths, I realize Sloan's right. Liam's sad and scared, and yeah, things are changing with me. Big time. "Thank you. You get big points for not trashing him. I appreciate it."

"Trashing him would hurt ye, Fi. And if ye remember, I swore to ye back in Ireland that first visit that I'd never hurt ye again if I can help it. I never want yer tears to be because of me."

I hold up my hand and let him pull me to my feet. After a quick hug, I step back and smile. "I can't believe I used to think you were such a haughty dickwad."

His mint-green gaze is lit with warmth. "As ye said once, I'm like a fungus. I grow on ye."

"You're a good friend. I'm thankful every day for that."

"Me too. Now away with ye. The man can only pace the back lane for so long before one of yer neighbors calls the coppers and reports him. I'd bet he'll want to right his wrongs and he's kickin' himself for upsettin' ye so."

I dry my tears and hug him again. "You're a good guy, Sloan Mackenzie."

"It's nice of ye to notice. Now go."

Sloan's right, as usual. I jog downstairs, hop off the back steps, and hustle past the grove to the back lane. Liam looks like he's fit to blow. "You're an idiot, you know?" I unlatch the fence and head out between the cars to the back lane. "You don't get to insult me and think that I'll throw away twenty-three years of loving you."

Liam meets me at the bumper of my car, and his eyes are far too glassy for my liking. "I am an idiot. No question."

"No question. But you're a damn fine idiot, and you make a mean cocktail."

He chuckles. "Tricks of the trade."

I squeeze his hand and fill my lungs. "I'm figuring things out as I go. I know I'm not a god, but I'm still me. I'd never knowingly put anyone in harm's way."

He pulls me in for a hug. "I know that Fi, but the stakes in your lives have been raised. You're reacting to your world crashing around you, and it scares the piss out of me."

"Hey, if it makes you feel better, it scares the piss out of me too."

His laughter vibrates against my chest as he pulls back. "No, actually, that doesn't make me feel better at all. I'd like the person with the magic to have a solid hold on the reins."

"Sorry. Should I fake it until I make it?"

"Nah. That's not your style." He steps back, and his smile drains away. "Be careful, Fi. The things that go bump in the night are scary and better left undisturbed."

"Agreed. I have no intention of stirring up trouble."

"No intention maybe...but you realize you were born a stir stick, right?"

"Har har, funny guy."

I say goodnight to Liam and stand in the back lane while he drives away. When his taillights turn, and he heads up Wellesley, I turn back to go inside the gate.

My shield fires to life, my early-warning system going off a split second before strong hands secure me from behind. Warm breath washes the side of my neck, and despite all efforts, I can't break free of the hold. "Loverboy is right about the things that go bump in the night, you know? You should've left us undisturbed."

CHAPTER TWENTY-ONE

I've portaled with Sloan enough times to understand the momentary disorientation that comes with being plucked out of one reality and deposited into another in the span of a racing heartbeat. Still, the wave of nausea and spinning head is new, and I'm not a fan.

I search for a point in the room to focus on while the squirrels in my stomach settle down. My eyes lock on the translucent glass wall at the other end of the large, rectangular room. It's backlit and illuminates the moving hands of a massive clock face.

Are we in a city clocktower?

A heritage building with a clock face?

I check out the modern chrome and black and white marble décor, and I've got nothing. Movement on the sidewall draws my gaze, and I see a man standing behind a well-stocked bar.

"Lady Druid." He holds the bottle tipped for a long pour. He's a burly, good-looking Jason Momoa kinda guy with nipple-length ebony hair, amethyst purple eyes, and enough sculpture in his abs and pecs to make the tailored black dress shirt work for him. He raises his glass to me, then takes a few deep swallows. "Thank you for accepting our invitation."

I pull at my captor's vice-grip hold banding my upper arm and get nowhere. Damn. This guy is ridiculously strong.

Bruin flutters within my chest. *Do you need me, Red? What's happened?*

Not yet. I've been kidnapped before. Let me see what this is about. No need to tip our hand.

I may be unable to gain my freedom, but there's no need to appear weak. Straightening, I lift my chin and meet the man's gaze with no fear. "Sorry, I missed the invite part of this get-together. It was more of a snatch-and-grab from my perspective."

My host smiles. I feel the pull of his charm as tangibly as the fingers banding my arms. I look down at the fingers gripping my dragon tattoo and wonder if manhandling assholes get transported into the Wyrm Queen's lair.

This guy would make a meaty snack for Her Scariness.

"Is there something wrong?" I say to my host, who is now staring at me with a screwed-up expression.

"What are you doing?"

"Me? Nothing." I return his assessing stare. "Why? What are you doing?"

He steps closer and chucks a finger under my chin. He's got a solid foot and a half on me, and an easy hundred and fifty pounds, but isn't trying to use his size to intimidate me. His expression holds genuine curiosity. "Why aren't you succumbing to my charms?"

I laugh. "My mistake. Is this you being charming? Sorry, I didn't realize it. Does the kidnapping and manhandling approach usually win you the favor of the ladies? If that's what you're expecting, you'll be disappointed. I'm more of a dinner and a walk by the lake girl myself."

He barks a laugh and steps back. "Well, the reports on you are certainly true. You are a mystery."

"You too. Could we solve that one together? Who are you and why am I here?"

"I am Garnet Grant, Alpha of the Toronto Moon Called and Grand Governor of the Lakeshore Guild."

"Uh-huh. Guild of what?"

He frowns. "Do you expect me to believe you haven't heard of us?"

I bite my lip and make a face. "Sorry. Is that a *faux pas* in kidnapping circles? I admit I'm new to the scene. I don't know all the social cues yet and haven't heard of much. Consider this a teaching opportunity. You are Garnet Grant, Grand Governor of the Lakeshore Guild of…artists, gamers, quilters? My next-door neighbor Janine belongs to the quilter's guild. Maybe you know her?"

"Empowered Ones." He scowls. "The Lakeshore Guild is a coalition that unites the most powerful species of empowered people under one ruling council."

"Oh, cool. I'm a huge fan of organized policing. You should know there is some crazy stuff going on in the city. I've been playing catch-up but would love to talk to you about it. I'm glad to meet you, Garnet."

His scowl deepens, and he grunts at me.

"Is that wrong? Shouldn't I be glad to meet you?"

He takes a step back and runs his fingers over his scalp, raking through his hair. "I wouldn't think so, no. Are you the one who drained all the magic from the city?"

"Oh, yeah. Sorry about that. A total accident, I assure you. I've taken steps to rectify that, and you should see the results very soon."

"Steps," he repeats and meets the curious glances of six newcomers. The large, black door to the room closes, and a grouchy-looking group joins us. They all have the same muscular physicality as Garnet, and something in me recognizes them all as Weres.

Oh, Moon Called. I get it.

Garnet swallows. "My people are having a hard time fighting

the pull of their beasts, and it's getting worse, not better. The full moon is in three nights, and without our powers, there's no amount of steps that can save us all from the inevitable bloodbath that will ensue."

Well, crap. "Again, I am super sorry. Honestly, I don't think it'll be a problem. My brothers and I have been working non-stop for two days to rectify the siphoning of power."

"But you and your brothers *are* the cause of the siphoning of power. I'm thinking the best way to rectify that is to eliminate you."

The guy squeezing my arms shifts his hold, and I frown. "Ow, dude. You seriously need to let go of my arm. And if I were you, I'd stay the hell away from my infinity dragon armband there… unless you're curious about visiting the treasure trove of a dragon queen."

I see the curiosity in his gaze a moment before he vanishes. Shaking out my shoulders, I run a hand up and down my arms as blood returns and pins and needles tingle in my hands. "Sorry about your guy."

The newcomers rush forward, but I put up my hand. "Are you sure you want to do this? I've been polite up until now, and would prefer to keep things friendly."

"Where is my man?" Garnet growls.

"I told you. He's visiting the treasure trove of a dragon queen. This armband is a portal."

"How does he get back?"

"He doesn't. I guarantee you that the she-dragon has eaten him by now and is feeding him to her babies."

The room echoes with the low rumble of growls.

I meet Garnet's gaze. "Hey. I warned him about not grabbing me there, and now he's dead. Let me go one further and warn the rest of your muscle—back the hell off me, or things will become a lot less cordial here."

Garnet raises his glass and takes another long sip of his drink.

"More than a pretty face. You surprise me, Lady Druid. It's been a long time since someone surprised me, especially a beautiful female."

I dip my chin and accept the compliment. "I'm much more than my packaging suggests. I can be an ally or an enemy. I would much prefer to be an ally. I love the idea of a ruling council. My family comes from a long line of law enforcement. I'm game to learn how it all works."

"Fuck that," a man shouts in the row of newcomers.

I turn in time to see him launch into the air. His clothes explode into tattered confetti as he flies at me, claws extended.

I release Bruin, and my bear roars out of me. He guts the attacking wolf mid-air. The beast falls to the polished marble floor as his blood splatters the other five men.

I call Birga to my hand and *Whirlwind* for effect. With my spear in my hand, I spin the weapon in my palm, and my hair flies around my face like I'm a badass supermodel. Bruin paces between me and the five, his canines exposed, his bloody claws clicking on the marble floor.

"It doesn't need to go this way, Garnet. Call off your dogs or they all die."

Garnet's smile grows, and he holds up his hand to halt the all-out attack of his remaining men. "You are a force, Lady Druid, and I am truly impressed."

"This isn't a show to impress you. I don't take life lightly, but I won't risk mine either. I am a woman of my word and have been straight with you. If your men attack me, my battle beast will eviscerate them. If they come against me directly, I am more than capable of defending myself."

"I believe you." Garnet finishes his drink and steps over to the wolf whining like a pitiful dog on the floor. He kneels, lifts the wolf's head, and twists. The snap of his neck ends the beast's suffering, and he points at two of the five men left.

"You two, take Jonas's body to the temple. You two clean this mess up. Trent, notify the Governors that I am escorting Miss Cumhaill home. They are to stand down on any further action unless I give the order."

"Alpha, you can't go out there alone. It could be a trap."

Garnet looks at me with a scrutinizing gaze. "Have you any intentions of destroying me or unseating the Lakeshore Guild, Lady Druid?"

I shake my head. "Nope. I'm happy to chat more if no one's trying to kill me or mine."

"Fair enough. If you would gather your beast, I shall take you home."

I nod at Bruin, and he dissolves into the air and returns to his place within me.

A moment later, Garnet and I are standing in the back lane, surrounded by a frantic and irate group of druids.

Garnet holds his ground, and I give him credit. In the face of six protective and angry druids, and after seeing what Bruin and I can do, he doesn't bat an eye. I guess that's an Alpha thing. Show no weakness.

I hold up my palms and step forward to act as a shield between my well-meaning protectors and our guest. Well, I don't suppose he's so much of a guest as a repentant kidnapper, but for the sake of turning over a new leaf, I'll go with guest for now.

"Stand down, you guys. I'm fine." I gesture at Garnet and commence with the introductions. "Everyone, this is—"

"Garnet Grant," Da snaps, his voice clipped. "I shoulda guessed ye weren't human by the number of times ye've walked out of police stations with yer goons and gotten off scot-free. So, what are ye then?"

I hold up my finger. "Let me see if I can get this right. He's the

Alpha of the Toronto Moon Called and Grand Governor of the Lakeshore Guild of Empowered Ones." I check with him, and when he nods, I smile and explain that to my brothers. "It's a local Justice League for gifted folks."

"So, yer a Were," Da says. "A wolf, bear, dragon?"

"Lion, actually." He flashes that goofy smile he tried on me when he first introduced himself. I feel Garnet's magic take hold. It tingles on my skin and makes my back itch.

Da and the others relax, and the tension in the back lane dissolves almost completely from one moment to the next.

"Stop that." I peg him with a glare. "You don't get to influence my family."

Garnet chuckles. "I influence everyone, Lady Druid. The question is, why don't my charms work on you?"

Sloan snorts. "Fiona views the world in a different light than most. She also sees through illusions better than most."

Garnet chuffs. "She tells me that you have all been working to restore the levels of magic you altered. Is that true?"

I don't want my trippy family to get into the fact that we can release unlimited amounts of fae magic. I don't know Garnet well enough to trust him with that info.

What if bad guys across the country take it upon themselves to start blowing up the Canadian Shield?

To cut my guys off from blabbing everything, I interrupt. "I told Garnet that we've worked day and night for the past two days to rectify the power drain we caused and that the city's ambient energy should return to previous levels very soon."

"And is that the entire truth?" Garnet asks expectantly.

"Not entirely," Da says. "We're optimistic the levels will be improved. The city's natural magic isn't enough to feed the cells. If our efforts are fruitful, that situation should improve."

I let out a huge sigh of relief and bat my eyelashes at the Alpha Were. "Happy?"

"I'm satisfied that you're making an effort to restore the magic. I won't be happy until I know that eight hundred Moon Called predators aren't going to stalk the city's innocents in a feeding frenzy in three nights' time."

I press my finger on my nose and nod. "I'm one hundy percent behind you on not wanting that to happen. We'll keep on it from our end, I promise. In the meantime, you gotta give us room to work."

"You have my word."

"Cool. And hey, if in three nights there's not enough magic for your people to control their urges, I have no doubt you'll set them on us first. Fair is fair."

"I'm glad we understand one another, Lady Druid. Until then." Garnet raises his fingers as if to tip an imaginary hat, then disappears.

Awesomesauce.

"He seemed nice," Emmet says, his eyes dreamy.

"Sexy as fuck," Calum adds.

The guys are all still smiling like lovestruck idiots, and I roll my eyes. "Okay, Sloan, do you have anything in your spellbook that counteracts an Alpha Were's power to influence? I think we might need that going forward."

After the third day of hiking, standing in icy streams, and drilling through stone to create passageways for the magic of the ley lines to reach the surface, I can't even think about it anymore. I suggest that those brothers of mine who aren't working the streets join me, Sloan, and Da for a night at Shenanigans for some let-loose recreation.

I'm on my third Redbreast when one of my favorite songs comes on, and I wriggle my butt in the booth while pointing at the dancefloor.

"But yer food just got here," Sloan says.

I laugh. "Food can be reheated, but Shenanigans prides itself on never repeating a song in a night's playlist. It's now or never, Mackenzie."

Emmet abandons the end spot in the booth, and Calum moves his chair back from the end. The moment I'm free, I check to see if anyone is joining me. No? I head to the dancefloor on my own. Fine. Sucks to be them.

I merge in with the regulars, happy to take advantage of my whiskey buzz and be among friends. As the tempo fills my ears, I close my eyes and let some of the stress from the past three days drain away.

A solid hand presses against the small of my back and I'm spun in place to face the cocky smile of one of the Weres I had the unfortunate pleasure to meet this afternoon.

I push back from his hold, but there's no getting free without causing a scene in front of a lot of innocent people I care about.

"Trent, wasn't it? If you wanted to dance, you could've asked. Like your friend learned this afternoon, manhandling me doesn't end well."

His grin widens as his grip grows bruisingly painful. "For you, maybe."

"Garnet won't like this. He and I are on good terms. You're supposed to leave us alone to correct our mistake."

"Why should I care what a fucking feline says? That male has forgotten what it means to be an Alpha. He's more interested in fancy titles and expensive wines than what it truly means to be a Moon Called warrior."

Crap. Hostile and disgruntled. That can't be good. "Have you forgotten about my ursine protector? If you get out of line, my spirit bear will rip you to shreds."

"But you can't launch your killer bear in here, can you, sweet cheeks? When you're in public, you're only a mundane girlie out for a night on the town, ain't that right?"

"Wrong again, asswipe." I give Bruin quick directions and release him. "You feel that breeze tugging at the nape of your neck? That's him. He doesn't have to take physical form to kill you. He can enter your body and stop your heart. No one would think anything weird about a guy having a heart attack on the dance floor. Sucks to be you."

"You're lying." Bruin swirls around the two of us, and Trent's gaze narrows.

"Am I? Okay, then, let's see how it plays out. Do I seem worried to you?"

He glares at me while gauging what I said.

I guess I'm a convincing liar because a second later his knuckles bury into my stomach with a solid punch. Shit, these guys are strong.

My vision fritzes and my breath rushes from my lungs.

I lose track of time and place for a moment, and by the time I blink past my watery vision, he's gone. Bowed at the waist and breathless, I stagger down the hall to the loo.

It takes me a few minutes to pull myself together, and when I head back out, I'm a little lost as to what to do about the assault. Garnet gave us a pass. Or did he? Maybe he's not as upfront as I took him for.

After apologizing to the two people I practically bowled over in my sucker-punched stupor, I head back to our booth.

Emmet stands when I arrive, and I slide back into my spot in the corner. "You okay, Fi?"

"Sure. A bit dizzy. I figure Sloan's right. It's better to eat when the food's hot. Besides, I don't want to miss any of the latest Cumhaill gossip. Calum, tell us, how are things with Kevin? Is your new Robin Hood status still driving the forgiveness train steadily down the tracks?"

As my brothers devolve into lewd comments about Calum making his man merry, I focus on my burger.

Maybe coming here was a mistake. Maybe Liam's right, and

we're not 'normal' people anymore. Am I putting people at risk? The idea that who and what I am endangers Auntie Shannon, Liam, or the clientele here is more than upsetting.

It robs me of one of my fundamental truths.

That Shenanigans will always be home to me.

CHAPTER TWENTY-TWO

Getting ready for bed two hours later, I unbutton my shirt and open the two sides to expose my ribs. My full-length mirror gives me a shocking look at the damage. "Oh, that's grisly." I test the bruising that runs from my hip to the underside of my boob and wince.

A sucker punch from a werewolf is like getting hit by a wrecking ball in full swing. "Asshole."

I let the shirt drop off my shoulders and twist my arm back to unhook my bra. The piercing pain that rips up my side brings tears to my eyes. "Screw that. If it hurts this much to take off tonight, odds are it'll hurt more tomorrow trying to get it back on."

I abandon the idea and grab Brenny's t-shirt off my pillow. It's awkward getting it over my head without raising my left arm, and freeing my hair from the collar doesn't go much smoother.

"Okay, I'm officially pissed."

I open the drawer to my bedside table, take out a bottle of Tylenol, and go for a twofer. When those are down, I exchange my water bottle for Beauty. Maybe there's an easy healing spell in her pages that will let me get some sleep.

I consider asking Sloan for help.

After all, he's the son of the Order's healer and has a strong affinity for it himself. I have no doubt he could patch me up, but I can't face him right now.

Trent's violence may have stolen my breath, but what knocked the wind out of me is the thought of bringing thugs like him into contact with people I care about.

Liam's right. I'm not the same person I was four months ago, and I'm not 'normal' like them anymore.

Does that mean me loving them puts them in danger?

A knock on my door brings Da's voice in the hall. "Are ye decent?"

"One sec." I bite my lip and climb into bed, holding my breath. I settle against my headboard as quickly as I can and try to breathe through the pain. "Coast is clear."

Da comes in, closes the door, and strides to the end of my bed. He studies me, folds his arms over his chest, and frowns. "Do you want to tell me what happened at the pub tonight, or do I have to go back and check the tapes?"

I chuckle. "Auntie Shannon doesn't let just any looker with a badge access her security footage."

His crooked smile is a relief. If he knew what happened, there would be no humor in him at all.

"What makes you think you'll find something?"

"Because I know my baby girl. Yer mood did a one-eighty after yer trip onto the dance floor. I'd like to know who blew out your candles."

I pull my quilt up, but it makes a flimsy shield against everything that hurts tonight.

Da sits beside me and tucks my blankets tight against my hips and legs like he used to do when I was little and scared. "Talk to me, *mo chroi*. It doesn't matter if yer twenty-three or sixty-three, ye'll always be my baby girl. As yer Da, I need to know yer all right."

"I'm all right." I meet his worried gaze and squeeze his hand. "One of Garnet's men caught me off-guard on the dance floor tonight. A wolf asshole."

Da tenses and his gaze clouds with a threat of violence I've seen enough times to know no good can come of riling him up and letting him loose. "Caught you off-guard how?"

I shrug and regret the movement immediately. Thankfully, Da doesn't seem to notice. "He wasn't happy that Garnet gave me a pass and wanted to put me on notice."

"And? What's the rest?"

"What makes you think there's more?"

"A threat from a mouthy asshole would raise yer ire and have ye swingin' mad and full of piss and vinegar. That's not what happened. He broke somethin' in ye. I want to know what, so I can fix it."

I stare at Da's hand in mine and smile. He's right. Whether I'm twenty-three or sixty-three, Da will always be my safe place. "He knew I wouldn't fight back or cause a scene because I wouldn't put Auntie Shannon or the regular crowd at risk. It got me thinking."

"Thinking what?"

I tell him about my fight with Liam and what he said about me acting like a god and endangering the 'normal' people. "It really hurt, Da. He drew a line between us like I don't belong anymore. I dismissed it as him being stupid, and how guys say the worst possible thing in a moment of anxiety but then, on the dancefloor, it hit me. Trent was there because of me. He was angry because of me. And if people got hurt, it would be because of me."

"Ye can't take on the responsibility for assholes who come at you determined to cause collateral damage, Fi."

"Maybe not, but it made me think that maybe I had no right to be there anymore."

He sighs and tilts his neck from side to side. The hollow *pop-*

pop-pop of his vertebrae makes me wince. "That's a tough call, *mo chroi*. On the one hand, Shenanigans is an extension of our home and our family. Ye belong there as much or more than anyone else. On the other, who you are now—who *we* are now—draws attention from bigger and badder people."

"It made me sad, you know? To think that Shenanigans might be better without me."

"And that's a very sad thought, indeed." He cups my cheek and kisses my forehead.

The pain from leaning forward is excruciating, but I do my best not to let on. "I want peace with the Lakeshore Guild and won't let one hot-headed, hairy dickwad ruin any chance of that happening."

He sits back and nods. "The arc of the moral universe is long, but it bends toward justice."

I run my fingers absentmindedly over the soft blue suede of Beauty's cover and think about the Martin Luther King Jr. quote. It's one of Da's favorites, and we've discussed it individually and as a family more than once.

He's telling me that change takes time, but it happens.

Each of us, fighting for social change, is part of the larger picture, a cog in the wheel of making the world better for all. "Nothing great was ever achieved without sacrifice, I suppose."

Da squeezes my hand and gets up. "Heavy is the head that wears the crown."

When Da turns out my light and closes the door, I slide down and stare at the ceiling. I don't like feeling like I don't belong in my life. It's lonely.

I'm lonely. Bruin went after Trent at the pub and hasn't come back. I miss his presence.

Even in a house filled with family, I feel separate.

I lay there another long while before I give up on sleep. My mind is spinning with too many thoughts to rest. After closing my eyes, I send my consciousness into the trunk of my body. Like

Myra's home tree, there is a hollow where those of us with magic hold and nurture our gifts.

Patty said it doesn't matter whether it's a magical fae spark like the druids possess, or an essence brought out by worship for the Wiccans or root power like the Tuatha De Danann. Fae energy is stored and protected somewhere within.

My happy place is even more special because I hold my brother Brendan's heritage spark. He may have been shot and killed being a hero, but he'll never be gone as long as his energy lives inside me.

I open my eyes and slide out of the booth I was in earlier at Shenanigans.

My big brother Brendan is behind the bar. He smiles at me when I get closer, and I climb onto one of the barstools. "Hey, baby girl. Why the long face?"

I look at his bright green eyes and smile. Even the sound of his voice starts the process of refilling me with joy. "Just hit a rocky patch. Do you mind if I hang with you for a bit? I could use the company."

Brendan winks and closes his hand over mine. "Whatever you need, sista. If you need me to hold the world back for you for a while, consider it done. I've got you."

I nod and squeeze his hand. "Love you too."

I roll over the next morning and gasp. My freaking ribs are killing me, and it's way past time for more painkillers. Calum is sitting on the chair by the window and frowning at me. What's with men sitting there watching me sleep?

"What's with the flinch and the gasp?"

"You scared me, bro." I lie and lock down my expression as I shift to sit up. "Howeyah?"

"Fast cars and orgasms. Can't complain."

Maybe he believes that I gasped because he scared me. Maybe not. Either way, he doesn't seem intent on pursuing it. He's in uniform and sipping coffee out of a Tim's cup, his feet propped up on the end of the bed.

On the little table beside him sits a drink tray with a medium tea and a bag with the Tim Horton's logo on it. I opt for a change of subject. "What's that? Did I place an order I don't remember?

"You were crying in your sleep last night, Fi. You haven't done that since we were kids. I was worried and went to Da. He told me about what happened with Liam, and with Garnet's man at the pub. I thought some pampering might brighten your morning."

"It definitely does." With deliberate care, I reach to claim the bag. "Mmm, warm apple fritters." I pull apart the fresh sugary delight and pop a chunk into my mouth. "This is very thoughtful. Thank you."

He frees the cup from the tray and sets it on my nightstand. "Anything for you. Anytime. You know that."

"Love you, too." I pull off another chunk of fritter and give him a reassuring smile. "Today will be better."

"Yeah? You sound sure."

"I am. I spent time in my happy place last night with Brenny. That always soothes my soul."

At the mention of Brendan, Calum's smile tightens. Brenny was our laughter—our no-hassle, good-time guy. We all miss him. We always will.

"I'd like to do a ride-along with you sometime and see him. You said you took Sloan there with you once, right?"

"I did. And yeah, anytime. You know it's not really him though, right? It's his spark and my interpretation and memories of him."

Calum nods. "I'm aware. At first, I didn't think I'd like it, but now, I think I would. I miss him something awful."

"Me too. It helps me to spend time with him. He helps me sort things out."

"And did the two of you come up with any epiphanies?"

"A few. More like new truths I needed to face."

"Anything you care to share?"

I claim my cup and pull back the tab to let out the steam. *Mmm,* a chai tea with vanilla and cinnamon. He really does want to spoil me this morning.

"Nothing earth-shattering. There have been a lot of major changes lately, and it's unrealistic to expect things to be both so different and remain the same. Shenanigans is special to me and always will be. No furry asshole can take that away, but if being there draws the wrong kind of attention to people I care about, I have to rethink."

"You're not rethinking being a druid are you?"

"No. Only what that looks like going forward. When Liam drew the line of normal people between himself and me, he wasn't all wrong. As much as it hurt, I *am* different now."

Calum's radio squelches and he stands. "Coffee break is over. I'll see you tonight. FYI, Kev's coming for dinner. I bought the stuff for chicken pot pie and put it in the fridge. If you're around and have time, great. If not, no worries, I'll throw it together when I get here."

"I should be around. Have a good shift. Safe home."

Calum kisses my forehead. "No more tears, Fi. It doesn't matter where we are, you and me and this family...we're all we'll ever need."

When Calum leaves, I take my tea and shuffle to the reading chair by the window. Bruin's out cold on the floor, his heavy breathing a steady, rumbling comfort. For the next half-hour, I flip through Beauty's pages and sip tea. I didn't have the clarity of mind to achieve a successful self-healing spell last night. Maybe I'll have better luck this morning.

Maybe I could swear Emmet to secrecy and let him try.

Maybe I should lump it and let Sloan do it.

My mind spins with the spinoff scenarios of riling up well-meaning men and opt against it. "Come on, Beauty. Girl Power time. Show me what you've got." As I skim the pages, I finish my apple fritter and sip my tea. Calum is not only thoughtful, but he's also right—and so is Da.

My happy place isn't a place. It's the people I love.

Shenanigans isn't going anywhere. I have time to sort it out, and once the changes settle, I can revisit the idea of where I belong without panicking. There will never be a line dividing me from Liam and Auntie Shannon. They are part of me.

I find a spell in the healing section that looks promising.

Taking a notepad from the drawer of my side table, I rework the wording. Powerful and practiced druids don't need spells or rhyme to focus their powers. I'm not there yet. I can't affect things solely through the strength of my connection to magic. One day I will, but today, I need the spell, my salted caramel candle, and my casting stones.

When my candle's flame is lit, I breathe in the sweet succulence, focus, and recite my spell.

Magic mend and candle burn,

Damage end and health return.

Strengthen that which needs to knit,

End the pain and leave me fit.

I sit there with my eyes closed and focus my intentions. Almost immediately, I can move without losing my breath. Yay me! Cautiously optimistic, I step into the shower and wash away the last of my heartache.

I told Calum today would be better, and hey, things are looking up already. Dressed, and with my hair blown dry and pulled back in a clip, I head downstairs to start my day.

The house is empty.

Vacation is over, and normal life reclaimed my brothers. Cops are cops, I suppose. As much as I love having everyone with me full-time, it's good to resume the routine of our life.

Fully charged for the day, I call down the basement steps and get nothing but echo back. I find a note from Sloan on the kitchen table saying to meet him in the grove when I'm ready.

Perfect. I take a picture of the grocery list on the fridge, slip my cell into my pocket, and slide my feet into my shoes.

It's a quarter to ten when I hit the back yard to track down Sloan. The day is crisp with the smell of autumn in the air but still clings to summer's last remnants. The sky is clear, not as blue as I like, but certainly not overcast.

I find Sloan swinging gently beneath one of the elm trees he contributed during the grove's expansion. He's meditating in a wicker basket swing chair. It looks roomy, fits with the grove's organic feel, and has a big, puffy brown cushion lining the inside. It seems like it would be super comfy whether sitting in it or lounging back.

His eyes are closed, and although I haven't made any noise on my approach, his expression softens to a smile. "Alive and well and wondering how to eject me from this fine furniture to claim it for yerself?"

I giggle. "Something like that."

His smile widens as he sits forward and climbs out of the hanging woven oval frame. I exchange places with him and tuck my feet beneath me. It's cozy, and I love it the moment I'm inside. "When did we get this?"

"I picked it up this morning when I was out. I remembered how ye hogged the hammock at Lugh's and Lara's and thought ye might enjoy it. I also remembered how tentative and awkward ye found it getting on and off the hammock, so I thought the chair might suit ye better."

I snuggle deeper into the cushion and sink heavy into the pendulum motion as it swings beneath the canopy. Sighing, I study the lush green of new growth in my trees. "It's perfect. I absolutely love it. Thank you."

"My pleasure."

"Is this a parting gift?" I sit up straighter. "I guess it's time for you to head home. You're probably fully recharged and eager to get back to your life, eh?"

"I am fully charged, although it's not necessarily a parting gift. I thought I might stick around for another day or two and help ye break in yer cushion."

I chuckle. "Break in my cushion? You're assuming I'd ever get out of it to give you the chance."

"Meals. Trips to the loo. I'm a patient man."

"And I'm a stubborn girl with a strong bladder. If you challenge me, I might cop a squat right here to defend my territory."

"Och, the things that come out of yer mouth." He laughs and grips the frame to give me a push. "In truth, I knew ye wouldn't be willing to share." He waves his hand in front of the tree opposite me, and another chair becomes visible. "So, I went ahead and got one for myself or the boys as well."

"Aww. You *do* get me."

"Despite all logic, I'm starting to." He sits in his chair, a mirror copy of mine, and leans back looking pleased with himself. He should. He gets a big point for understanding how I work. Most don't.

Or don't take the time to try.

We swing for a little while, and I watch the Spriggans flitter around. The stag comes by to tilt his rack in greeting, and I bid him a good morning in return. It's incredible how centered I feel here—my connection to nature fulfilled and at ease.

After a long while, I break the silence. "You know, you claim it's the allure of lounging in my grove that's keeping you here, but I can read you too."

He opens one eye and grins. "And what do you think you see, Cumhaill?"

"You want to stick around until you're sure our work with the ley lines has taken hold and you know we're in the clear. You're worried about me and know you'll worry more if you go home and can't just blink back here."

He shrugs. "Why not take the extra days and be sure, if I haven't worn out my welcome?"

I run a loving hand over my new chair swing and smile. "After this, your welcome is in mint condition."

"Then my evil plan has worked."

I laugh while lounging back into the cushion. I may have joked about never getting out of this swing, but I genuinely don't want to. "Besides, why should you leave when there's potential for us to get attacked by a horde of angry preternatural beings? You'd miss all the fun."

"Fun, ye say? You have a warped sense of self-preservation." He stretches out his long legs, and I do the same. The soles of our shoes meet, and we use them to push off one another and swing.

"I also thought we could train. We've been so busy with the magic shortage and establishing the grove and yer fae that we haven't worked on yer skills. Yer stronger every day, but there's always someone stronger."

I hear the worry in his tone and appreciate it. "How about we take the books back to Myra, make a few stops, grab some lunch, then we can face off for the afternoon?"

"That works. It so happens I'm free."

CHAPTER TWENTY-THREE

Myra is busy with one of her repeat customers when we arrive at the bookstore. She waves us off, so we take the books we borrowed into the home tree part of the bookstore and replace them on the shelves. Once that's taken care of, we search for the healing reference textbook Sloan's father Wallace wants to add to his collection.

Myra doesn't have *Ancient Aztec Healing Rituals,* but there is another book by the same author called, *Healing with Herbs and Rituals: An Exploration of Mexican Traditions.*

Sloan selects it as a close runner-up, and we lounge on the leather sofas until the brass bell over the door chimes and tells us the coast is clear.

"Sorry about that, kids." Myra accepts the book and scans it into the computer. "If your father has specific titles he's looking for, Sloan, I'm happy to search for them in the future. Are you sure this one will do?"

"Och, ye never can tell with Da. If ye can have a look for the exact one he wants, that would be much appreciated. I'll tell him I got this one in the meantime."

"That works." Myra opens her big leather ledger and starts a page for Sloan/Wallace Mackenzie.

"Look at that." I waggle my eyebrows and tap a finger on the parchment. "You've made it now. You have a page."

Sloan chuckles. "Yer a nut."

"Nice of you to notice." When Myra's finished writing down the title of the book Wallace Mackenzie wants, I gesture at the ledger. "Is Garnet Grant one of your regular clients?"

Myra casts me a sideways glance. I can't tell if her smile tightening is personal or professional, but something about my question annoys her. "What makes you ask about Garnet Grant?"

"He had her kidnapped yesterday," Sloan answers.

Myra puffs up like a black cat on Halloween. Yep. Without a doubt, something about Garnet Grant rubs Myra the wrong way.

I hold up my palms to allay her panic. "Technically that's true, but we got it sorted."

"For the moment," Sloan adds.

"For the moment, we came to a tentative truce while we await the return of ambient magic."

Myra places the book in a singing bowl and cleanses its energy before wrapping it to go. "And how goes the quest to restore the city's power?"

"Good, I think. We figured out the problem and spent three solid days working on fixing it. I think we're in good shape. We were able to tap into the ley lines and free up some of the magic flow. I think once things settle you'll find there's *more* magic than there was."

She looks skeptical. "I don't feel it yet."

"No, but ask your tree later if he can feel it in his roots. Like the ley lines in Ireland, there is power coming from beneath the ground. We simply needed to release it. If things pan out like I think they will, the fae magic will flow into the water table and Lake Ontario. We expect it to build naturally around the city. Then everyone will be happy again."

Myra seems appeased by our progress and lets out a heavy breath. "Good. I'm relieved for you."

"We're not out of the woods yet."

"What do you mean by that?"

I explain to her about my visit with Garnet and his concern that those affected by the full moon won't be able to fight their beastly side tomorrow night. "I'm not keen on the streets turning into a raging bloodbath."

Myra frowns. "Likely no one is."

"Except maybe the vampires."

Sloan and Myra both flash me a disapproving look.

"I'm not wrong. If there are vampires in the city—and I know there are—a bloodbath in the streets would be right up their alley. Their plasma-sucking disgusting alley."

Myra blinks at me, then changes the subject. "So, you're on the Guild's radar, are you?"

I push down the images polluting my daymare and focus. "Is that a bad thing? I kinda liked the idea of a policing organization watching over magically powered people in the city."

"It depends who's watching and why," Myra says.

"And how effective they are," Sloan adds.

I shrug. "Garnet spoke like we should be impressed. I got the feeling the Guild is a big deal."

"A lot of good they did ye with Skull Trim. That lunatic and his men nearly killed ye. More than once, and in very public parts of the city."

"True story."

Sloan accepts the brown bag once his purchase is wrapped and ready to go. "My thought is that ye shouldn't put yer faith in an organization ye know nothing about. The Lakeshore Guild of Empowered Ones is an unknown player and yer not yet familiar with the rules of the game. They could be good or bad depending on where ye fall on the scale of their goals. Maybe they know what the Black Dog is up to and are helping them, or maybe they choose to turn a blind eye and not interfere."

"I couldn't have said it better myself." Myra closes her ledger and stashes it beneath the counter. "The thing with powerful people is sometimes they don't want to take on other powerful people for fear of physical or political blowback."

I frown at them both. "But isn't that the whole idea behind the policing power of a Guild? The power of many controlling the unwanted actions of the few?"

"In theory, yes," Myra cautions. "But not all things play out as well in practice as they do in theory."

"Huh. Well, that sucks. I hoped the Guild would offer us a few answers, not add more questions."

Myra's electric blue hair swings loose as she shakes her head. "Your fresh and hopeful outlook is admirable, if not somewhat unrealistic. Still, go out into the world and form conclusions for yourself. Don't get jaded by the old girl you work for."

I blow Myra a kiss and wave over my shoulder as we head out. "I happen to adore the old girl I work for."

Sloan and I emerge onto the sidewalk and cross through the pedestrians to my SUV parked at the store's curb-front. No one takes notice of us because very few people take note of much in the city and because Myra's Mystical Emporium is spelled to blend into the background and mask its clientele's comings and goings from those who don't need to see. It's her way of ensuring that only those who need her can find her.

"Do you think we should be wary of the Lakeshore Guild?" I hold out my fob and unlock the Hellcat.

"Unfortunately, I do. I love that it's yer first instinct to accept new things, but it might prove prudent in the magical world to flip that on its head. In theory, you can hope everyone is what they seem, but in actuality, it's important to remember that illusion is real in this world. Things usually *aren't* what they seem."

He slides his hand into mine and laces our fingers. It looks innocent enough to strangers on the street, but I recognize it for what it is. He wants me to see what he sees.

Even after swapping spit with the elf in the Doyle grove, I don't see as much as he does with his enchanted bone ring. I get to see the fae in my grove, which is great and what I'd asked him for, but Sloan sees everything.

The aura of people. The true faces of creatures and beings who use illusion to blend into everyday life.

And who or what is that?

Sloan spins me in his arms and pushes me up against the passenger side door. Feigning an affectionate touch, he brushes a long strand of hair away from my face and tucks it behind my ear. "Don't stare, Cumhaill. Ye gotta work on yer subtleties."

I chuckle. "Subtle isn't my best event."

"I have noticed that a time or two."

I smile at him, keeping up the pretense of a girl admiring her yummilicious man. It's not a hard sell. This close, my traitorous heart starts pumping wildly although my head knows this is staged. "So, what is that thing across the road? Is he watching us or did he simply notice us?"

"He's watching and cloaked to avoid detection. I've only seen pictures in books, but I believe that's a hobgoblin."

"I thought they were little, dumb, and slightly green."

"That's a goblin. Hobgoblins are their larger, smarter, and much more vicious cousins."

Oh, goody. "So, why is he watching us? Who do you think I pissed off this time?"

"There's no telling." He leans closer, changing his position to get a better view. The shift of his shoulders brushes my arm, and I remind myself yet again that this is staged.

"Get a room," someone hollers as they pass.

"Get a life," I shout back while throwing up my middle finger.

When I look back up at Sloan, he looks baffled. "What was that?"

"Normal city interaction. Why?"

He shakes his head and steps back, putting more space between us. "I thought you were a live and let live person."

I chuckle, round the hood of my truck, and climb in. "Live and let live goes both ways. So does get in my face, I'll get in yours."

The engine stirs to life with the turn of the key, and I check that the way is clear. "Is he still watching?"

Sloan stretches his hand behind my headrest and twists to face me. "Nope. Whoever he is, he's gone now."

I pull into traffic and let that rattle around in my head. "Do you think he might've been on the street, spotted us, and simply been curious?"

"Maybe, but knowing that yer stalker from the woods at Ross Castle had contact with a species that lives down in the subway tunnels, I'm pretty confident that would be a no."

"Too bad. A coincidence would be nice for a change, wouldn't it?"

Sloan chuckles and adjusts in his seat to face the front. "It would. Although, even if something seemed innocuous, I'd still find it suspect if yer involved."

"Paranoid much?"

"Until recently—no. That has changed, however. Seems prudent now though."

The traffic on Queen Street is always steady, but that's what you get in a city with three million citizens. "Crap. There are no spots." I pull to the curb and pull my wallet from my purse. I give him the claim ticket for the tailor and forty bucks. "That should be plenty. Make sure she gives you two jackets and three pairs of pants. Mrs. Allison is an amazing seamstress, but she's old and forgetful. Oh, and if she asks to measure your inseam the answer is not today, you're in a bit of a rush."

The horrified gaze Sloan hits me with is too funny. "She's going to try to touch my pants?"

I laugh. "It's not your pants she'll try to touch."

His frown darkens. "Maybe you should go in."

I laugh harder and slip it into Park. "Scaredy cat. Fine, hop in the driver's seat. If a cop comes up behind you and bleeps his siren, go around the block and pick me up. Or if a spot opens up—"

"I know how to drive in a city, Cumhaill. I lived in Dublin for four years, remember?"

"Actually, I didn't know that. I figured you *poofed* home. I'm glad to hear you got the whole experience." We get out and meet at the front grille as we trade places. "I'll be quick."

And I am.

As it turns out, Mrs. Allison is home with a sick cat so her niece is minding the store. That makes picking up the tailoring that much simpler. When I get back out front, I'm met by an empty curb and three still-full parking spots.

Yep. I saw that coming. He got looped. I step over to the bus shelter, lean on the glass, and wait for my ride to circle back around.

With the zippered clothes carrier draped over my arm, I pull out my phone and check if anyone needs me.

Nope. S'all good.

I glance up the road to my left but there's no sign of my truck. I pull up the shopping list and start reading it over. If Kevin's coming over, I should pick up the spinach salad he likes with the berries and nuts.

Despite him insisting all is forgiven, I'll be taking special care of him for ages. I can't believe how close I came to breaking him and Calum up.

It hurts my heart to even think about it.

My shield tingling brings my head up fast. I slide my phone back into my pocket and scan the street up and down. I can't see half the stuff Sloan can, and from what I see, nothing seems out of the ordinary.

Except, I know better.

Red? You all right? Do you need me?

Just a bad feeling. So far so good. No need to cause a citywide panic.

The deep rumble of his laughter eases my stress a little. *Better that than you getting dead.*

True story.

My Hellcat pulls up in front of me, and I jump in, clothing bag and all.

"What's wrong?" Sloan takes the bag off my lap and flings it into the back seat. "What happened?"

"Just my Spidey-senses telling me that something wicked this way comes. Is my hobgoblin friend here?"

Sloan swings a nonchalant glance across the windshield's span, then launches out the driver's side door.

"Shit on a stick." I jump out of my seat, but by the time I get around the fender, Sloan's doing a damned good impression of Usain Bolt, sprinting across the street.

A taxi honks at my open driver's side door and I run to get into the SUV.

"Where is he?"

In between the cars and buses passing, I catch snippets of Sloan in the alley across the way. He has a homeless lady—or what appears to be a homeless lady—by the shoulders of her ratty shawl and is shaking her.

Concerned citizens are closing in, and there's a cruiser on the other side of the lights. "Fuck a duck."

As a dump truck passes, I focus on the load heaping above the top of his vehicle. *"Dirt Devil."*

A gust of wind picks up, and Queen Street is suddenly swirling in a dust cyclone that rivals any desert storm. As cars screech to a halt, I check that the way is clear, pull away from the curb, and make a reckless U-turn across the four lanes.

At the curb across the street, I honk my horn and hit the button to lower my window. "In the car, crazy man. Now. The coppers are coming."

Sloan looks up and notices the angry citizens. He curses, releases his hold, then jumps into the Hellcat. Before the door closes, I hit the pedal and gun it down the first street to get out of sight.

"Seriously? You lecture me about subtlety, then shake the stuffing out of an old homeless lady in broad daylight in front of twenty people?"

"Feckin' hell. Is that the glamor he had on?"

"Yep."

Sloan sinks low in the seat and points at the street on the right. "Take us around the block and back again. I'll cast a bafflement spell and wipe whoever's there."

"Good plan. Otherwise, dinner will be very interesting tonight when five cops come home from their shifts with your description in their daily sheets."

He winces. "Yeah, let's try to avoid that."

CHAPTER TWENTY-FOUR

Our next stop of the day takes us to the Queens on Queen nightclub. I park in one of the public spots on the street out front and pass Sloan a few coins for the meter. As I step onto the sidewalk, the loud *cacaw-cacaw* of a raven draws my attention skyward.

I stop beside the parking meter and stare up as one, two, then a dozen blackbirds fly in a circle above. No. Not a circle. As they arc and glide through the air between the towering glass buildings, the lead birds shift toward the center of the ring, and it becomes a moving spiral.

The hair on my arms stands on end, and I wince. "Well, that's not something you see every day."

Sloan follows my pointed finger and frowns. "That's not something you see *ever*. Not naturally, anyway."

"Sooo, cryptic. What unnatural catalyst or omen do you think will top our daily sundae of stalking and assault?"

Sloan feeds the coins into the meter's slot. "With you here and everything we've done the past three days to stir up the magical world, there's no telling."

"Right? If the universe is flipping us the birds," I raise my hand

and point at the freakshow above, "you'd think it could at least give us a clue of what we're in for."

He grips my elbow and gives me the bum's rush across the concrete walkway and into the drag queen club owned and operated by my magical ink master—Pan Dora.

"Pushy much?" I wriggle in his hold, and he lets me pull away the moment we're inside. "Yes, the day seems to be going to shit, but let's not get our thongs in a bunch. Maybe that flock of birds is only a flock of birds. There's a chance they're merely acting weird. Or maybe they're trained birds, like homing pigeons or something."

"Are ye serious? Yer a feckin' druid, Cumhaill. Reach way down deep into yer instincts. Do animals simply go off script and act weird?"

"Is this a lover's spat or can I welcome you in?"

We turn to where Dora stands inside the open second door that divides the breezeway from the club proper. She's wearing fishnets, stilettos, and a wildly bright fuchsia wig, but the rest of her usual outrageous fashion sense isn't currently in play. She has an old Metallica t-shirt tied at her hips over a pair of Daisy Duke cutoff jean shorts.

"We're fine." I take the interruption as an opportunity to gain a bit of distance from Sloan's intensity. "It's been a day. Sloan got spooked by some birds and is a bit wigged out."

Sloan rolls his eyes and explains the raven weirdness to Pan Dora. He looks out to see if they're still out there, but apparently, the show is over.

Dora swallows and runs a hand over her Adam's apple. "I'm with the Irishman on this one, girlfriend. That sounds like a portent. Come inside. Let me finish my numbers with our lighting guy, and we'll go upstairs and consult the cards. If it's answers you want, Tarot will help you find them."

"That would be wonderful. And, of course, finish what you were doing. Sorry, we didn't mean to interrupt."

She ushers us inside the club's dining area, and Sloan and I shuffle off and settle at a four-top. When we get there, I lay my head on the table. "And my day started so nicely. Our mistake was leaving our swings. I told you we should never get out of them."

"If only life were so simple."

Dora hustles her butt back to the stage and takes the stairs like a sprinter despite the four-inch, spiked heels. *Cray-cray*. "All right, Kenny." She strikes a pose and nods toward the control booth in the corner. "Take it from the bridge."

As the music comes up, the lights go down, and Dora picks up her number. She finishes the song we interrupted, then does an amazing rendition of *Burlesque,* performing the movie's title song as well, if not better than Cher did.

"Have you seen this movie?" I ask Sloan.

The look he flashes me is too funny. "No."

I can't help the grin that takes me over. I grab my phone and start texting. "Tonight. Kevin is coming over, and he owns it. I'm telling him to bring it with him. Oh, it's so good. You're gonna love it."

"I'm smart enough not to argue."

"But not smart enough to steer clear of her altogether." A man steps from the shadows and Sloan and I launch to our feet. He's a fit, blond surfer-dude wearing a sleek silk suit. By the way it clings to the musculature, it's tailored to his frame. "Netflix and chill must wait. If I were you, I'd head home for a go-bag and run. Your lot is marked, Cumhaill. Time to get outta Dodge."

I stiffen as he tosses an envelope onto the table. Unfolding the flap, I pull out a folded sheet of paper and open it. After a quick scan down the legal-sized page, I start at the top again and then read it over, trying to make sense of what I'm holding.

It reads like a court document, but it's not a subpoena. It's a warrant for justice. It's written in legalese and names me, Da, and the boys as offenders. "What's a Vow of Vengeance?"

I pass it to Sloan. He looks at it and shrugs. "I've never heard of it. Trumped-up bullshit, I'd guess."

Surfer Dude shakes that off. "No. A Vow of Vengeance is a legal and binding warrant that gives an offended party the legal right to hold the named party responsible for personal loss and hardship."

Something about this guy triggers my survival instinct. Reaching out with my senses, I try to recall why he looks or feels so familiar. It's not a good kind of reminiscence. My guts are twisting, and I'm fighting the urge to run out of the club screaming. "Sorry. Have we met?"

"Not officially." A sly turn curves his grin. "More like two ships passing in the night."

Red? What's happening? Do you need me?

Stay ghosted and gather intel. Who is this dickwad? I draw a deep breath and release him. My hair tickles my cheeks as the breeze of Bruin's exit stirs the air around me.

It's him. The male from the forest in Ireland. The one who tried to reel ye in with the poison vine.

Okay, that's unsettling. "So, are you from Toronto and followed me to Ireland, or are you from Ireland and followed me here?"

The narrowing of his gaze suggests my question caught him off-guard. "What are you going on about?"

"You're the shadow lurker in the woods at Ross Castle. The night we busted up the Black Dog sacrificial pot-luck party, you cast a Creeping Vine spell and tried to drag me into the darkness. The invisibility and paralytic in the thorns combo was a creative touch. Too bad it didn't work."

He has the nerve to glare at me and look angry. "What are you playing at?"

"You're stalking me. Isn't that my line?"

The music cuts off, and a moment later, Dora's voice echoes all around us. "You're not welcome here, Droghun."

Our surfer dude intruder leans back against the table behind him and crosses his arms. "Your hostility is unwarranted. I came in an official capacity to convey a message to our mutual friend. I'm not causing trouble. I'm well within my rights to be here on Guild business."

"Ye flat-out threatened her and ye belong to the villainous group that tried to kidnap and kill her on three different occasions since her druid powers unlocked."

Droghun frowns. "You've got me mixed up with someone else, Irish. I arrived in town two days ago and haven't been to Toronto in almost a year before that. I'm not sure what happened, but I assure you I had nothing to do with it."

"Still, ye don't deny being part of Barghest, do ye?"

"Why would I? I'm proud of it. Barghest was founded by a visionary group of druids not afraid to step off the Emerald Isle. Your fiery flame isn't the first to strike a different path. Barghest has evolved over the decades and has roots around the world. Your venom against us is unwarranted, I assure you. The organization is a powerful and respected pillar in the magical community."

I raise my hands. "Unwarranted? In the past couple of months, we've tied Barghest to fae massacre, exsanguinating innocent humans, dark magic, necromancy, murder, kidnapping, ensorcelling, and enslaving vampires…"

"And that's just off the top of her head," Sloan says. "If ye've been at it for decades like ye say, there's no telling what other vile things yer dippin' yer wicks into."

He shakes his finger like we're naughty children. "You two need to be careful about slandering Barghest. There are powerful members of the organization who won't appreciate you painting us as magical mobsters."

"But that's what you are." I look from him to the Vow of Vengeance warrant, my mind spinning. How could *we* possibly be considered the bad guys here?

Barghest is evil incarnate.

I snatch up the warrant, fold it back together, and slip it into the envelope. "I'm sure the Lakeshore Guild will be interested in what I have to say. I'll take this to them, and we'll see who's left blowing in the wind."

The cocky smile that he flashes makes my stomach twist. He pulls out his phone and takes a picture of me holding the warrant. "You have twenty-four hours to counter the charge from the time you are served. The contact information of the Guild Governors involved and website are on the bottom of the page."

There's a website to fight scum-sucking criminals?

I take a closer look at the watermark stamp at the bottom of the warrant. Droghun's signature is listed as the representative of Toronto druids. It strikes me then, his confidence and Myra's warning about powerful people.

"You're one of the Guild Governors? Barghest holds a seat in the Lakeshore Guild of Empowered Ones."

He dips his chin and smiles. "I was named the interim Toronto representative of druids yesterday. I've been told my predecessor was brutally attacked and slain by a rogue family of druid startups intent on claiming Toronto as theirs. My first act in my position was to launch a full investigation."

My mouth falls open. "Bullshit. That's not even close to the truth."

He shrugs. "As I said, I'm looking into it. I encourage you to respond to the claims. I look forward to hearing your side of things. Oh, that is if Clan Cumhaill is still around by the end of the week. Like I mentioned earlier, the Vow of Vengeance has been filed against your family."

"By who?"

"The hobgoblins."

"And what's the offense?"

"I believe it was something about siphoning off the city's ambient magic for personal gain."

Cat hack on the rug.

"I take it you plan to fight the charge?"

"You bet your tailored ass we're going to fight—"

Before I get the words out of my mouth, Droghan the Black Dog douche is gone.

Pan Dora lets out a low curse in some forgotten language I've never heard before and glares at the warrant in my hand. "Did you siphon ambient power?"

"We did…well, sort of… It's a long story."

"And did I hear you correctly? Droghan tried to drug and capture you in Ireland?"

"Yeah, I hadn't even met him then. I know the Black Dog hates me and I've killed a few vampires they considered assets, but why the hell would the hobgoblins come at me like this? I never even laid eyes on one of them until today."

Dora shakes out her hands and magic sparks off her fingertips. "One of the closest allies to the necromancers you call Barghest is the Emperor Hobgoblin, Kartak of the Narrows. On a scale of freaks and creeps, he tips the scale of don't wanna go there territory. If he's part of this, you really should consider running as fast and far as you can."

I press my hand against my chest and try to draw breath past the lead weight pushing on my lungs. "Leaving the city isn't on the table as an option. If their beef with me is written out in legal terms, I'll prove them wrong. If there's one thing my family knows like the back of our hands, it's the law. Emperor Hobgoblin creeper can kiss my Irish ass."

Pan Dora's apartment is located over the club and is an eclectic mashup of old-world ancient meets bedazzling bathhouse meets brash and sassy drag queen delight. Sloan and I follow the zebra-print runner into the studio apartment living space and are momentarily stunned by the overwhelming Pan Dora-*ness* of it all.

"Oh, wow."

Dora smiles adoringly at her home and sweeps her hand through the air. "I know. Takes your breath away, doesn't it? I could spend every waking hour here. Doesn't it exude homey comfort?"

It exudes something.

"It's…amazing. Truly amazing." My gaze bounces from the peacock velvet lounger to the black and white glossy of a male orgy above the couch, to the feather boas used as drapery ties and valance accessories along the window wall. "I've never seen anyone decorate with such…"

"Passion and personality," Sloan suggests.

"Definitely. Passion and personality."

Dora beams and gestures toward the teak table heaped with glitter and sequins. It seems that not only does she own the club and perform, as well as possess the unique ability to ink magical druid spell tattoos, but she also Martha Stewart's costumes in her spare time.

Talk about a triple threat.

"Clear yourselves a spot. I'll get my deck, and we'll figure out what the hell has skewed your juju. Myra mentioned you were a magnet for drama and disaster. Being on the watch list of an Emperor Hobgoblin, the Guild, and Barghest certainly solidifies that."

"The Alpha Were, Garnet Grant, and his Moon Called have issues with me too."

Dora's glossy painted lips fall open. "My good gracious, I underestimated your talent for pissing off the wrong people."

I chuff. "Yeah, it's a talent. Mind-boggling, isn't it?"

Dora slips into one of the back rooms and comes back a moment later wearing a velveteen cheetah-print sheath dress.

She stops in front of an ancient apothecary cabinet and pulls open one of the drawers.

Detecting someone's aura isn't something I do frequently or purposely. I get little glimmers of color now and then, but the moment she takes hold of her Tarot cards, Pan Dora's aura bursts off her like nothing I've ever seen.

Unlike the usual reds, oranges, greens, and blues, her aura is an amazing bronze color with silver swirls in it that twist and turn like wispy ribbons. I've never seen anything like it.

It makes me wonder what Sloan sees.

I reach across the table and take his hand. As I suspected, Pan Dora isn't at all that she appears. Whatever or whoever she is, her existence goes way beyond my realm of experience and likely my understanding.

"Is it rude to ask what magical sect you belong to?"

She eases down into the embroidered chair opposite me and shuffles a well-worn deck of Tarot cards. "Not rude, girlfriend. A bit cheeky, because we don't know each other well yet, but not rude. But, considering the forces gathering against you, whether it's curiosity or caution behind you asking, I don't hold it against you in any way."

When she doesn't say any more, I figure that's as far as I'm getting with that. I release Sloan's hand and return her privacy to her.

"I don't usually get involved in magical mayhem, but Droghan came into my sanctum and pissed me off. I'm also no fan of hobgoblins. How about we play a little game of quid pro quo?"

"Sure, what do you have in mind?"

She arches a dramatically penciled brow. "I sense a great spirit with you. It's either tethered to you or haunting you. It feels familiar to me, and I'm wondering about it."

"Oh, that's not even cheeky. That's my animal companion. Would you like to meet him?"

She dips her chiseled jaw. "I would."

I look around her loft and point at the coffee table. "Sloan, will you help me move this so it doesn't get crushed?"

When the area is clear, I invite Bruin to take form and meet a friend. When he manifests into his full, furry frame, Dora surprises me by approaching him with a smile.

"Killer Clawbearer, I thought that was you. It's been an eternity, my friend."

Sloan looks at me. I shrug.

Like she pointed out, I don't know the woman well. Myra put us together and Dora's spent more time with my brothers to record their mastered spells than with me. I've chatted with her when our paths have crossed, but I can't say I know her.

Bruin cants his head to the side and looks confused at first, then he lumbers closer and sniffs. "An eternity doesn't begin to describe it. You look different these days."

Her laugh is deep and genuine. "Life's too long not to live authentically."

Seeing how my bear is the actual Bear of lore, I wonder how old Pan Dora is *and* who she used to be *and* how they know each other. I try to bite my tongue and mind my own business. Can't. Stop. Too. Much.

Yeah, I don't know why I even tried. "So, you two know each other from back in the day? Another life?"

"Another life, to be sure." Dora looks unsettled by my question. She studies me again and must see something she trusts because she relaxes and presses her hand over her chest. "Over time, I've worn a great many titles, Fiona. Some I am proud of, others, I am not. Wizard. Prophet. Drunk. Confidant. King's advisor. Mentor. Your friend Killer Clawbearer and I met a very long time ago. And while I believe we learn from the past, I don't enjoy looking back. I believe how we handle the present dictates if you live long enough for a future."

"Preach." I hold up my knuckles for a bump. I give up on the curiosity and resolve to bombard Bruin with questions later. If she doesn't like to remember a painful past, I'm certainly not going to make her relive things.

Reclaiming my seat at the table, I gesture at the Tarot deck. "So, speaking of living long enough to have a future, explain to me how this works."

Dora sits opposite me once again and shuffles a little more. Then, she fans the deck face down in a sweeping arc in front of herself. "Without touching the cards, scan the deck, and one by one, pick out nine cards for me to place in what's called a spread."

"And this spread will tell you what's going on?"

"The cards will tell a story, which we will interpret together. Some images will relate to you and your journey of past, present, and future, while others might represent the people and forces surrounding you. Your dark mocha manliness, here, will take notes and you can review them and think about possible deeper meanings over the next hours and days."

I waggle my brows at Sloan. Dark mocha manliness suits him. If we are going that route, I'm a chai tea latte girl, extra cream, with cinnamon garnish freckles.

Dora waves her hand over the fan of cards. "Point to the ones that hold energy for you. You don't have to go left to right or right to left. Pick and choose as inspiration strikes."

"All right." I focus on the backs of the cards and try to connect. I study the triple goddess moon symbol glowing against the galaxy pattern of constellations. It's easier to choose than I thought. As I stare at the deck, the card I'm meant to pick practically vibrates on a frequency that sings to me. I point at the first one, then rinse and repeat from my second through to the ninth.

When that's done, Dora gathers the cards not chosen and sets them aside, then places each one of the nine face-down in a deliberate pattern on the table.

"There are seventy-eight cards in a standard Tarot deck. There are fifty-six cards in the Minor Arcana and twenty-two in the Major Arcana. The Minor Arcana consists of four suits—

swords, cups, wands, and pentacles—that range from the ace to the king, much like mundane playing cards."

Okay, that I understand. Brendan and Calum went through a big Texas Hold'em phase. They bought clay chips, and we play cards all the time.

"Ace through king reflect a journey—the ace being one and symbolizing the beginning of something new and untested and the king signifying mastery or completion."

I groan. "Why do I suddenly feel like I'm going to get a lot of low cards?"

"Your journey is new, that's true, but the Tarot tells us more than that. By what I've witnessed, I'll bet the Major Arcana will weigh in heavily, and the cards will have plenty they want to say."

I hope so. "Will it explain why the ravens were flying weird outside? And maybe what I should do about the Vow of Vengeance leveled against us?"

"If it matters, it will. Now, stay with me. The Major Arcana provides twenty-two different cards that symbolize the fool's journey."

"Am I the fool?"

Sloan snorts. "Can I answer that one?"

I stick my tongue out at him. "Pretty men are better seen and not heard."

His dark mocha manliness crosses his buff arms over his chest and continues to laugh at me.

Dora points at the deck, and I give her back my full attention. "Card zero is The Fool and shows him beginning his quest. He's young, carefree, and happy. By the time he's worked his way through the Major Arcana, our traveler is older and wiser. When we see him reflected in the final card, The World, he has embraced the challenges and mysteries of his path and fully evolved."

"Okay, it all seems simple enough."

Dora chuckles and flips the first card. "If it were simple, it wouldn't have stumped and terrified the masses since the fifteenth century. For now, I'll help you read the signs. You'll want to find a deck that speaks to you and start learning to read them yourself. Even if you start with pulling one card a day, eventually you'll get the hang of it."

"Well then, if it's going to take that long, I'm glad to have you on my team."

Dora nods. "Deep breath. Positive energy. Open mind. Are you ready to begin?"

"Let's do this." Jazzed, I look down at my first card. My enthusiasm gets knocked on its ass, and I throw up my hands.

Death. My first card is Death.

"Are you fucking kidding me?"

CHAPTER TWENTY-FIVE

Sloan walks tight to my ass as we make our way from the nightclub to my truck. I have my keys out and my sights set on my vehicle. He has his palm up, and his eyes scan rooflines, pedestrians' faces, and moving vehicles.

"There's no need to panic." I'm not sure if I'm trying to convince him or me. By the shaky tone of my voice, I think mostly me. "She said interpretation is key. Maybe it's not as bad as it seemed. And nothing is set in stone. She said that a bunch of times. We all have the power to change the course of what's coming at us."

"Oh, we're changing it." Sloan snatches the keys from my hand, clicks the fob, and opens the passenger door. After he has me in my seat and checks that my seatbelt is buckled and secured, he closes the door.

Locking the doors while he walks around to the driver's side seems slightly over the top, but I won't argue. Growing up with Da and five older brothers, I'm well-versed in overprotective males. I know when to push for independence, and I know when to shut up and let them do what they need to do not to lose their shit.

We are squarely in shit-losing territory.

"Can you even drive here?" I suddenly feel nervous for entirely different reasons. "Canada roads are opposite, right? This is my new SUV. Please don't kill my Hellcat."

"I won't kill yer truck. For fuck's sake, would ye try to worry about the right things for once?"

"Testy much?"

I want to remind him that Death doesn't mean death, the Hanged Man doesn't mean I'm trapped and stuck, and the Tower's shocking and dramatic upheaval doesn't have to be negative. It won't help.

Dora tried, and he swelled up like a pufferfish.

"Is there anything I can say that will defuse the bomb ticking inside you?"

"No."

All righty then. I search on my phone to find the grave of John Ridout, a teenager shot in the throat and killed in a duel in 1817. When the search comes back, I nod and relax a little. "I know exactly where the St. James Cathedral is. At the second intersection, turn right on Parliament. Three city blocks after turn right again on King."

"Before ye traipse around out in the open, are ye sure Pan Dora's magical knowhow and support is worth a side trip now? Yer in the crosshairs of everyone in sight. Is this the right time to do the woman a favor?"

"Are you familiar with the term quid pro quo? She's going to approach the Lakeshore Guild on my behalf, and I'm going to fetch her lost trinket."

"We don't even know who or what she is. We can't be sure we can trust her."

Ye can, Red. Without a doubt in yer mind.

"Bruin says we can."

"And what makes ye so sure, Bear? This is Fiona's life we're talking about. Does Pan Dora have the goods to risk her safety for an errand?"

There's no one I would trust more for magical support. If she says she'll help in exchange for the amulet, get it for her.

When the light flips green, Sloan makes the first right, and we head south. "So, don't keep us in suspense then. Who was Pan Dora when you knew her way back when?"

I won't say. There's honor in giving those of us with long lives privacy and anonymity.

"A fat lot of help that is."

"Easy." I peg Sloan with a stink-eye. "Bruin's on our side, remember? If he's not comfortable telling Dora's story, that's his choice."

Sloan draws a deep breath and nods. "My apologies, Bear. It's been a day."

Besides, she basically told ye herself.

I relay that to Sloan, and he frowns. "Okay, what did she say? A wizard, prophet, drunk, mentor, and king's advisor. And ye think we'll know, so she is someone we've heard of."

Without a doubt.

I'm mulling over the clues in my mind and thinking about Bruin's declaration that there's no one he'd rank higher than Dora for magical support. I cast a sideways glance to Sloan at the same time his brow comes down and he looks at me. "No way."

Sloan shakes his idea off at the same time. "That can't be right. Impossible."

I think about the clues again, and my hamster is spinning in its wheel. "Is anything impossible in this world? A goddess made a bird into a rabbit who crapped out a turd that made a forest in my backyard. That's pretty impossible."

"That's a deity."

"The ghost of my great-granda warrior sucked me back in time to feed me an enchanted fish with all the Fianna fortress's answers. Does that sound possible?"

Sloan stops at the corner of King and Parliament, and we wave away the window-washing panhandler. "I get that ye don't want to betray the woman's confidence, Bear, but are ye tellin' us what we think yer tellin' us?"

I told you nothing. She did.

When our path is clear, Sloan turns right, and we pull away from the corner. "Right. But we're not crazy for thinkin' what we're thinkin'?"

Yer not crazy. In another lifetime, Pan Dora navigated castles and dragons. She was renowned by some and feared by a great deal more. That she found happiness in this life by reinventing herself is a well-deserved blessing. If ye want to see her smile, the next time ye see her, Red, mention ye spent more time with the Queen of Dragons. It'll mean a great deal to her to know they thrive.

I repeat that for Sloan's benefit, dazzled by the whole thing. "Pass the cathedral and turn right on Church Street. There's parking on the left off Court."

He follows my instructions, and we enter the parking lot and pull into a vacant spot.

"We can't tell my brothers. They'll make a huge deal of it, and she'll be uncomfortable. Bruin's right. If she wanted people to know, we would've known. We won't tell anyone."

"Tell anyone what?" Sloan runs his hand over the steering wheel, much calmer than he was a moment ago. "As Bruin said, there's honor in giving a person their privacy."

"Then it's agreed. Pan Dora's secret is safe with us."

I thank ye, Red. And thank broody too.

"Of course," he says after I relay the info. After turning off the engine, he hands me my keys. "It's a fun secret even if only the three of us know."

I giggle and stomp my feet against the floorboard like a maniac. "I'm trying to play it cool—seriously, I am—but I'm fighting down an OMG, screaming girl, freakout dance."

Sloan laughs. "Yer not winning the fight. It's leaking out. How about ye save the big finale until we get ye home and into the grove? That way, no one in the outside world has to bear witness to yer particular brand of insanity."

I slip my cell into my purse and smile. "And *you* won't be embarrassed? Is that what we're really talking about here?"

"Something like that." Sloan adjusts the rearview and does a three-sixty check to ensure the coast is clear.

"Well, you're not launching off to attack homeless people heading into the mission. That's a good sign."

He ignores the jibe. "Now that we've established that Pan Dora knows what she's talking about and we can trust her, what's our plan for retrieving this trinket of hers?"

I sit back in my seat and look at the massive Gothic Revival cathedral across the road. "Ask nicely?"

"Try again."

"Wait until tonight when it's dark and abandoned?"

Sloan shakes his head. "According to Droghan, Emperor Creeper and his minions are coming for ye. No. I think we need to get it now and have Dora solidly on our side."

"Bam. Sloan Mackenzie, all fired up."

He points at the people entering the grand entrance at the south end of the church. "I looked it up while ye thanked Dora for yer reading. At one o'clock, there's an organ performance. The concert keeps everyone in the nave and draws enough attention that we should be able to work without unwanted attention to us performing a felony."

"All gung-ho and ready to go. FYI, grave robbing is not a felony. It's a misdemeanor punishable with a fine or short-term imprisonment. As long as we don't do anything gross with the body or bones, at worst, we'll be charged with possession of property obtained by crime and/or mischief over five thousand dollars. Do you think an ancient amulet from a certain wizard would be valued over five thousand dollars?"

Sloan is busy watching the people entering the church. "That ye even know that is both bizarre and endearing. And yes, I think an authentic piece of history from that particular wizard will be valued at more than five thousand dollars, more likely five million dollars."

"Holy crapamoly. Yeah?"

The two of us bail out of my truck, and I eye the almost two-hundred-year-old church's architecture. "It's in better shape than the last cathedral you took me to."

"This one is seven hundred years younger."

"*Annnd* has a roof and all its walls. That Ardfelt Cathedral is a bit of a fixer-upper."

Sloan presses a gentle hand against the small of my back and urges me toward the main entrance. "Don't tell me that I don't show ye a good time."

We stop at the bottom of the stone steps below the south porch and nod to a busload of blue-haired old ladies wearing regrettable floral dresses and bad shoes.

"Hopefully, we get done here without someone hexing me, and you forcing me to drink liquid manure."

"Och, I believe ye poured a foul concoction of yer own down my throat the other day. Kevin told us before ye topped it with coffee that it smelled like festering maggots."

I frown. "Loose lips sink ships. I'll talk to Kevin about what we share with the impaired. Besides, the two of you were on your feet and ready to take on your day before Emmet got hold of you. That's worth a few gulps of festering maggots. Trust me. You got the better end of that deal."

Sloan presses his back against the stone of the wall, and I can tell by his expression that he's scanning for hobgoblins, weres, fae, or any other weirdness we should be aware of.

Thankfully, for once, there's nothing.

"Score one for the good guys." I raise a hand in the air. "Can I get an amen and hallelujah?"

Several of the old ladies shuffling up the stairs peg me with a scowl.

Save the celebration, Red. First, we have to make sure this amulet is still here. Dora said she stashed it in the grave in the 1800s. There's no guarantee someone hasn't found it and taken it since then.

"It's here." I breathe to the depths of my lungs. "Positive thinking. It's here somewhere. We won't have a problem."

Sloan arches a brow. "How can ye be so sure?"

"Because the rest of our day has been a bubbling cauldron of monkey shit. As Calum would say, we're due for some fast cars and orgasms."

Sloan bursts out laughing, and we draw more geriatric disapproval. "I'm with Calum. That would be a nice change over bubbling cauldrons of monkey shit. Okay, I'll take yer word for it. It's here."

"Forget what I said before. It's not here."

I roll my eyes and give Sloan the most disdainful stink-eye I can muster. "No shit, Sherlock. But the gravestone is here. Why wouldn't his grave be attached to it?"

I read the commemorative plaque on the stone wall of the St. James Cathedral and paraphrase the highlights. "In July 1817, Samuel Jarvis and John Ridout got into a scafuffle about Sam's gambling debts owed to Johnny's daddy. Yadda yadda. Social privilege. Upstanding families. When cornered to pay up, Sam challenged the kid to a duel. They stood back-to-back, took eight strides, and were supposed to shoot on the count of three."

"But they didn't?" Sloan shifts closer to read.

"No, the kid spooked and shot on two. So the Seconds witnessing the event decided Johnny would stand unarmed while Jarvis took his shot. He caught it in the neck."

"That sucks."

"Yeah. It says here that dead Johnny's gravestone was removed from the old cemetery to be displayed here on the south porch wall as a tribute to rich daddy who donated a chunk of change to the diocese."

"So his grave is at the old St. James cemetery, which isn't at the old St. James Cathedral?"

"That's my take on it, yeah." I pull out my phone and do another search. "We're definitely in the wrong place. Our dead guy's dirt isn't here. But hey, you got to see another historical old church."

"It's lovely, but I'm not interested in churches at the moment. We're a little busy for sightseeing."

"Maybe, but I thought you, the history snob elitist, would still appreciate the historic significance. See, Toronto has history too, and it doesn't even smell moldy or look crumbly."

"Is this you focusing?"

"As close as it gets when I'm stressed and hangry, yeah." We turn and head back to the parking lot across the road. I spot a street meat truck parked on King. I detour and point. "Sausage dog me, Mackenzie. I'm about to turn into a gremlin, and I can't be held responsible."

He looks from me to the food truck and back again. "Now? The magical world is closin' in on ye. Yer aware of that, yeah?"

"I'm aware. But if the hobgoblins descend, I don't want to be weak and faint. Sausage dog… Saaausssage daawwg."

He curses and relents, grips my elbow, and turns us up the road. "Ye'll be the death of me, I swear."

"Then it's fitting that we'll be at the cemetery."

My street meat sausage is utterly amazeballs, and by the time I pull into my spot in the back lane, I'm catching my second wind.

Sloan looks at me sideways and shrugs. "I thought we were headed to the cemetery next. Ye told Pan Dora we'd get it done straight away."

"We are and we will." I turn off my truck and crank the handle to get out. "Wanna hear something cray-cray?"

He rolls his eyes. "Not really, no, but I have a feeling it's coming my way regardless."

I laugh and point across the side lane at the trees. "The crazy thing is, the old St. James Cemetery is part of the wildlands that border my house. I figured we'd be less conspicuous if we walk. There are always people exploring the gravesites and making etchings of the mausoleum inscriptions. We can walk around, find poor dead Johnny Ridout, and walk on out. Besides, you wanted to get some exercise this afternoon, didn't you?"

He follows me across the dirt side lane and into the trees. If we went right, the forested area would take us deeper into the Don River System, but the left is less than a hundred meters until the cemetery's paved pathway. We wander side by side, exploring the grounds and working our way through the aisles of tombstones and commemorative plaques.

"This is taking too long." Sloan blows out a breath. "As lovely as this place is, we don't have time to sightsee today, and there are too many choices. We need to cast a scrying spell or something."

I snort. "Or, we could *ask* someone. Crazy, eh? You can't always think like a druid, Mackenzie. Sometimes the easiest answer is the way to go."

I scan the landscape and find a groundskeeper who's finishing up with an elderly gentleman. "Excuse me," I say once he's alone and free to talk. "My friend and I were over at the Cathedral earlier and read about John Ridout and his duel. They moved his gravestone to the church's south wall, but we were curious about where his grave is."

The groundskeeper—Perdeep, it says on the embroidered patch on his shirt—points back the way we came to a cream mausoleum. "The Ridout family has a large plot. There's a crypt, and a few memorial trees and plaques. I expect that's where you'll find him."

"Thanks for your help."

I hustle to collect Sloan, and we make our way to the square, stone building. We split up and start searching the gravestones and markers.

"It'll be one of the oldest ones." Sloan rubs leaves off the surface of some old markers.

"This is a beautiful building." I track the names and dates on the plaques and make my way around the back. The square structure has the family's dead listed on all four sides, and I track them one by one. "You know, I might be developing a soft spot for historic buildings. I admit, knowing that these structures have stood the test of hundreds of years is fascinating and admirable."

"I think so too." He moves from gravestones to tree plaques while I round another side. "Although, I'd never want to be placed in a crypt. Burn me and give me back to nature. Even being buried would be better. Being stuck in a stone casket in a building for hundreds of years is horrifying to me."

"My mam was cremated. I've honestly never given it much thought."

"Here."

When I round the corner, he's kneeling on the grass and blowing debris off the stone. He must have cast a spell to help because I doubt he has that much wind power.

"John Ridout, 1817." I kneel beside Sloan and look around to see if anyone's watching us. "Now what?"

Sloan takes my hand and presses it firmly against the ground. "Cast a spell and bring the amulet to the surface."

"Me? You're better at casting than I am."

"And this is a perfect chance for ye to practice. No one's watching, we don't have to rush, there's nothing distractin' ye from yer task."

I chuckle. "Except for death threats and the promise of total annihilation of everyone and everything I love."

He nods. "Except for that."

"Well, if that's all, then what am I complaining about, right?" I take out my phone, open my notes, and come up with a few lines of rhyme that I think might work. I realize it's not very impressive that I need to work it out on a notepad, but hey, whatevs. With my spell fresh in my mind, I close my eyes and plant my palms heavy onto the grass.

Ancient treasure of power and past,

Yer owner claims you back at last.

Beneath the soil, so dark and tight,

Work yer way up to the light.

I wait, projecting positive thoughts and my intentions.

"Come on, magic amulet. Your owner wants the two of you reunited."

I send magic down into the ground below, inviting the amulet to rise and join us. The tattoo on the inside of my right arm burns, and I look at Birga inked on my skin. I'm not calling my spear, but she's reacting to something.

"Sloan? Birga's enchantment is partly based in necromancy, right?"

"Right."

"Do you think she can sense or call the dead?"

He pops one eye open and frowns. "Why do you ask?"

"Oh, no reason. It's probably nothing." I push away thoughts of zombie resurrection and focus on the ground beneath my palms again.

Pan Dora's amulet has been dormant for a long time.

Maybe it needs help to wake up and make it to the surface. Or, perhaps instead of calling the amulet, I should connect with the soil and ask it to give up its guest.

Ancient treasure in your clutch,

Sits below where none can touch.

Wriggle, push, and lift to light,
Work it up to see the light.

I send my energy into the soil and envision the earth doing my bidding. Before long, I feel a gentle *pop* of magic released and open my eyes. On the grass, sitting equidistant between Sloan and me is a starburst amulet with a rearing dragon breathing fire depicted on it.

"Hello there." I collect the treasure, touching it only with the gentle touch of my fingertips. I fight the urge to brush it clean. I've seen Aladdin. I know things can happen when you least expect them and considering the owner of this trinket, I'm not willing to take any chances. "Okay, wrap this baby up, and I'll text her that we've got it."

I give the amulet to Sloan and brush the soil off my hands and knees. "Damn. It's only three o'clock, but it feels like bedtime. I need a nap in my forest swing."

The two of us are making our way back home when my shield lights off, and I tense.

"What is it?"

"If I were to guess, I'd say hobgoblins." I glance back at the cemetery, but we're out of sight and lost in the trees close to my house. It galls me to think that my stalkers are loitering around my home. Then again, it wouldn't be the first time.

When my shield burns, I call my armor and Birga. The tree tattoos cover my arms at the same time my flesh hardens. Birga practically vibrates in my grip as I search my surroundings.

"Come out, come out, wherever you are."

Sloan opens his palm, and a thick branch lifts from the scrub and heeds his call. Swinging his makeshift club, he closes the distance between us. "Yer jumpin' the gun, assholes. The Guild Governor, Droghun, gave her twenty-four hours from the time she was notified of the complaint. I would bet if you attack before that, you lose ground. Actually, why don't ye take a swing at us? I'm sure yer Emperor fella won't care if ye foul up his plans."

Now that he says it out loud, I kinda hope they do attack. Wouldn't it be nice if the whole hobgoblin complaint got thrown out of court? Hells to the yeah.

Before I figure out how to incite them to overstep, the tingle on my back subsides, and Birga falls still.

"They're gone."

"Are ye sure?" Sloan is still searching the woods surrounding us and the leafy canopy above. "They're tricky assholes."

"Maybe, but they're gone. I'm sure."

I release the Tough as Bark and put Birga away until the next time. Which, who are we kidding, will be within the next day or so.

"Okay, I've had enough bullying and intimidation for one day. Let's go home and figure out how to put these bastards in their place. I'm sick of being reactive. It's time for proactive. If the hobgoblins want a piece of me, let them come to claim it."

"Don't tempt them. You're tired and cranky."

"Damn straight I'm tired and cranky. All I want to do is spend an hour or two napping in my grove, then watch a great movie with you and my family. Those stupid hobgoblins are ruining everything."

CHAPTER TWENTY-SIX

"Hey," Dillan greets when Sloan and I get home. "How was your—okay, wow—what's that face?"

Seeing Dillan and Emmet coming out of the family room brings it all crashing in on me. I kick off my shoes by the door and push my sneakers to the side. "It's been a day, D."

"And I'd ask what kind of day, but I'm afraid."

"Good instincts," Sloan says.

"Give us the highlight reel." Emmet gives me a wide berth as he passes me to get to the kitchen. "Is anyone dead?"

"No, but Sloan shook the shit out of a homeless woman on Queen Street this afternoon."

"That was you?" Dillan busts up. "I responded to that. Frustrating as hell. No homeless woman. Everyone had a different story to tell. And I was choking on dirt for the next two hours. What the hell, Mackenzie?"

"It was a hobgoblin with an illusion," Sloan snaps. "I'll take responsibility for the confusion, but the dirt storm was yer sister, not me."

I hang the strap of my purse on my hook and chuckle at Sloan's righteous indignation. "Okay, that was pretty funny."

"So, if that wasn't the worst of your day, what was?"

"Oh, that we're being *stalked* by hobgoblins. I found out this afternoon that they filed a complaint against us for siphoning magic. The Guild served me with this. It's a Vow of Vengeance. We have to look into it more, but I'm pretty sure it gives them the right to attack us and exact their pound of flesh."

"And the Guild sanctioned that?" Dillan takes the warrant and opens it up.

"Yeah, the druid rep served the notice himself. He happens to be the Black Dog prick that Creeping Vined me and tried to drag me into the woods at the fae slaughter site."

Emmet brings an armful of Guinness into the hall and starts handing them out. "How did the Black Dog get involved in serving a warrant?"

Sloan accepts two beers and gestures for us to move out of the back hall and into the family room. "Because the Black Dog holds the druid seat for the Lakeshore Guild and has for decades. Apparently, they're very well respected."

"Fuck that." Dillan twists the cap off his long-neck. "That can't bode well for us."

I beeline it across the family room and sit in my blue lady chair in the corner. "Nope. The douche druid let me know that he's launching a full investigation into the family of violent upstart druids who slaughtered his predecessor. We have that to look forward to as well."

"Double-fuck."

"Pretty much... But wait, there's more. I also had my first Tarot reading today."

Dillan takes a long swallow and lets out a deep breath. "I'm cluing into a pattern here, but I'm a sucker for punishment. Hey, Fi, how'd that go?"

"Better, once I learned that the Death card doesn't mean I'm going to die."

Emmet holds up his bottle. "Sunshine and strawberries. Things are looking up. What else did you learn?"

I hold up my fingers to count off. "One, our quest with water is not complete. Two, beware the stranger with ill intent. And three, there are trials on the horizon."

Dillan scowls. "I thought Tarot readings were supposed to be fun. Like, you're about to come into money or meet your soulmate or something."

"For other people, maybe. I got Death and lots of blindfolded ladies with swords pointing at them and a powerful magician who poses a threat."

"That's considerably less fun."

"Right?"

Dillan finishes with the warrant and hands it off to Emmet to look at.

I take a swig of my beer and point at the Vow of Vengeance. "There's a website on the bottom of the page. We have twenty-four hours to contest the charges before they come at us."

My reminder to get dinner started goes off on my phone. I leave them to study the Vow of Vengeance warrant and abandon my chair. In the kitchen, I open the fridge and pull out the chicken and veggies Calum left for the pot pie. Then I take out potatoes from the pantry, and the plaid recipe box that belonged to our mom.

When I turn around, they've all joined me.

"Em, we need a best guess on how precisely the wording ties them down. They named the six of us, but not Sloan and not our fae. I want to know that they're in the clear. I'll have Sloan portal them all back to Ireland if there's a chance they could be held responsible and hurt."

"Agreed," he and Dillan both say.

"And see if you can figure out the wiggle room to disprove them and revoke their right to annihilate us if the magic is returned to their satisfaction."

"On it." Emmet takes the paperwork and heads into the dining room.

Dillan plunks heavily into his chair at the table. "Da's going to blow a gasket when he catches wind of this."

"That's why we have to have as much intel gathered as possible before he gets home. Oh, I did learn another interesting factoid. Pan Dora doesn't like the hobgoblins or the Black Dog any better than us."

"Respect. I knew that female has amazingly good taste."

I snort. "Did she flirt with you?"

He chuckles. "Maybe."

I grab my peeler and start on the carrots. "Anyway, she agreed to help us sort through some of this chaos. Sloan and I did her a quick favor this afternoon, and in return, she's meeting with the Guild Governors to speak on our behalf."

Dillan's eyes go wide, the bright green of his irises dancing in the light. "No kidding? I did not see that coming. I didn't know she had that kind of sway."

"Right? So, everyone is going to be extra nice to Dora."

Dillan nods. "What else can I do?"

Sloan takes the potatoes I pulled out and heads to the sink to rinse them. "During the Tarot reading, the important message that came through several times—and with several cards—is that the quest with water is not complete."

I nod and accept the washed spuds. "I'm pulling dinner together, then Sloan and I are headed to the lakeshore to both figuratively and metaphorically test the waters."

"I'll go change and join you. If there will be blindfolded ladies and evil magicians, I don't want you going into Guild territory alone."

Sloan frowns. "Ye realize there aren't any real blindfolded ladies, don't ye?"

I pull the pastry shells out of the freezer to thaw and start peeling the potatoes. "He does. He's just coddin' ye, Mackenzie. Ye can't keep fallin' for every bit of blarney ye hear."

Dillan chuckles. "Especially in this house. Okay, I'll go change and grab my hood."

I laugh. "Oh, you're going to wear your hooded cloak of awesomeness. I would never have guessed."

Dillan points at me and grins. "Envy green looks good on you, sister. Goes well with your orange hair."

"*Oh!*" I throw an oven mitt at him, and he runs, laughing all the way up the stairs. "You'll pay for that, Dillan James. You'll rue the day."

Sloan retrieves my quilted mitt from the hall and hands it back to me. "What was that about?"

"Orange. Seriously? Whenever my brothers wanted to tease me and make me cry when I was little, they'd say I have orange hair. It's one of my buttons. I always wanted raven black hair like our mom."

Sloan shakes his head. "Yer hair is lovely the way it is. It's russet and mahogany and has copper highlights running through it, but no orange."

"Oh, I know." I pull a knife from the block and point it at the stairs. "I also know all of Dillan's buttons, so it's game on. You're my witness. He started it."

Sloan scratches his head. "Why do I feel like this will end badly?"

I snort. "It likely will, but that's nothing new."

Once the pot pie is assembled and in the oven, I call Da and let him know what time dinner will be ready and that we're headed to Sugar Beach to check on the arrival of magic.

Then I check with Emmet to keep an eye on dinner.

When everything is taken care of, we take our leave.

"Ye know," Sloan gestures toward the scenery passing Dillan's truck, "as much as I love Ireland, I think I'm developin' a soft spot for yer city."

I lean forward and grab the two seats ahead of me. "How can you not? Toronto is charm, wrapped in history, decorated with everything you'd ever want, and topped with great people."

"Not that she's biased." Dillan hits his indicator and takes us straight down Sherbourne Street.

"Oh, I never claimed to be objective."

"Why do they call it Sugar Beach?" Sloan asks.

"Because it's right next to the Redpath Sugar Refinery. It's been part of our waterfront since the 1950s."

"And people swim in an industrial area right next to a refinery?"

"Swim, no, but it's a beautiful beach with a splash pad and umbrellas and places to sun and have fun."

Dillan turns right onto Queen's Quay, then a quick left into the parking lot at Sugar Beach. "It's also really damn close and won't be busy at this time of year."

The three of us bail out of his truck and jog down to the water. The closer I get to the shoreline, the more my nerves take hold. I can feel the warm tingle of fae power, but it's not ambient and flowing through the air like before.

It's concentrated in the lake.

"Well, crap." After toeing off my shoes, I pull my socks off and roll my pants up to my knees, then wade into the freezing water and sigh. "The power is here." I point at the surface.

"But it's not here." Dillan waves his arms through the air. "So how do we get it airborne? Sloan, do you have any aerosol spells up the sleeve of your designer shirt?"

Sloan frowns. "Not off the top of my head, no."

"Would a Naiad know how?" I think about Iridan and his nasty little otters. I'd rather not have to speak with that twerp again, but I can deal if it saves our lives.

"Likely, but we're druids." Sloan stares across the water toward the lights of the Toronto Islands. "Nature is our wheelhouse. I'm sure we can figure it out."

Sadly, instead of getting our groove on after dinner and watching *Burlesque* as I wanted, it's family druid meeting time. We're all back in the dining room trying to figure out how to make the magic now building up in Lake Ontario more readily available.

"Who says it has to be airborne?" Emmet asks. "Can't people go to the waterfront and dip their toes to get powered up? If they drink the water, won't they get it that way? Toronto water is good."

Da twists the top of a fresh beer and frowns. "Do ye think that the oldest and strongest of the empowered folks will thank us for the disconnect between them and their skills? I doubt it. We already have a complaint lodged against us. Our best chance at fighting it is to put things back the way they were so no one can complain."

Calum sighs. "And in what kind of system does lodging a complaint include lodging a blade between our ribs?"

"That's how the game is played here, it seems."

"Granda?" I focus on the video screen and try not to imagine the mass slaughter of my family. "Anything?"

"One second, *mo chroí*." He and Gran are talking about something off to the side. When he comes back on screen, he smiles. "We have an idea. It's a simple solution, but with a bit of smoke and mirrors, we think it might not only satisfy yer ambient magic problem but also make magic-powered folks think twice about coming at ye from all sides.

"Wouldn't that be a nice change of pace?" Dillan says.

"I could get behind that," Kevin adds and squeezes Calum's arm. "I've only been in the loop for a few days, and I'm exhausted worrying about all of you. I can't imagine what you go through."

Aiden holds up his beer to salute Kev. "We're getting good at watching our six. I'll tell you that."

For the eleventeen-millionth time, I regret how my actions have impacted my family's life and safety. I'd apologize again, but it solves nothing. I need to fix the problem. "Okay, let's hear your plan, Granda. We're game to try anything."

The Toronto Island Ferry system is a unique and rather ingenious way to deliver our aerosol spell. When Gran and Granda ask if there is regular traffic in the harbor, it's our first thought. "Yeah, we have ferries that run every day of the year from the Toronto port across to Ward's Island, Centre Island, and Hanlan's Point."

"And they run often?"

Calum has his phone up and is searching. "Yeah, every half-hour in peak times and every hour all other times. Three hundy and sixty-five days a year."

"As well as the other water traffic," Aiden adds. "There are also regular dinner cruises and party boats that people book for large groups."

"Good." Gran looks relieved. 'That's exactly what we were hoping for. The idea is to enchant the boats so that they churn the water when they travel through the harbor and the spell converts the magic into airborne energy."

"Will a spell like that last indefinitely or is it something we'll have to maintain?" I flip through Beauty, looking for possible spells to use.

"A bit of both," Granda says. "Yer going to anchor the spell at the island docks to recharge and refresh when the ships dock to let the passengers and cars off and on, but yer also going to check on it now and then. If it means yer lives, it's worth a quick trip down to the shoreline."

Aiden nods. "Kinu and I take the kids to Centreville on

Centre Island once a month when the amusement park is open. I can check then."

Emmet nods. "And between patrols and beach events, I'm down there a lot too."

"It's doable, Mam. Thank ye both for the help."

CHAPTER TWENTY-SEVEN

Our Toronto Island tour is complete by nine o'clock, and the aerosol spell is active and anchored to the docks. We've enchanted all the ferries, and the party cruise boats and landings as well. By midnight, it's now time for the smoke and mirrors portion of the evening.

While standing at the stone altar in the center of the druid circle, I breathe in and feel the released power of the ley lines misting in the air. The stage is set.

My father, my brothers, and Sloan stand at attention around me. In their druid garb and with their weapons in hand, they are truly a sight to see. We lit candles atop the seventeen stone pillars, so the golden glow of flickering flames bathes the whole scene.

I call my Tough as Bark armor forward, have Birga in my hand, and Killer Clawbearer at my side.

This will work. It has to.

The itchy tingle on my back signals the arrival of our guests. Garnet Grant arrives with a posse of four. I give him points for keeping his party small enough that he's not overtly threatening us or accusing us of being untrustworthy.

No doubt, he has more Moon Called Weres close by if he needs backup—but he won't. This isn't an offensive.

The Grand Governor of the Lakeshore Guild steps into the ring of druid stones, and I smile. His swagger boasts of the confidence of his life experience. He's the shit, and he knows it. For sure, he's a predator and can defend himself and take lives. The promise is there in his muscled frame and the primal strength glittering in his amethyst eyes.

But what impresses me more than his strength and sass is that he came here hoping for good news.

By now, he and his Justice League of Superpowers must know that we're new druids on the scene, but that we also have a vast history and a strong foundation.

The Cumhaills are not only part of the original Fianna Warriors of the seventh century—Fionn was their leader. That was before the Viking raids, the Crusades, the Black Death, and before Charlemagne began his quest to wipe out Paganism and bury the powers and beliefs of the Celtic people.

Before all of it, there was us.

Those are deep roots, and druids are all about them.

"Thank you for coming." I dip my chin and spread my palms out toward the ring of stones. "May I introduce Clan Cumhaill, the direct descendants of Fionn mac Cumhaill, leader of the Fianna and rightful heirs of that honor."

Garnet seems to appreciate the flair for drama. "It's nice to meet you all again." Influence seeps off him as he speaks, but this time, neither my father nor my brothers fall under his hypnotic spell.

A quick family visit to Dora's club after dinner took care of that. She was thrilled to have her amulet returned to her. In return, she took care of any Alpha influence Garnet Grant held over them.

Garnet's grin widens as he realizes they are now immune to his suggestion. "Like that, is it?"

I offer him an unapologetic smile. "If we are to be friends, I'd much prefer our relationship to be genuine. That's a stronger foundation to build on, don't you think?"

He dips his chin again. "It'll never be boring with you, will it, Lady Druid?"

My brothers and Sloan all chuckle at that.

I shrug. "I am me, and I refuse to apologize for it. I don't conform well, but I also don't play games. If I have something on my mind, you'll always know it. I don't mince words, and I often offend people who prefer social graces and subtext."

Garnet raises his palm to halt his men and stalks forward to stand directly in front of me. "As I said, it'll never be boring. Besides, subtext and social graces are best reserved for dinner parties. In the real world, it's best to put it all out there so there are no misunderstandings."

"I'm glad we agree."

"And to that end, why am I here?

Here goes everything. "Well, to start with, since you're breathing, you can tell the ambient magic is back."

He tilts his head back and pulls a deep breath into his lungs. "It is. Though it's not the same as before. There's a different taste to it."

"It comes from a different source, which I believe you'll find more powerful."

"And is this source sustainable or is this a stop-gap to keep us from killing you for siphoning off the power we had before you interfered?"

"You say interfered. I say utilized during an unplanned period of transition. Or, if you like, you could consider it payment for services rendered."

"How so?"

"The different taste, as you put it, is our druid contribution. You see, before the Barghest group targeted me and tried to offer me up as a blood sacrifice, we weren't aware of other druids in our city. Da and my brothers are police officers, and our family has long held to a code of Protect and Serve. To know that our magical sect has bloodied the streets of our city with not only dark magic but death magic is vile and offensive to us."

"So, you disavow the Barghest?"

"We do."

"What does that have to do with the ambient magic?"

"We reject their practices of necromancy and blood sacrifice. Their moniker praises a mythical black dog of death. It's fitting because they are dogs, mongrels in the streets. If there are druids in this city, they should be held to our sect's standards and principles. If they turned to necromancy out of desperation for magic, that's over now. We've amped up the magic available in the city, and if everyone behaves and lives in accordance with the laws of decency, we have the power to increase it more."

Garnet frowns. "And where exactly are you getting this magic? That's what I can't figure out. Where would six local druids get enough magical energy to power the city?"

I draw a steadying breath. "From the fae ley lines."

I expect the rolling laughter from Garnet and his men. In fact, I'm counting on it. "Come, Lady Druid. Do you think the magical shortages of the city are new to me—to the Guild? We've studied every source of power available to us and ley lines have never been one of them."

"Until now."

He stares at me. At first, he seems to expect me to explain, but I don't. If he wants answers he can ask for them. "You're serious?"

"As serious as a Moon Called mass killing in the streets of my city. Druids are the keepers of nature and the champions of the fae. It's not surprising that the Black Dog couldn't access the local ley lines, but we can."

"And did," Da says.

"And did," I repeat. "We have picked up the mantle of our ancestors and will live by the tenets of our sect. Empowered

Ones in Toronto who can utilize fae energy no longer have an excuse to torture and kill for their power. It's readily available."

"There are magicians, witches, and druids alike who choose blood and death magic. It isn't out of necessity. It's a choice of their craft."

I nod. "And if they target innocent civilians, we have a problem with that."

"Is that a threat?"

"No. It's us saying that our dedication to serve and protect extends beyond human boundaries. If empowered folks choose to prey on innocents, we will fight to end that practice."

"And are you blackmailing us with ambient magic?"

"Blackmail, no. Cautioning, yes."

His brow pinches. "Explain."

"It took seven of us three days to open the conduit to access the ley lines. What the Guild and others before us haven't accomplished in centuries, we did in days."

"What's your point?"

"I was chosen by Fionn mac Cumhaill himself to resurrect the Fianna and lead the druids into a new era. I'm not expecting that to be well-received by everyone."

"And?"

"*Annnd* our efforts to establish stable access to the ley lines are ongoing. The potential for more power is real, but we won't amp everyone up until we ensure the safety of the city's citizens."

"She's fucking spoon-feeding us," Trent snaps. "I say we slaughter the lot of them and amp up the power ourselves."

I point at his man. "My point exactly."

Garnet frowns. "There's no need to take a defensive posture. I will declare you and your efforts protected. No one will touch you."

I ruck up my shirt and wait until he gets a good look at the black and green bruising across my ribcage. It's the second day, so the bruising has spread. It looks gnarly. I ignore the intake of breath from my family and stay focused on Garnet. "And why should they listen to a fucking feline who's forgotten what it is to be an Alpha Warrior of Moon Called?"

Garnet's eyes flip gold and his muscled frame swells. "Who? Who fucking did that and spoke those words?"

The circle of men, mine and his, tenses with the promise of a fight. If I point my finger at Trent, Garnet will slaughter him—I have no doubt about that—but will that bring the others in line or create animosity with more of them?

I drop my shirt and draw a deep breath. The power of the ley lines is gaining strength. It's nowhere near the levels of Ireland, but it's a solid start.

"My point is, there are dangers to us from those who don't like us joining the party. I'm sure you're aware that Acting Governor Droghun awarded the hobgoblins a Vow of Vengeance against us."

He nods. "And you should know, I opposed it."

"The Black Dog targeted us the moment we claimed our heritage and allied with the hobgoblins against us. If that's how your grand organization establishes order, we have very different ideas of what law and justice means."

Garnet frowns. "I'll look into it."

"Thank you. And, am I correct in assuming that since the ambient magic is restored and improved within the twenty-four hours allotted to contest the Vow of Vengeance judgment, that the warrant will be rescinded?"

"Consider it null and void."

Yee-fucking-haw. I nod and breathe to the depth of my lungs for the first time in almost a week. The biggest fires are now out. We're safe, our fae are safe, and our grove will continue to thrive.

That's a win-win-win.

I'm about to end our meeting when I notice how unsettled his men seem with the outcome of things tonight. "Again, I am sorry for the siphoning of power and any impact it may have had on your people. There is time to build trust. For now, the ambient power is returned and upgraded. The Moon Called should be able to control themselves for the full moon tomorrow night, and the immediate crisis is averted. Let's please call Phase One a win, and everyone goes home."

Garnet is still pissed and vibrating with a lethal threat. Thankfully, it's not aimed at me. Still, when he manages to calm himself enough that his eyes flip back to purple, he bows at the waist. "Phase One is a win. Go in peace, Lady Druid. I look forward to when next we meet."

"Did it work?" Gran asks.

"She was amazing, Mam." Da winks over Emmet's head at me. "I'm sure that Fionn himself was there and guidin' her. By the end of it, she had *me* convinced that we're an indispensable link in the ambient power supply chain."

"And the power is stabilizing?" Granda asks.

I shake my head. "Not yet. It's still increasing in the lake, but we're controlling how much of it gets airborne. I just don't think it's wise to give people who have scrounged and killed for magic for centuries an abundance all at once."

"Yer not wrong," Granda says. "Besides, it's in the water now, so it'll be in the taps and water parks and public fountains. With ground seepage and raincloud dispersion, it won't be long until that entire area pulses with magic."

"And yer sure the aerosol spell will continue to extract the power from the lake water and circulate it into the air?"

I nod. "We did the spell just like you instructed, Gran. Da and Sloan worked on the tethering and tying it off and had no problems. As far as we can tell, the spell will continue to convert the ley line magic into ambient energy, and it's anchored off the Toronto Islands like a ship in the harbor.

"That's good," Gran praises. "Ye don't want powerful people to know how easy it would be to up their dose of magic."

"Agreed," Da says. "I can see people blowing up huge chunks of the Canadian Shield and altering nature in all the wrong ways."

"But for now, yer all safe and ye think yer in the clear?"

"For now, at least."

After the debrief on the ambient magic is over, I bring up a debrief of another sort. "Gran, have you got a good potion or spell for poison ivy? Emmet ran into a few bumps in the woods and is suffering pretty badly."

"Och, my dear, show me the rash, *mo chroí*."

I bite my bottom lip, but I'm the only one in the room who even tries to hold back the laughter.

"Yeah, show her your rash, Em," Calum jibes.

"Fuck off, you guys." Emmet's cheeks are bright red. "I can't show you, Gran. The rash isn't anywhere you want to see."

"True story." I offer Emmet an apologetic wince. I can't look back at the rest of them because they're all buckled over at poor Emmet's expense. "Needless to say, he's uncomfortable and would like for the torture to end."

"Don't forget that Sloan's here." Calum points at where he's standing at the end of the table. "If he has to do a bit of touch healing, I'm sure the two of them could getter done."

Sloan arches a manicured brow. "You first, buddy. I'm not the one who touches man junk."

Calum laughs. "I don't touch my *brother's* man junk, you perv."

As the room devolves into ribald remarks and general mayhem, Gran says she'll get straight to work. I let them go. I leave my brothers to their playground bullying and head outside for some fresh air.

"Yer Da's right, ye know." Sloan follows me out into the crisp night air. "Ye impressed that man, and I get the sense that he's not so easily impressed."

We walk together across the back lawn and into the grove. I sit in my basket seat and use my toe to swing. "I'm glad things worked out. We have our sacred grove, our fae are safe, and who knows, maybe if Garnet and the Lakeshore Guild find value in our contribution to the magical cause, they'll live and let live."

"That would be nice, wouldn't it?"

I chuckle. "Yeah. Unusual, but nice."

"And the bruising on yer stomach?"

"It's nothing."

Sloan shakes his head and moves to stand in front of me. He grips both sides of the wicker seat I'm suspended in and stops my motion. "Last I checked, yer natural affinity for healing was one of your lowest scores. How about you let me make that decision?"

I wave him off, but he drops to his knee and points at my shirt's hem. "Let me see."

"You really don't—"

"We can heal yer side with or without a fight, but the result will be the same. I'm not lettin' it go, and yer not movin' from my sight until I assess the damage that fuckin' wolf did to ye at the pub."

"How do you know—" The violence in his glare cuts off my denial. "What? There was nothing to be done. I didn't want to make a scene, and by the time I got back to the table, he was long gone. I don't want to make it a thing. I don't want bad blood with Garnet and the Moon Called. We already have enough of a fan club building in the wings."

"Fine, but I could've eased yer sufferin'. Yer not indestructible, Cumhaill. And no matter how tough ye are, ye need to fall back on yer family and those ye trust to help ye out when the world closes in."

"You sound like Da."

His touch eases around the ribs banding my side. The contact of skin-on-skin warms, and I almost groan as the low-level ache I've suffered for two days eases and dissolves.

He must read the relief in my gaze because he frowns and shakes his head. "Nothing was broken, but they were bruised. Don't be such a hero. If yer hurt, ye have to tell one of us. Otherwise, how will we know if ye need help?"

Mention of a hero brings images of Brenny to mind and my eyes sting. It's stupid how that loss sneaks up on me at the most inopportune times.

"Am I interrupting?"

I stiffen and blink fast, searching for the intruder. "Mr. Grant." I abandon my swing and step out of the grove to find him standing at the back gate. "Twice in one night. To what do I owe the honor?"

Garnet looks from me to Sloan and back again. "I owe you a serious apology."

"You? Why?"

"I declared you free to go about your business in restoring the ambient magic. I never thought any more of it. If one of my men hurt you, it's on me."

I shrug and pat my side. "Sloan patched me up, so you're off the hook."

"Who did it, Lady Druid?"

I check his eyes. They're still amethyst purple, but I sense his lion's primal nature close to the surface. "I'd rather build relationships, not tear them down. Eyes on the horizon, and all that."

"I appreciate that, and from a political standpoint, I respect it. But as an Alpha of the Moon Called, if someone disrespects my leadership, I need to know who. Doubt and mistrust are cancer in the animal kingdom. The same goes for the Were kingdoms."

I shrug. "Not my monkeys. Not my circus."

Sloan frowns. "It was yer man Trent."

"*Et tu, Brute?*" I peg Sloan with a glare. "What happened to me not wanting to cause bad blood with anyone else in the magical community?"

Sloan shrugs. "You might not want to cause bad blood, but I

don't give a flying fuck. That animal cornered ye on the dance-floor at a pub to intimidate ye. He knew ye couldn't defend yerself in public without causing a scene and he took advantage. It was cowardly and deserves to be addressed."

I look from Sloan to Garnet and shake my head. "I never told him any of that. He's guessing."

"Yer not that complex a book to read, Cumhaill. I was there. I saw how hurt and shaken ye were when ye came back to the table. Ye told yer da one of Garnet's men caught ye off-guard. It's not rocket science to put the two things together."

Garnet nods his thanks to Sloan, then smiles at me. "Don't be too hard on your man, Lady Druid. That's what I expected to hear. I'm sorry for your suffering. Be assured I'll deal with him."

When Garnet flashes away, I'm left looking at an annoyed and guarded Sloan. "Why are *you* pissed off? I'm the one who should be mad."

"Call it preventative ire. I know where yer headed, and I'll not apologize for hangin' the beast out to dry. Ye fuck with the lass, ye get put on yer ass."

Despite wanting to stay mad at him, I have to laugh. "Did you just make that up, or have you been saving it?"

"It came to me just now, although I'm thinkin' of gettin' t-shirts made."

I close my eyes and shake off my night. "Gawd, when did I become fodder for t-shirts?"

Sloan shrugs. "I have no idea. I've only known ye four months. I'd bet, however, it was long before then."

CHAPTER TWENTY-EIGHT

In the spirit of entertaining our fae with music, we rig up the basement TV in the grove and watch *Burlesque* as a group. Kevin and Calum are in the Adirondacks, Sloan and I are in our fancy new basket chair swings, and Emmet is on the ground buried under fae creatures happy to snuggle with him.

Sloan thought I was crazy when I suggested it, but hey, why walk the path everyone else walks, amirite?

"Man, Christina Aguilera killed that number," I say.

Pip and Nilm are dancing, and the Spriggans and Ostara rabbits are flitting and fluttering around. The purple lady with the white wings nods. "Is most good."

Ow, shit. I sit up, my back on fire. "My shield lit up, boys. Something's amiss."

We all jump to our feet in the next second. Emmet phones Dillan inside the house. "We've got trouble. Grab your hood and get out here."

Calum flexes his fists and calls his bow and quiver.

Kevin growls. "So fucking hot."

Calum chuckles and plants a kiss on him. "Stay inside the grove. It's warded. You'll be safe in here."

"Be safe out there," Kev says.

"Bear, you're up, buddy." I step out toward the edge of the trees and scan the back yard.

Emmet looks back and frowns. "Our fae are scared."

I offer them a genuine smile of reassurance. "Don't be. We are your druids. We won't let anything happen to you."

Dillan launches off the back porch with Da following him at a dead run. Emmet bolts out to join them, and I frown. Em's weapon is amping us up for a fight. He shouldn't be at the front of the pack.

I feel his fury, though, and share it.

Whether it's the Black Dog or hobgoblins or maniacal shifters, they have no business anywhere near our home or our sacred grove. Thundering footsteps beside me bring me the comfort of knowing we're facing this together.

Whoever dares to challenge us has no idea what an ass-whooping they're in for.

Chaos explodes the moment my brothers reach the back lane. Whatever illusion the hobgoblins glamoured themselves with to hide their presence drops once we're all out there.

We're surrounded.

"That's the way ye want to play it, is it?" Da has his staff out and starts cutting through intruders.

"Damn." Emmet dives out of the strike zone of a hobgoblin's sword. "We need to fumigate. Our back lane is lousy with pests."

Birga sings in my hand, happy to taste blood. There's not enough space to get our groove on, and we're in full view of our neighbors. *"Obscure Vision."*

Hopefully, my privacy spell keeps Janine and Mark from noticing a bloody battle in the back.

Bear roars near the back fence and rears up on his hind feet. Swinging his massive claws through the night, he minces and mulches with each swipe of his mighty paws.

A solid strike to my shoulder sends me spinning, and I scowl.

It doesn't hurt. My armor is in place and working perfectly, but it does knock me for a loop. "Striking a lady is rude. You should be ashamed."

"Stealing from others is rude," says the hobgoblin coming at me hard. "You should be punished."

I step back to absorb his next attack and deflect the blade of his short sword with my arm guard. With his sword pushed to the side and his core exposed, I bury Birga's green marble spear-head into his belly. "Swipe left."

My opponent falls to the ground, and I spin to take on the next one. I catch sight of an asshole creeping up behind Sloan. He's busy with two and facing the other direction.

He doesn't see the attack coming, and I won't get there in time. Lifting Birga over my shoulder, I throw my spear the thirty feet to catch the third man in the back of his neck.

The green Connemara speartip buries into the guy's flesh and pierces his neck through to the front. He falls lifeless at Sloan's back, and he twists. Seeing my handiwork, he goes back to his two and I collect my spear and back him up.

When we polish off those two, we spin for the next incoming. Only, there is no one still standing.

"Is that it? Are we done?"

"Seems so." Dillan wipes his dual blades clean on a dead guy's shirt. "For now, at least."

I lower Birga and pull out my phone. My text to Garnet is short and sweet. His response is immediate.

"Hello again, Lady Druid." He materializes behind the back bumper of Dillan's truck. "Had a bit of excitement tonight, did you?"

"Imagine our surprise." I wipe the blood spatter on my face with the back of my sleeve and realize I've likely smeared one helluva mess across my face. "I thought you said you called off the Guild hit."

"Harsh. The Guild hardly put a hit out on you."

"Semantics. You put out an 'it's okay to annihilate them' on us before asking us what happened, and before giving us the chance to prove we were making things right."

"Our experience with your family up until that point had been reports of rogue slaughter. A colleague of ours is dead."

"You mean the Skull Trim bastard who came at me the minute my powers were unlocked? The bastard who tied up my family, stabbed my brother, and intended to sacrifice me on a stone altar in front of thirty freaks in robes? Should I have played passive on that and let them have their way because they have more important friends in the community? Fuck that."

Garnet chuckles. "Point made."

"So, back to this attack. You said you called off the Vow of Vengeance."

"I did."

"So, what? These guys don't respect the authority of the almighty Guild? That doesn't instill confidence. Maybe you and your playmates aren't all that after all."

Garnet's purple eyes flash gold. "Careful, Lady Druid. If they were informed, they wouldn't have attacked. There must've been a break in the chain of communication."

I roll my eyes. "Are you honestly saying they didn't get the memo?"

Emmet snorts behind me. "That's lame."

Garnet frowns, scans my family's disbelieving faces, and the heaping mass of dead in my back lane. "I assure you, I'll look into it."

As much as I want to flip him off, I have enough self-preservation to realize that having at least one person in a position of authority who doesn't want to kill us is a good thing.

"We would appreciate that. And what about the bodies? Do you want them? Do you need to identify them? How does the Guild handle an exposure scene like this?"

Garnet waves toward the side lane and two men in a box

truck turn in. "We'll take care of this. You and your family are free to resume your evening."

Dillan stands tall and scans the back lane. When he gives us the nod that he senses nothing more out there, I relax and back away. "All right. Have yourselves a good night."

"You all as well."

When I wake the next morning, there is a massive bouquet of four dozen white tulips on my bedside table and Sloan sitting in the chair with his socked feet on my bed. He looks deep in thought, and I almost feel bad about asking him what the hell he's doing. Almost.

"Hello? Ever heard of boundaries? I was sleeping, and this isn't the basement pullout."

Sloan's smile is unrepentant. "You talk in your sleep, you know?"

Oh, gawd. Yes, I know. My brothers have tormented me with things I've said my entire life. "What did I say? Dammit, broody, I can't be held responsible for things my brain barfs out when I'm unconscious."

He chuckles. "Relax. Ye didn't divulge anything salacious, although that would've been nice. Mostly ye gave yer brothers hell for one thing or another."

"Mostly?"

His smile fades. "The other night, ye cried quite a bit. I popped in to check on ye after ye acted strangely at the pub. I wasn't tryin' to invade yer privacy. I worry."

I wave that off. "Calum mentioned that too. Sorry. It's been years since I did that. It happened a lot after Mam died. I'm sure it's because I'm missing Brenny and was panicked about all the changes in my life."

He points at the flowers. "These were on the doorstep this morning when yer father and Calum left for their shifts."

"Who are they from?"

He stands and pulls the card from where it's nestled in the sea of white petals. "Despite yer outburst to the contrary, I respect yer boundaries. I didn't read yer card. However, tulips are symbolic of new beginnings and peace. White tulips signify a request for forgiveness. My guess would be Garnet Grant. Or Liam perhaps, if he's still conflicted about upsetting ye earlier in the week."

I accept the card and rip it open. "Four dozen seems like overkill. Think of all the pretty tulips that gave their life to assuage manly guilt. I would've been fine with a bottle of Redbreast Whiskey with a happy-face Post-It on it."

Sloan chuckles. "Not my proudest moment."

"But one of my favorites. You should let loose more often. You and Calum had a good time, no one got hurt, and you came up with the answer to our problems. No fault. No foul."

I open the card, read it, and tuck it back into the envelope. "Right you are. Garnet Grant regrets Trent's behavior and the attack on us last night, and how it might have tarnished our view of the Guild. He sends his sincere apologies."

Sloan nods. "As he should."

I lean back into my pillow and take in the view. I may not be hopping into Sloan's bed, but he sure is nice to look at. "So, I guess now that the magic shortage is taken care of and s'all good here, you're heading home?"

He shifts to sit on the edge of my bed and points at the duffle on the floor. "I'm sure there are a dozen things Da and Lugh have waiting for me."

"Well, as always, I'm sad to see you go. But my loss is their gain. I'm sure everyone will be thrilled to have you back, especially Manx. You should bring him next time. I'm sure he and Bruin could get into trouble in the Don."

He chuckles and rolls his eyes. "And I want my animal companion to get into trouble, why?"

I wave that away. "And hey, by leaving this morning, you'll be home and ready to roll for the next heir drink night. Tons of craic, that group. I bet Tad's less of a dick now that you've battled together, and I'm sure Ciara misses you."

Sloan tilts his head into my line of sight and his gaze narrows. "What are ye babbling on about? Ye know I have zero interest in Ciara. Or at least, ye should. I've made it clear enough."

"Yeah, I know. I was razzing you."

He shakes his head and takes my hand. "I'm headed home. I'll work with Lugh and the Order in the capacity of my apprenticeship. I'll help Da with his patients. And, I promised Manx I'll make up the time I've missed with him when I get there. Nowhere in there is there any intention to cozy up with Ciara Doyle. Ye have nothin' to worry about."

"Worried? I'm not worried. I was teasing."

He nods. "Och, I know. But as they say, there's a little truth in every jibe."

I grip the quilt pooled around my waist and pick at a loose thread. "Sloan, I told you…"

He catches my hand and squeezes my fingers. "I'm not makin' a play, Cumhaill. I'm simply sayin' Ciara's not the one for me. The girl I have my sights set on is going through a lot. She needs time to find her balance. I respect the hell outta that. No rush. No expectations. But she needs to know, while I may step back to give her the space to grow, I'm never far away. With one text, I'll cross the ocean and be at her side. All she has to do is say the word."

I swallow, my bedroom suddenly feeling very small and warm. "And what's the word the girl is supposed to say?"

"Lady's choice. Yes. Come. It's time. S'all good. I need ye. I'm horny." He shrugs. "I honestly don't care what the word is. Someday, she'll tell me it's *that* day. She'll look around and realize we're a great team and she's stronger with me at her side. When that day comes, things will truly start to get interesting."

"What if that doesn't happen?"

"It will. I have no doubt. However long it takes. Until then, we'll keep pretending we're only friends."

I pull in a deep breath and sigh. "We *are* only friends."

He winks, and his smile melts my heart. "Whatever ye say, Cumhaill. Stay safe. Text me when ye need me, 'cause we both know ye need me."

With that, Sloan kisses my hand, picks up his duffle, and portals away.

Cocky jerk.

I chuckle and get out of bed.

Super-sexy, cocky jerk.

And yeah, Emmet's right. With his wayfarer gift, he *does* kick ass on the dramatic exits.

In an effort not to dwell on Sloan Mackenzie, I snatch up Garnet's note and reread it. "Friday, noon. Lunch meeting with the Guild Governors. Business formal. A car will pick you up at 11:45."

Friday, eh? I suppose I can take time out of my busy schedule to make myself available.

With images bouncing around inside my cranium of what a meeting with the Governors of the Lakeshore Guild of Empowered Ones might look like, I get out of bed and decide to spend a few hours with Myra at the bookshop.

After that, I might swing by the Eaton Centre and shop for a Druid Lady power outfit. Ooo, I'll find an emerald green blouse that sets off the red of my hair and black pants that hang loose in case I need to fight. I'll pass on shoes and go with boots. Yeah, a good pair of black leather ass-kicking boots with buckles.

Picturing the outfit in my head, I hustle to the bathroom to start my day. A lunch meeting with the Guild...

I can't wait to see the cyclone of chaos that stirs up.

Thank you for reading – ***A Sacred Grove***

While the story is fresh in your mind, click **HERE** and tell other readers what you thought.

A star rating and/or even one sentence can mean so much to readers deciding whether or not to try out a book or new author.

And if you loved it, continue with the Chronicles of an Urban Druid and claim your copy of book three – ***A Family Oath***

IRISH TRANSLATIONS

Arragh – a guttural sound for when something bad happened
Banjaxed – broken, ruined, completely obliterated
Bogger – those who live in the boggy countryside
Bollocks – a man's testicles
Bollix – thrown into disorder, bungled, messed up
Boyo – boy, lad
Cock-crow – close enough that you can hear a cock crow
Craic – gossip, fun, entertainment
Culchie – those who live in the agricultural countryside
Donkey's years – a long time
Dosser – a layabout, lazy person
Eejit – slightly less severe than idiot
Fair whack away – far away
Feck – an exclamation less severe than fuck
Flute – a man's penis
Gammie – injured, not working properly
Hape – a heap
Howeyah/Howaya/Howya – a greeting not necessarily requiring an answer.

Irish – traditional Irish language (Commonly referred to as Irish Gaelic unless you're Irish.)
Knackers – a man's testicles
Mo chroi – my heart (pronounced muh chree)
Mocker – a hex
Och – used to express agreement or disagreement to something said
Shite – less offensive than shit
Slan! – health be with you (pronounced slawn)
Gobshite – fool, acting in unwanted behavior
Slainte mhath – cheers, good health (pronounced slawn cha va)
Wee – small

The story continues with A Family Oath, coming soon Amazon and Kindle Unlimited.

Pre-order now to have it delivered to your Kindle on midnight November 29, 2020.

AUTHOR NOTES - AUBURN TEMPEST
OCTOBER 16, 2020

Thank you so much for reading ***A Sacred Grove***.

And what more can I say but thank you again for the love Fiona is receiving. When I submitted the manuscript for *A Gilded Cage* to Michael, we knew we had something special. The dynamic of the Cumhaill family is honest and imperfect and I hoped the mayhem of their lives and unbreakable love would translate on the page and resonate with the readers.

We got our wish.

At the time of me writing this, *A Gilded Cage* has been Amazon's #1 New Release in Historical Fantasy Fiction for almost three consecutive weeks since it's release. That's all because of readers like you. The reviews are so positive and we couldn't be more thrilled that readers love Fi and her family.

In truth, we love them too.

Michael and I have lots of laughs and adventures planned for future pages, so we hope you stick with Fi as she continues to find her footing in the druid world. With new friends, magical creatures, and ancient lore to keep her on her toes, Fiona has only begun to grasp her destiny.

The next installment of Chronicles of an Urban Druid, ***A Family Oath***, is written, and being polished by Michael's team. You can expect it out in the world on November 29th.

Wishing you all lives filled with a bit of magic.

Hugs,

Auburn Tempest

AUTHOR NOTES - MICHAEL ANDERLE
OCTOBER 20, 2020

It's all about Family with a capital "F" ;-)

And a huge thank you for reading this story and to the back of the book and these *Author Notes*.

At the time of me writing these author notes, there are at eighty-one reviews (go 100! 1000! Hehehe), and the notes are uplifting and really helpful as decisions were made to figure out just how many books we would commit to.

Because of your early and ongoing support, we now have six books planned from three when we started.

THANK YOU SO MUCH!

I believe you will enjoy what we have going on, how we intend to enrich Fi's life with both joy and trouble, all wrapped up in the same package of fun.

Baby! (No, not really...exactly...no human babies involved in the making of this story, babies are both incredibly hard to audition, insure, and then you need twins. Wait. That's if you are doing a TV show or movie...)

Seriously, she is NOT having a baby, and Auburn will likely call me up when she reads this part.

Damn.

I think she is having to drive some distance for family at the moment. Let's just all pretend this wasn't mentioned, and she won't be the wiser. Right?

Right?

<Sigh.> Here's hoping.

Ad Aeternitatem,

Michael Anderle

ABOUT AUBURN TEMPEST

Auburn Tempest is a multi-genre novelist giving life to Urban Fantasy, Paranormal, and Sci-Fi adventures. Under the pen name, JL Madore, she writes in the same genres but in full romance, sexy-steamy novels. Whether Romance or not, she loves to twist Alpha heroes and kick-ass heroines into chaotic, hilarious, fast-paced, magical situations and make them really work for their happy endings.

Auburn Tempest lives in the Greater Toronto Area, Canada with her dear, wonderful hubby of 30 years and a menagerie of family, friends, and animals.

BOOKS BY AUBURN TEMPEST

Auburn Tempest - Urban Fantasy Action/Adventure

Chronicles of an Urban Druid

Book 1 – A Gilded Cage

Book 2 – A Sacred Grove

Book 3 – A Family Oath

Book 4 - A Witches Revenge

Misty's Magick and Mayhem Series – Written by Carolina Mac/Contributed to by Auburn Tempest

Book 1 – School for Reluctant Witches

Book 2 – School for Saucy Sorceresses

Book 3 – School for Unwitting Wiccans

Book 4 – Nine St. Gillian Street

Book 5 – The Ghost of Pirate's Alley

Book 6 – Jinxing Jackson Square

Book 7 – Flame

Book 8 – Frost

Book 9 – Nocturne

Book 10 – Luna

Book 11 – Swamp Magic

Exemplar Hall – Co-written with Ruby Night

Prequel – Death of a Magi Knight

Book 1 – Drafted by the Magi

Book 2 – Jesse and the Magi Vault

Book 3 – The Makings of a Magi

CONNECT WITH THE AUTHORS

Connect with Auburn

Amazon, Facebook, Newsletter

Web page – www.jlmadore.com

Email – AuburnTempestWrites@gmail.com

Connect with Michael Anderle and sign up for his email list here:

Website: http://lmbpn.com

Email List: http://lmbpn.com/email/

Social Media:

https://www.facebook.com/LMBPNPublishing

https://twitter.com/MichaelAnderle

https://www.instagram.com/lmbpn_publishing/

https://www.bookbub.com/authors/michael-anderle

OTHER LMBPN PUBLISHING BOOKS

For a complete list of books published by LMBPN please visit the following page:

https://lmbpn.com/books-by-lmbpn-publishing/

Printed in Poland
by Amazon Fulfillment
Poland Sp. z o.o., Wrocław

30297165R00179